*Look what people are saying about
these talented authors...*

Jacquie D'Alessandro

"Ms. D'Alessandro's books are not only
keepers—they are treasures."
—*Affaire de Coeur*

"*We've Got Tonight* is super-sexy
and peppered with clever dialogue."
—*Romantic Times BOOKreviews*

Jill Shalvis

"Shalvis' talent for penning excellent stories
has never ceased to amaze me."
—*A Romance Reader*

"Jill Shalvis is a breath of fresh air on a hot,
humid night."
—*The Readers Connection.com*

Crystal Green

"Be prepared for some torrid encounters!"
—*The Best Reviews* on *Born To Be Bad*

"This is very much a guilty pleasure read."
—*All About Romance* on *Playmates*

ABOUT THE AUTHORS

USA TODAY bestselling author **Jacquie D'Alessandro** grew up on Long Island, New York, where she fell in love with romance at an early age. She dreamed of being swept away by a dashing rogue riding a spirited stallion. When her hero finally showed up, he was dressed in jeans and drove a Volkswagen, but she recognized him anyway. They are now living their happily-ever-afters in Atlanta, Georgia, along with their son, who is a dashing rogue in the making. Jacquie writes both contemporary and Regency-era historical romances filled with two of her favorite things—love and laughter. She loves to hear from readers and can be contacted through her Web site at www.JacquieD.com.

Bestselling, award-winning **Jill Shalvis** believes that it's great karma that's helped her write over three dozen romances for Harlequin Books. Barring her own Valentine's Day curse, she intends to spend the day eating chocolate given to her by her husband and kids.... Look for her next Harlequin Blaze novel, *Shadow Hawk* out in June 2007.

A fan favorite, **Crystal Green** lives near Las Vegas, Nevada, where she writes Harlequin Blaze and Silhouette Special Edition novels, plus vampire tales. She loves to read, overanalyze movies, practice yoga, travel and write about her obsessions on her Web page, www.crystal-green.com. Unlike Wes and Erin in "Tall, Dark & Temporary," Crystal has never suffered a Valentine's Day curse—though, having said that, she might have just jinxed herself....

Jacquie D'Alessandro
Jill Shalvis
Crystal Green

Jinxed!

A Valentine's Day Collection

HARLEQUIN®

TORONTO • NEW YORK • LONDON
AMSTERDAM • PARIS • SYDNEY • HAMBURG
STOCKHOLM • ATHENS • TOKYO • MILAN • MADRID
PRAGUE • WARSAW • BUDAPEST • AUCKLAND

ISBN-13: 978-0-373-79307-5
ISBN-10:   0-373-79307-3

JINXED!
Copyright © 2007 by Harlequin Enterprises Ltd.

The publisher acknowledges the copyright holders of the individual works as follows:

BLAME IT ON KARMA
Copyright © 2007 by Jacquie D'Alessandro.

TOGETHER AGAIN?
Copyright © 2007 by Jill Shalvis.

TALL, DARK & TEMPORARY
Copyright © 2007 by Chris Marie Green.

CONTENTS

BLAME IT ON KARMA

Jacquie D'Alessandro

This book is dedicated to Jill Shalvis and Crystal Green for making this such a fun project, and to my fabulous editor Brenda Chin for bringing us all together. And, as always, to my wonderful husband, Joe—Karma was smiling on me the day I met you; and our terrific son, Chris, aka Karma-was-smiling Junior.

Prologue

ISABELLE GIRARD, AKA The Legendary Madame Karma, sat at her fortune-telling table and observed the crowds wandering through the spacious courtyard. It was a perfect sun-drenched southern California day for the outdoor Valentine's Day party, thrown to celebrate the recently completed renovations to the upscale Fairfax building complex. The event was in full swing and clearly a huge success. People of all ages, families with children, couples, singles, groups of teens meandered along the flower-lined walkways or on the meticulously manicured grass, sampling food from the cafés in the complex as well as from the numerous booths featuring foods from local restaurants. Many party goers carried shopping bags bearing the logo of a Fairfax shop while others toted artsy items ranging from paintings to ceramics purchased at one of the craft booths set up for the occasion. Entertainment in the form of face painters, jugglers, wandering magicians and Madame Karma herself added to the festive atmosphere. There was even a band, complete with a small dance floor, set up in a corner of the courtyard, a popular attraction based on the number of couples currently dancing.

Isabelle drew in a contented breath. She enjoyed participating in events like this. Not only did they provide extra income and allow her to increase the customer base for her fortune-telling business, but she loved being outdoors. The fresh air and sunshine rejuvenated her, recharged her "psychic batteries." And after telling fortunes for more than six decades, Madame Karma welcomed the occasional change of scenery.

Her gaze shifted to the huge fountain marking the U-shaped courtyard's center, where a rainbow of sunshine-gilded droplets cascaded from the shooting streams of water. A profusion of colorful flowers and neatly trimmed dark green hedges encircled the area. Numerous inviting wrought-iron benches dotted the courtyard, some situated in the sunshine, others resting in the shade provided by soaring elms. It was the perfect place for shoppers visiting the complex's stores to rest and enjoy a snack, or for the workers in the offices above the retail spaces to enjoy a casual, outdoor lunch.

Or, based on the number of couples currently seated close together on the benches, it was also the perfect place for a bit of romance. Especially with today being Valentine's Day.

Isabelle's gaze settled on one of the couples, a pair she judged to be in their early forties, and her psychic instincts tingled. She clearly sensed the couple's deep love for one another. Isabelle focused her energies—or as she called them, her "cosmic feelings"—on the couple, and then a smile tugged at her lips as the reason for their obvious happiness became clear to her. A much-wanted, long-awaited-for baby was on the way. She hoped they would visit her table so she could confirm her feeling.

She resumed her perusal of the numerous other party goers, a number of whom possessed bright auras and evoked a strong psychic reaction in her, again filling her with the hope that those individuals would take the time to visit her table. Whether it was because of Valentine's Day or due to the planets' current alignment, or a combination of both, she strongly sensed love and romance in the air. In her experience, however, many people fought the forces of fate. Didn't believe in destiny. Or karma. Walked right by or completely ignored their perfect match because of preconceived notions. Focused their attentions on people who, in the long run, wouldn't make them happy, when the person who would make their lives complete often stood right beneath their noses.

Foolish people. If only they would accept their karma, their path. In her experience, those who did always fared well in matters of the heart. Those who didn't…well, as she knew, fighting fate was like trying to push back the ocean with a broom—you were doomed to fail.

Well, perhaps today, with all these romantic currents all but snapping in the air, she could set some of these party goers on the right path. Help them find their soul mates. Or at least keep them from choosing the wrong person.

She straightened in her chair as a smiling young woman approached her—a young woman whose aura was particularly bright. Isabelle's instincts tingled with anticipation.

Karma and Fate were about to be predicted.

1

HOLDING A STEAMING container of freshly brewed tea in one hand and an oversized frosted cookie in the other, Lacey Perkins walked toward the fortune-telling table.

Bright afternoon sunshine warmed Lacey's skin and, unable to resist its alluring heat, she paused for several seconds to savor the sensation. Closing her eyes, she tipped back her head and drew in several deep, appreciative breaths of fresh air redolent with the delicious scents wafting from the various food tents set up around the courtyard. She'd been cooped up in Constant Cravings since early this morning, and as much as she loved her coffee shop, she welcomed this momentary respite.

She opened her eyes, then blinked against the sun's glare. Based on the crowded courtyard and the nonstop stream of customers who had filed into Constant Cravings from the moment she'd opened the doors this morning, the Valentine's Day party celebrating Fairfax's renovations was a huge success. Certainly her sales thus far today had exceeded her expectations. Throughout the course of the hectic day she'd recognized the faces of many of her regular customers—Baxter Hills locals and workers whose offices were located in the complex. Everyone from executives to the landscapers who kept the courtyard in pristine condition had dropped into her shop.

But she was even more encouraged by the number of newcomers, many of whom reached for one of the business cards she kept stacked by the cash register. Hopefully those first-timers would come back for more of her specialty coffees, teas and fresh-baked goods. Check out her Web site. Hire her to bake custom items for their next special occasion or party.

She'd worked long and hard to make her dream of running her own store a reality, and all she'd accomplished with Constant Cravings—the personal touches she'd put into the decor and the menu items—filled her with pride. While you couldn't swing a stick and fail to hit one of the coffee-house franchises that occupied space in nearly every block in the Los Angeles area, she'd worked to make Constant Cravings different in every way, from setting up her store in Baxter Hills—an up-and-coming area on the outskirts of the city—to the decorations, to the desserts she served, to the colorful napkins she used. She hoped the exposure from today's party would lead not only to those new faces becoming regular customers but to them telling their friends about her shop. Which would lead to even better sales.

Which might finally get Evan Sawyer off her back.

As if the mere thought of Fairfax's building manager—who, by virtue of that title was unfortunately her landlord—could make him materialize, her gaze happened upon him standing across the courtyard. His features were set in their usual scowl, and she wasn't in the least bit surprised to note that despite the warm weather and the fact that it was a Saturday *and* this was a party, he wore one of his uptight business suits complete with a perfectly knotted maroon tie.

Annoyance rippled through her. The man *always* looked perfect, as if he'd just stepped from some *GQ* photo shoot—dark suit perfectly fitted, dress shirt without a wrinkle, shoes buffed to a glossy shine. Even though the breeze currently ruffled his dark hair, he somehow managed to look *perfectly* windblown.

Yes, his was the sort of irritating perfection that always made her feel gauche, messy, wilted and somehow undone—like an unmade bed. Made her want to smooth her hands over her own wrinkled attire, wish she'd taken more time with her out-of-control curly hair and surreptitiously check her teeth to make sure no remnants of her spinach salad remained.

Which was completely ridiculous. What did she care if he found her physical appearance lacking? While she grudgingly admitted that he'd never *said* such a thing, he *did* have a way of looking at her that made it clear he didn't approve of her. Certainly he'd made no secret of the fact that he didn't approve of the way she ran Constant Cravings.

She'd been a Fairfax tenant for nearly eight months, and her every interaction with Evan Sawyer had proven frustrating. He was more rigid than a concrete pillar, repeatedly complaining about the lingerie-clad mannequins she re-dressed bimonthly for her quirky window displays. Said they were "too suggestive," as were her best-selling cookies in the shapes of men's and women's torsos. Her latest idea she'd run by him—to expand Constant Cravings into one of the storefronts on either side of her should they come up for lease—had been met with all the enthusiasm of having his innards ripped out with a rusty knife.

Sheesh. You'd think the man would be thrilled that she wanted to expand since her store generated such solid sales figures, a percentage of which were paid to Fairfax. But no, all he did was complain. He was an uptight, unbending, workaholic thorn in her side. One of those all-work, no-play types she called Soulless Clones. And given what was clearly his strong aversion to anything the least bit sensual, she suspected he was a dead bore between the sheets.

Which was too bad, because he was *very* easy on the eyes— if you cared for that buttoned-down corporate type. Which she most emphatically did not. Good thing, too, because she'd be a complete idiot to find attractive a man who was so ridiculously not her type in any way. So what if he filled out those uptight suits very nicely? Who cared if his eyes were the most amazing shade of blue she'd ever seen? Big deal. Lots of men had great bodies and beautiful eyes. Most of those other men probably also knew how to smile. And laugh. And take a few minutes to stop and smell the roses. And didn't mind cookies that looked like torsos.

Determined not to allow the irritating man to disrupt this fabulous day, Lacey was about to turn away and continue toward the fortune-teller when Evan's gaze zeroed in on her. Inexplicably feeling as if she'd been caught in a sniper's crosshairs, she froze, and for several seconds they simply stared at each other. An odd warmth tingled down Lacey's spine—no doubt aggravation brought on by the fact that the man really was undeservedly handsome. Why the good-looks gods had so abundantly blessed him when he should resemble a troll was a shining example of utter unfairness, one she put right up there with the fact that males didn't suffer from cellulite. And that crow's feet made men look distinguished and women look old. And that every bite of chocolate didn't permanently attach itself to the male ass. It just wasn't *right*.

Yanking herself from her frozen state, she inclined her head in greeting and forced a half smile. But did he even attempt to do the same? Noooo. Instead, his gaze flicked over her and then his frown deepened into a downright scowl. She looked down at her white short-sleeved shirt, which bore the Constant Cravings logo, her plain black pants and comfy black ballet flats, mystified as to what he could possibly have seen to inspire such a thunderous expression. Talk about a grouch.

Raising her chin, she deliberately ignored him and approached the table with a huge sign announcing that she was in the presence of the renowned Madame Karma. After introducing herself, Lacey said, "I saw that you had a free moment and thought you might enjoy a snack." She set her offerings—the cookie and the tea—on the corner of the brocade-covered table.

Madame Karma's dark eyes sparkled. "Thank you, my dear. That's very thoughtful." She picked up the cookie, her expression turning amused at the confection, which looked like a side view of a woman's curvy leg. The intricate frosting made it appear as if that curvy leg was encased in fishnet stockings and the dainty foot slipped into a sexy, red, high-heeled shoe.

"Wish my legs still looked like this," Madame said with a sigh. "They used to—when I was your age."

"I call that cookie For Your Thighs Only. It's one of my best-sellers."

Madame bit off the bright red shoe, then slowly chewed. After washing down the morsel with a sip of the tea, she said, "Absolutely delicious. How much do I owe you?"

"It's on the house. I would have brought it out to you sooner, but it's been crazy in the shop."

"Well, if you won't let me give you any money, you must allow me to read your fortune as payment for what is, without a doubt, the most delicious cookie I've ever eaten." She shot Lacey a wink. "And believe me, I've eaten a lot of cookies over the years."

"That sounds like a fair exchange."

"Please, sit down," Madame Karma said, indicating the chair opposite her with a wave of her heavily be-ringed fingers. After Lacey was settled in the chair, Madame leaned forward. Her sharp gaze seemed to penetrate directly into Lacey's soul.

"Your aura is very bright, my dear," Madame said in a low, husky whisper. "I'm feeling a very strong psychic connection." Without breaking eye contact, Madame reached into an ornately carved wooden box and pulled out a deck of cards. "For you, I will use these cards. For a special reading. One that will offer deep insight."

Lacey pulled her gaze away from Madame's and looked at the deck. It looked like a regular deck of playing cards to her. She watched Madame fan the cards, facedown, on the table.

"Please choose seven cards, using your left hand, then pass them to me."

Lacey followed the instructions, then repeated the task twice more at Madame's bidding. After turning up the cards into three rows, Madame pointed to the first group. "These represent your past." She studied the cards in silence for nearly a minute, then said, "I see two women with you. Your mother and sister. There was a man, your father, but his presence was dim and then gone." She looked up and her gaze locked with Lacey's. "He is dead, yes?"

Lacey blinked in surprise at the accuracy of Madame's words, then a lump tightened her throat. "Yes," she whispered.

"He died young," Madame continued, studying the cards. "From trouble with his heart."

An eerie chill swept through Lacey. How could Madame Karma have known something so personal? An image of her father, always so serious, always so consumed with his career, flashed through Lacey's mind. She had to swallow to locate her voice. "A heart attack," she concurred. "When I was fourteen."

Madame nodded. "I see the sadness from his death. The hardships it caused your family. But I also see your love of life. Your determination to succeed, yet not at the expense of your health, as was the case with your father. Your resolution not to make the same mistakes you feel your mother and sister made."

Another odd chill crept down Lacey's spine, and she had to fight the urge to fidget. It was as if Madame could truly see into her soul.

"These cards represent your present," Madame Karma continued, indicating the middle row. "Your professional life is going very well, although I do see a…presence. Someone or something that is frustrating you and is, for lack of a better term, a thorn in your side."

Thorn in her side? An image of Evan Sawyer instantly materialized in Lacey's mind, and she found herself gritting her teeth and narrowing her eyes. "What about this thorn in my side? Will it—he—go away?"

"Patience, my dear," Madame said, looking up briefly. "I will know more after I read the last row, which represents your future. Now, back to the present. While your professional life is progressing nicely, your personal life is decidedly lacking. I see…loneliness. No male companionship, although…" She frowned.

"What?" Lacey asked, leaning forward.

"Someone is looming on the horizon."

A fissure of hope filled Lacey. "A *nice* someone?" A nice someone would be…nice. A non-whacko, non-self-absorbed, non-jackass someone. She hadn't had a date in over a month. And the last three dates she'd gone on... A shudder ran through her. Those dates could be summed up in three words: stink, stank, stunk.

"A someone who is somehow related to the shadow hanging over your professional life. Let us continue on to the last row of cards, which represent your immediate future." After studying the seven cards, Madame Karma pursed her lips. "Regarding this thorn in your side, I can see clearly in this grouping of cards that it is a man. A man who is close to you, although only in prox-imity, not in a sexual way. Perhaps a coworker." She looked up and her dark eyes locked with Lacey's. "You know to whom I am referring."

"I can think of someone who I'd describe as a thorn in my side," Lacey said slowly. "He's the man who manages this building complex."

Madame Karma nodded solemnly. "Yes, that fits perfectly, as your cards indicate he is a man of power."

"Right. A powerful pain in the butt."

"What is this man's name?"

"Evan Sawyer." She nodded toward the cards. "So, is Thorn-in-My-Side Sawyer about to leave Fairfax?" Lacey asked in a hopeful voice. "Get transferred to Siberia?"

"No. Indeed, just the opposite. The manner of his proximity to you is about to change. From nonsexual to...can't get enough of him."

Lacey actually felt her jaw drop open. A strange tingle, sort of like a slow-motion pulse of static electricity, eased through her. Then a short huff of laughter escaped her. "There must be some other thorn in my side because I can assure you, *that* is not going to happen."

"My dear, I assure you that it is. The cards plainly say so and you cannot fight karma. Cannot deny your fate. To do so will bring the wrath of both upon your head, the equivalent of being cursed. Trust me, that is something you do not want. Your luck will change from good to bad like *that*." Madame snapped her fingers and her multitude of metal bracelets jangled with an ominous clang. She then reached out and clasped Lacey's hands. "This Evan Sawyer…you think he is all wrong for you, but he is, without a doubt, Mr. Right."

2

EVAN SAWYER STARED across the bright courtyard at Lacey Perkins and felt every muscle in his body tense. Something about the woman unsettled him in a way he neither understood nor liked. Surely the tension that gripped him whenever he saw her—hell, whenever he so much as thought of her—was nothing more than severe irritation. It definitely rankled that she pushed the envelope with her coffee shop's window displays and sensuously named products. Who the hell sold baked goods named Chocolate Orgasm and coffee drinks called Hot, Wet & Wild?

The woman and her eclectic shop were a major headache and had been since Constant Cravings first opened. He'd stopped in early on the shop's opening day, looking forward to bringing a cappuccino to his office. Before he could place his order, however, a smiling Lacey had asked him if he'd like to try the opening day special—A Slow Glide into Pleasure. That had been eight months ago, yet he recalled the moment and the fire that had raced through him so vividly it might as well have happened eight seconds ago. Even now, all these months later, the memory of her asking him that question, in her smoky, husky voice, her eyes twinkling with mischief, had him clenching his hands to keep from yanking at his suddenly too tight tie. He couldn't recall ever being so flustered by a woman.

And no wonder. His and Lacey's personalities were like oil and water, leaving them constantly at odds. If Constant Cravings wasn't one of the most income-producing stores in the Fairfax complex, Evan would have terminated her lease months ago. She continually tested him, seeing how much she could get away with, how far she could push the boundaries, a trait that totally rubbed him the wrong way. Why couldn't she simply follow the rules like all the other tenants?

No doubt because she was one of those artsy-fartsy, free-spirit types who believed rules were made to be bent, twisted or downright broken to accommodate her "creativity." She simply didn't grasp the fact that Fairfax projected a certain upscale image, and that her suggestive window displays and product names did not fit that image. No, she scoffed whenever he reminded her of that. She insisted that her displays were tongue-in-cheek, and that since sales were on the increase, obviously sex *did* sell.

While Evan couldn't argue with her financial success, damn it there were *rules* to be followed. Unfortunately the wording in her tenant agreement regarding the appropriateness of her store's decorations gave her enough wiggle room to make his job of enforcing the dictates difficult. So far no one had complained, but he suspected it was just a matter of time, especially since she kept pushing the sensuality factor with every new display.

Just then she turned and their gazes met. He stilled, feeling the impact like a sucker punch. Although he couldn't see the color of her eyes from this distance, they reminded him of caramel, the irises dotted with lighter flecks of gold and surrounded by a dark ring that resembled melted chocolate. Every time he looked into them he felt an inexplicable craving to indulge in something sweet.

The breeze teased her wildly curly hair, which she'd clearly tried to tame into a ponytail, with limited success. He tried to look away, but as always seemed to be the case when he saw her, his eyeballs failed to cooperate with his brain. Instead of looking away, his gaze flicked down her form. There was nothing overtly provocative about her white short-sleeved shirt and plain black pants. Certainly nothing that should have tightened his jaw further.

But there was just something about the way her clothes

hugged her figure that rendered it…spectacular. And rendered him speechless. Damn it, every time he looked at her, in his mind's eye he saw her lips—her full, glistening lips—forming the words, *Would you like A Slow Glide into Pleasure?* He found himself shifting to relieve the sudden discomfort in his pants, and irritation yanked down his eyebrows. How damn annoying was it that his body reacted so strongly to a woman he didn't even like?

Pretty damn annoying.

She inclined her head and offered him a tight-looking half smile, a greeting of sorts he supposed, but before he could respond, she lifted her chin in that aggravating, stubborn way she had, then turned away and approached the fortune-teller's table. He tried his damnedest to pull his gaze from her, but again failed, his attention riveted on her walk. She might be an artsy-fartsy, rule-breaking pest but there was no denying that she walked like sin in motion, with a slow, sensual, hip-rolling stride that made it seem as if the small patch of grass he stood on had suddenly moved closer to the sun.

Clearing his throat, he finally managed to force his gaze away from her, only to have it fall on her shop's window. His teeth clenched at the provocative display. A mannequin couple stood in what was supposed to be a cozy kitchen. The oven door was open, and the female mannequin, dressed in a short, slinky, fire-engine-red dress, held a cookie sheet in one oven-mitted hand. In the other hand she held an oversized heart-shaped, pink-frosted cookie. With her glossy scarlet lips parted and her eyes half-closed, she was lifting the cookie toward the male mannequin that stood behind her.

Dressed in a black satin robe and matching boxers decorated with small pink hearts, the male mannequin's hands rested on the female's hips, his head bent toward the curve of her neck. Across the top of the window, painted in bold crimson script were the challenging words, Taste Me…Then Just *Try* To Walk Away.

An image of Lacey, her curves encased in that sexy red dress, offering him that cookie, flashed through his mind, leaving a trail of heat in its wake that had nothing to do with the bright sunshine.

"You planning to visit the fortune-teller, Evan?"

Evan blinked away the distracting, disturbing image and turned to look at Paul West, an attorney who'd been his best friend since college and who'd moved his office into the Fairfax building only last week. With his brain still not fully recovered, he managed only to grunt, "Huh?"

"The fortune-teller. By the number of people I've seen stop by her table, I'd say she's the hit of the party. You going to get your cards read?"

"Me?" Evan asked, raising his eyebrows. "You can't be serious."

"I am, the operative word being *serious.* Which is what you've been too much lately. Loosen up a little. Relax. This is a *party,* remember?"

"Of course I remember." How could he forget? The party had been his idea, and the hefty price tag for it was being picked up by the company he worked for, GreenSpace Property Management—money well spent as the party was clearly a success, drawing a large, diverse group of visitors to Fairfax's mix of retail stores. From the array of mid to high end boutiques to the cafés, there was something here for everyone, and pride filled Evan at the fact that the retail spaces were currently one hundred percent leased. Now that the renovations were completed, his goal was to see that the office spaces, currently leased at eighty percent, were also at one hundred percent by year's end.

Paul nudged him in the ribs, then nodded across the courtyard. "Looks like Lacey Perkins is having her fortune told."

Evan's gaze snapped around and zeroed in on Lacey, who sat with her back to them at the fortune-teller's table. "You know her?" he asked, a note of surprise creeping into his voice.

"Hell, yeah. You think I wouldn't know the owner of the

coffee shop nearest my office? I met her last week on my first day here, when she made me the best double shot no-foam latte I've ever had. She's really nice."

"Nice?" Evan shook his head. "That's not the word I'd use to describe her." No, *annoying, irritating, aggravating*…those words were much more accurate.

"Hmm. Maybe you're right. Something like *sizzling hot* is probably better."

Evan whipped his head around and found himself staring at Paul's profile. His friend's attention was riveted across the courtyard on Lacey. A fissure of something that felt exactly like jealousy but couldn't possibly be snaked through Evan. "Hot? You think?"

"Are you kidding me?" Paul turned and shot him an incredulous look. "You manage this place. Have you never *seen* her?"

Oh, he'd seen her all right. More times than he cared to remember. "Of course."

"And you don't think the woman could set the Pacific Ocean on fire?"

The question caught Evan off guard in a way he neither understood nor liked. "Any attractiveness she might possess is completely cancelled out by the fact that she and her innuendo-laced displays and products are a major pain in my ass."

"Yeah, well those 'innuendo-laced products' are absolutely delicious. I tasted her Sugar Lips crumb cake yesterday and…wow. The things that woman can whip up in the kitchen could make a grown man weep." Paul grinned. "I'm hoping next week's cookie is named something like Wild Sweaty Sex in the Backseat. Would love to get me some of *that*—with her."

Something cramped Evan's insides—and apparently his facial muscles as well—because Paul blinked, held up his hands and said, "Whoa, sorry. Didn't realize I was stepping on your toes."

"What are you talking about?"

"That laser-beam death stare you just sizzled at me. You never mentioned having a thing for her."

Evan wiped his face clean of expression, irked to realize he'd been scowling. "No doubt because I don't." Really. He didn't. That steaming heat she inspired? Nothing more than severe annoyance.

"Uh-huh. Then why haven't you been able to stop staring at her? Not that I blame you—Lacey is certainly something to look at."

"If I *was* staring, it's only because I was trying to figure out what she's going to do next. She's always bending the rules."

"Ah. So she challenges you."

"No, she *annoys* me."

"She's not the sort of woman you usually go for."

Evan shook his head and looked skyward. "I'm *not* 'going for' her. In fact, I'd like her to move out of Fairfax when her lease is up. But instead, she's talking about expanding. Wants me to let her know if the storefront on either side of her comes up for lease."

Paul studied him for several long seconds, the scrutiny making Evan feel as if he were a germ under a microscope. Then Paul grinned. "Oh, you've got it bad, man. And what's so funny, is that you—Mr. 4.0, MBA, top-of-his-class smart guy— don't realize it. Gotta say, I'm torn—half of me is glad that you're finally showing an interest in a woman who's not the uptight, high-maintenance, boring type you've been wasting your time on, but damn, I wish I'd seen Lacey first. She is *fine.*" His grin flashed wider. "Maybe she has a sister."

"You're welcome to her," Evan said, pissed—and alarmed— that he actually had to force out the words.

"If I thought for even a nanosecond that you meant that, believe me, I'd go for it."

"And I don't usually go for uptight, high-maintenance, boring types." A frown pulled down his eyebrows. Did he?

"Maybe not recently, but only because you've been living like a freakin' monk. Before that? Nearly every woman I've seen you with for the past two years has been a carbon copy of the other— and they've all been uptight, high-maintenance and boring."

Was Paul right? Surely not. He'd have to think on that. But later. "Lacey Perkins is certainly a high-maintenance tenant."

"That doesn't mean she's a high-maintenance woman. And she sure as hell doesn't strike me as uptight or boring. But just a warning—I think you have your work cut out for you. Since I didn't know you'd already staked a claim, I flirted with her every morning this past week. And while she's been friendly, that's all she's been. She definitely throws out a strong 'hands off' vibe. Probably has a boyfriend."

The profound sense of relief Evan experienced that Lacey hadn't caught any of the flirtatious balls Paul had tossed her way utterly confused him, as did the cramping at the thought of her having a serious boyfriend. What the hell did he care if she flirted with Paul or anyone else? Who gave a rat's ass if she had a boyfriend or even a husband? Not him. In fact, he hoped she *did* have a boyfriend—one on the verge of being transferred to another state, who'd take her with him when he moved.

"C'mon, let's go get your fortune read," Paul said. "See if it's in the cards for you and Lacey to—"

"I assure you it's not."

"Okay, then maybe the fortune-teller can tell you if you're gonna get lucky with *anyone* anytime soon."

"Why don't you have *your* fortune read and she can tell you if *you're* going to get lucky anytime soon?"

"I already know." Paul gave a wolfish grin. "I have a date tonight with this babe named Melinda, who I met yesterday at the supermarket. We bonded over broccoli."

"You don't like broccoli."

"True. But I really liked the steaming-hot woman who was picking some out, so it was well worth the three bucks I spent on the gross stuff."

"Seems like you're with a different woman every week."

"I am. And you know why? Because I actually *go out.* To places where women are. Women who want to meet men. It's called *dating.* You should try it sometime."

"I date." Although admittedly not very much lately. And the last series of dates he'd gone on? All empty evenings spent with women he'd found physically attractive, but who had proven ultimately un-interesting—usually after less than two hours in their company.

"Don't you ever get…" Evan hesitated, not sure how to express the perplexing discontent he'd been feeling the past few months "…*tired?* Of going to clubs? Of awkward first dates? Of trying to find a woman you can actually *talk* to?"

"*Talk* to?" Paul shook his head. "You sound more like ninety-two than thirty-two. I knew you'd buried yourself in your work lately, but I hadn't realized the situation was this dire. When's the last time you got laid?"

Too long ago. Yet even the last two times, which had satis-fied him physically, had still felt somehow…empty. In a way he didn't understand himself, and definitely had no intention of trying to explain to Paul. "I'm not having this conversation."

A flicker of concern flashed in Paul's eyes. "Ever since you and Heather split up you've turned into a work-obsessed maniac. It's been six months—time for you to come out of mourning over a relationship with a woman who was all wrong for you."

"I'm not in mourning. I'm just busy. Overseeing the Fairfax renovations has taken an enormous amount of time."

"No guy is too busy to get laid."

"Who says I haven't gotten laid?"

"Have you?"

"Of course."

Paul's eyes narrowed. "Since you and Heather broke up?"

"Yes."

"Well, that's a relief. How many times?"

Evan blew out an impatient sigh. He considered lying, just to end this conversation, but he was a lousy liar, and Paul knew it. "Twice."

"Twice? In the past six months? Holy crap, your dick is gonna fall off." Paul shot him a look Evan was sure had swayed more than one opposing counsel to agree to his terms. "The renova-tions are finished and it's time you started living again."

"I never stopped."

"You certainly stopped having fun." He hesitated, then added quietly, "Heather's moved on, Evan. You need to as well."

Evan dragged his hands·down his face then drew a deep breath. "Look, I appreciate the concern, but this isn't a case of me not moving on. Believe me, my heart's not broken."

"She cheated on you."

"Which pissed me off. But it didn't break my heart. The job's just kept me crazy busy and, frankly, I haven't met a woman recently who's interested me enough to make more than a token effort. But as soon as I meet one—and now that I finally have more time I'm sure I will—believe me, I'll go for it."

And he meant every word. He supposed that his ego should have been bruised by Heather's betrayal, but in truth, after the initial shock of anger, he'd been more relieved than anything else. Heather had been one of those women who in theory should have been perfect for him. She came from a good family, had attended all the right schools, was successful in her management position with Neiman Marcus, and very attractive. They hailed from similar backgrounds, had a lot in common, and the sex had been good. In reality, however, they'd crashed and burned. All Heather's outward perfection and fabulous credentials had just cleverly hidden an inner character lacking in honesty and integrity.

"Well, glad to hear you're ready to jump back into the dating waters," Paul said. "And the timing's perfect. Since today is Valentine's Day—aka the biggest get-lucky occasion of the year—we're going to make certain you don't spend the night alone. C'mon. We're heading across the courtyard. If the sexy Lacey isn't the woman to jump-start things and end your dry spell—"

"She's not—"

"Then maybe the fortune-teller will clue us in to who is. There're hundreds of women roaming around here."

"Are you nuts? I don't believe in that fortune-teller nonsense."

"Fine. I'll ask her for you." He grinned. "Right after I tell Lacey you're insanely hot for her."

Evan rubbed his temple in a vain attempt to stem the throbbing there. "Cripes, you're like the pesky little brother I've never had. Or wanted. Have you always been such a pain in the ass?"

Paul's grin merely widened. "You won't think I'm a pain in the ass after you get laid. And I'm willing to bet you'll be in a much better mood afterward, too."

He could have protested but what was the point? Paul could argue the paint off walls—it's what made him such a good lawyer. And besides, much as it galled Evan to admit it, Paul was right. A good sweaty romp between the sheets would surely cure him of this discontent and the tension plaguing him. But enlisting the help of a fortune-teller? Ridiculous. He'd just head out to one of the dozens of L.A. clubs tonight and see what was out there.

You know what's out there, his inner voice whispered wearily. *You've seen it and dated it, dozens of times.*

Right. And the thought of doing so again didn't fill him with any anticipation. But unless he wanted Paul to carry out his threat—and he knew from experience his friend wouldn't hesitate to do so, and he saw Paul was already striding across the courtyard—he needed to get his ass in gear.

Against his better judgment and feeling uncharacteristically out of sorts, Evan jogged to catch up. As they approached the fortune-teller, who went by the totally absurd name of Madame Karma, Lacey rose from the chair, then turned. Her gaze collided with Evan's and his brisk footsteps nearly faltered at the impact. Her eyes narrowed on him with clear annoyance, and he bit back a grim smile. Good. Why should he be the only one out of sorts?

She then switched her attention to Paul, and her chilly expression instantly melted to a warm smile. "Paul, how nice to see you," she said, lifting one hand to shade her eyes. "Are you craving your usual double-shot, no-foam latte?"

"That, and one of your delicious cookies." He rubbed his hand over his stomach. "Best I've ever tasted."

Her smile outshone the bright golden sun, drawing Evan's gaze to her full lips and the pair of shallow dimples flanking them. Damn, he'd always had a thing for women with dimples. How unfair that such a sexy pair was wasted on this particular woman. Her smile faded, and feeling the weight of a stare, he raised his gaze to find her glaring at him. "Evan."

As far as enthusiastic greetings went, it wasn't much, but that was fine by him. His every muscle tensed and his suit suddenly felt as if it had shrunk. "Lacey."

Her gaze bounced between him and Paul. "You two know each other?"

"Best friends since college," Evan said.

Her eyebrows shot upward. "You two?" Her gaze remained steady on his, but her fingers waved back and forth between him and Paul.

He wasn't sure if he was more irked or amused at her obvious disbelief. "You seem shocked that I'd have a friend."

"I suppose I am, at least a friend who's so personable."

"I'm extremely personable—toward people who don't constantly wear on my patience."

"Perhaps you're just an impatient person. Maybe you should switch to decaf. It might help you relax."

"Actually, I consider myself a very patient man, considering all that I've had to put up with lately," he replied, his gaze resting significantly on her.

"Patient? Now that's not a word I would associate with a man so opposed to the tongue-in-cheek playful tone of my window displays."

"Obviously our definitions of *playful* aren't the same. Pushing the envelope toward nudity goes beyond what is appropriate for Fairfax."

Color rose in her cheeks. "My mannequins are fully clothed."

"Right—in a way that's as obvious as a slap in the face."

"Slap in the face…" She smiled sweetly. "Is that an invitation?"

He made a *tsk*ing noise. "I didn't know you harbored violent tendencies."

"Only toward people who constantly wear on my nerves."

"Speaking of wearing on my nerves…" He jerked his thumb toward her shop. "That window display is, um…"

"Provocative? Interesting?"

"I was thinking more along the lines of 'over the top.'"

"Thank you. I accept your compliment."

"I didn't pay you one."

"The fact that you noticed the display is a compliment in itself."

"Obviously our last conversation regarding toning down the displays fell on deaf ears."

"No, I heard you."

"Ah. Then this is a problem of you not knowing the difference between *hearing* and *listening*."

"I know the difference. But I also know the meaning of *ignoring*."

"Obviously."

"And this is a problem of you not knowing the meaning of the word *playful*. I suspect you wouldn't know playful if it jumped up and bit your butt."

"Undoubtedly because you don't know me."

"I don't? That's odd. I feel as if I know you very well."

She didn't add the word *unfortunately*, but it was clearly implied. "As I feel I know you," he murmured. "How…lucky for both of us."

"Hmm. Not certain *lucky* is the word I'd choose, but then, we don't agree on much, do we?"

"I think the next time we agree will be the first time."

"At least we can agree on *that*. And in that spirit of peace-making…" She nodded her chin toward the crowds of people. "The party is a huge success. Whoever planned it did a great job."

"Thank you."

Her eyebrows rose. "*You* planned all this?"

"You sound surprised."

"I am. You don't strike me as the party-planning type."

He was tempted to ask what type he did strike her as, but decided he didn't really want to know, especially as he doubted it would be complimentary. Instead he smiled, a gesture he knew didn't reach his eyes. "Managing property isn't the only thing I do well."

"I know. You're also adept at aggravating the tenants. And apparently you also know the name of a good party planner."

"Part of being a good manager is the ability to delegate."

"Uh-huh. So, will you be stopping in for a coffee? We have a special Valentine's sugar cookie you might enjoy. It's in the shape of lips." She shot him another sweet smile. "I call it Bite Me."

Paul made a choking sound, indicating a smothered laugh, and Evan turned toward his friend. Damn, he'd completely forgotten Paul's presence, and Madame Karma's as well, an oversight he blamed on the thoroughly irritating Lacey.

"Thanks, but I'll delegate coffee duty to Paul." Evan then turned toward the fortune-teller, who he noticed was studying him with undisguised interest. Holding out his hand, he smiled. "Madame Karma, I'm—"

"Evan Sawyer," the gypsy-garbed woman said in a low, compelling voice. Before he could recover from his surprise that she knew his name, she clasped his hand firmly between both of hers while her eyes, so dark he couldn't discern the pupil from the iris, seemed to bore into him. "Your aura…" she murmured, sandwiching his hand tightly between hers "…it is exceptionally bright. And strong. You will allow me to read your fortune?"

"That's why I'm here," Evan said politely, ignoring the smirk on Paul's face he saw from the corner of his eye.

Madame's gaze bounced between him and Lacey several times, then she nodded solemnly. "Excellent. Let us begin." She released his hand then made a shooing motion toward Lacey. "Off with you, my dear. Mr. Sawyer and I have much to discuss."

Evan couldn't think of a single thing that he and Madame Karma would have to discuss, but since it seemed there was no avoiding it, he might as well get this fortune-telling hooey over with. He'd listen and nod, then thank her and escape.

How bad could it be?

3

IT WAS NEARLY MIDNIGHT WHEN Lacey locked the door to Constant Cravings and headed across the courtyard toward the multilevel parking garage. The damp scent of rain still lingered in the air from the sudden bursts of storms that had blown through earlier, complete with thunder and lightning. Luckily the party had been winding down by then. In fact, the storm had helped her sales, as many party goers had sought refuge from the weather in Constant Cravings.

In spite of her aching feet and back after the long, hectic day, she couldn't help but feel exhilarated. Today's Valentine's Day party had resulted in record sales as well as three orders for party-themed cookie platters, with potentially more to come.

At 9:00 p.m., after setting the Closed sign in the window, she'd spent the rest of the evening baking crumb cake and cookies for tomorrow and doing paperwork—maybe not the most romantic way to spend Valentine's Day night, but in her experience a lot less trouble than men.

If only crumb cake, cookies and paperwork kept a girl warm at night, it would be a perfect world.

And speaking of warm… It could stand to be a little warmer outside. An unseasonably chilly breeze brushed across her bare arms and she quickened her pace, wishing she'd brought a sweatshirt from home.

After entering the ground floor of the parking deck, she headed for the elevator and pushed the up button, then leaned wearily against the wall. She heard an engine rev to life and seconds later saw a cream-colored SUV heading toward the exit. As the car drove past her, she realized the driver was none other than Evan Sawyer.

"Good riddance," she murmured to the fading glow of his taillights as he disappeared around the corner. It figured a workaholic like him had been slaving till midnight on a Saturday, and Valentine's Day no less. Certainly no surprise that a pest like him didn't have a date on the most romantic night of the year. *You didn't have a date on the most romantic night of the year, either,* her pesky inner voice reminded her.

Okay, fine. But she *could* have had a date if she'd wanted. Barbara had wanted to fix her up with a marketing executive at her office, but she'd turned down her best friend's offer. She just hadn't been in the mood to suffer through what would likely turn into yet another awkward first date, especially with an executive type whose first priority was undoubtedly his career, as was the case with nearly all the executive types she'd ever met. Which made him, sight unseen, *not* her type. While her state of datelessness was dragging on far longer than she'd anticipated, she simply hadn't met a man recently who interested her enough to break the cycle. And speaking of far longer than she'd anticipated, what was with this elevator?

She pushed the button again, but after waiting another two minutes decided it must be out of order. "Great," she muttered. Hiking her purse's shoulder strap higher, she pushed open the door leading to the stairwell and proceeded to climb six flights of concrete steps to the rooftop level, then continued across the freakishly cold, windy lot to her parking spot at the far corner.

By the time she sank behind the wheel of her car, she was cold, exhausted and impatient to be home. She slid the key into the ignition and turned her wrist.

And heard nothing.

She tried again, and only silence greeted her. Not even a tiny growl of life emitted from the engine.

Damn. She'd had a similar problem last summer and the

culprit had been a dead battery. Suspecting that was the case, she flipped the switch for the interior light. Nothing.

"Ugh," she moaned, flopping her head back against the leather headrest. First the elevator, now the car. And talk about lousy timing. Not that there was ever a good time for a dead car, but c'mon! Midnight, after an exhausting day, when your teeth were chattering from the cold, was a particularly sucky time.

Drawing a deep, weary breath, she dug through her purse for her cell phone and wondered how long it would take her roadside service company to arrive. No point in calling one of her friends instead—unlike her, they all had dates for Valentine's Day. And while she didn't doubt one of them would come to her rescue, she didn't want to disrupt anyone's romantic evening.

But when she found her cell, she discovered, much to her aggravation, that her phone was suffering from the same fate as her car—a dead battery. How was that possible? It had been fully charged just this afternoon.

Well, *how* both batteries had gone kaput at the same time didn't really matter. What mattered was now she was going to have to hoist her tired ass out of the car and trek all the way back to Constant Cravings to use the phone there. Muttering hostile and uncomplimentary words under her breath toward all things mechanical, she trudged back toward the elevator, only to recall that it wasn't working.

"Perfect. Just perfect. Could this night get any worse?" She stomped down the six flights of stairs, and the instant she exited the stairwell and stepped onto the sidewalk she was hit by a blast of chilly air and the undeniable realization that, yes, this night could indeed get worse. Because the first thing she saw was Evan Sawyer, standing next to his car, which was stopped in the fire lane. He'd removed his suit jacket, loosened his uptight tie, unfastened the top button of his dress shirt and rolled back the sleeves. She'd never seen him so casually undone. By damn, he looked almost…human.

He was frowning at his cell phone with a ferocity surely

meant to set the instrument on fire. The stairwell door slammed shut behind her and his head snapped up. His eyebrows rose at the sight of her, and then he once again frowned.

"What are you doing here?" they asked in unison.

Lacey wrapped her arms around herself to ward off the chill and continued toward him. "My car battery's dead. You?"

"Based on the reading on my gas gauge, it appears I'm out of gas. Which is odd since I just filled the tank yesterday."

"Probably the work of gas thieves."

"Gas thieves?"

Lacey nodded. "There was a news story about it just last week on TV. They hit crowded parking lots and siphon gasoline out of tanks. With prices at the pump rising so high, it's becoming a widespread problem."

He raked a hand through his hair. "Great. Just great."

"I have gas in my car."

"Do you have a siphon?"

"Of course not. Do I look like a gas thief?"

"I don't know. To the best of my knowledge I've never met one. And since you don't have a siphon, the gas in your car isn't going to do me much good. That's like me saying I have a perfectly good battery in my car, but unless you have 900-yard-long jumper cables, that's not much help to you."

"Jeez, you are such a grouch."

He pinched the bridge of his nose and blew out a long breath. "Sorry. I'm just tired. It's been a long day, one that unfortunately is getting longer."

A humorless sound escaped her. "I hear ya. Weird that we both had car trouble."

He lifted his hand and waggled his cell phone. "You can add phone trouble to my list of woes. My cell's battery is dead."

Her eyebrows shot up. "Really? Mine, too."

"Even weirder."

"Yeah. It's like we're cursed or something…"

Her words trailed off, and she suddenly recalled Madame

Karma's words during this afternoon's card reading. *You cannot fight karma. Cannot deny your fate. To do so will bring the wrath of both upon your head, the equivalent of being cursed…your luck will change from good to bad…*

Ridiculous, she scolded herself. Just as ridiculous as Madame's prediction that Evan was Mr. Right. She looked at him and noticed his odd expression. He was looking at her as if antennae had sprouted from her head.

"Something wrong?" she asked.

"No. I was just thinking…something that crazy fortune-teller said…" He shook his head. "Never mind."

Something Madame had said? *Oh. Dear. God.* Had Madame told Evan the same absurd things about her as she'd told Lacey about him? That she was The One for him? A heartfelt nooooo rose in her throat. That would just be too humiliating. Even though she was pretty sure she didn't want to know the answer, she couldn't stop herself from asking, "Evan, did Madame Karma mention me when she read your cards?"

His gaze immediately turned wary, confirming her worst fears. "Why do you ask?"

Might as well get this over with. She drew a deep breath, then said in a rush, "Because she mentioned *you* during *my* reading. Talked about our auras matching and…stuff."

His eyes narrowed. "Stuff? What kind of stuff?"

She raised her chin. "Ridiculous stuff. Like that we were compatible."

"And perfect for each other? Meant for each other?"

"Exactly."

"What a bunch of crap."

"Well, yeah." That was obvious. But sheesh, he didn't need to be so insulting about it. Not to be outdone, she added, "Biggest bunch of crap I've ever heard in my life."

"Exactly. She tell you that if you fight karma and fate you'll be cursed?"

"Yes." She tried for a smile, but her face felt tight. "Do you suppose broken cars and dead cell phones fall under the heading of 'cursed'?"

"Absolutely not. I don't believe in that nonsense. Nor do I believe anything that crazy woman said. She's nothing but a fraud."

"Actually, I recently read an article about her in *The Times,* describing how she successfully assisted the police on several cases. She apparently has a sterling reputation. But based on her telling me that you're Mr. Right, I'd have to say she's lost her touch."

"Since she told me the same off-the-wall thing about you, I'd say she's *really* lost it—assuming she ever had it in the first place." He dragged a hand through his hair. "Listen, I'm going to head back to my office to use the phone."

"I was about to do the same."

He hesitated, then cleared his throat. "Pretty silly for us to go to separate places. Why don't you come with me to my office to use the phone?"

"What's the matter, afraid of the dark?"

"Nooo. Actually, I was thinking of your safety. It's late for you to be walking around alone. Especially if there're gas thieves running around."

"That's unexpectedly chivalrous of you."

"I'm not the big bad wolf you seem to think I am."

Right. And she was Little Red Riding Hood. Still, she had to admit she wasn't keen on wandering about by herself. "Thanks for the offer, but how about we use the phone at Constant Cravings instead? I'll make some coffee and break out the cookies while we wait for the automotive cavalry to arrive."

"That sounds…nice. Thanks."

"You don't need to sound so shocked that I'd do something nice."

"Oh? You mean the way you didn't sound shocked that I'd do something chivalrous?"

To her surprise, a laugh tickled the back of her throat. "Exactly."

"Well, in that case…sorry."

She studied him for several seconds then a grin tugged at her lips. "No you're not. Jeez. You're a terrible liar."

"So I've been told."

"You must stink at poker."

"That's why I prefer blackjack."

They started across the courtyard, cutting across the wide expanse of lawn as a shortcut. Lacey kept her arms wrapped around herself and walked as fast as she could, hoping the exertion would warm her. They were less than halfway across the grass when a series of clicking sounds broke the silence.

"What's that?" Evan asked, pausing.

"I'm not sure," Lacey replied, stopping as well. Suddenly dozens of slim metal pipes popped up from the ground. Realization hit her at the exact instant her midsection was blasted with a spray of icy cold water.

Frozen in place by shock, she sucked in a breath, then gasped. "It's the—"

"Sprinklers. Got it. Got it right in the ass, actually. Cripes. Could this night get any worse?"

"Please, do *not* ask that question. I did earlier and found out that, yeah, it could." She hissed in another sharp breath as a barrage of frigid water slashed across her midsection like a wet machine-gun blast.

"Well, let's not stand here and get even wetter." He grabbed her hand and started across the lawn at a brisk jog.

Lacey did her best to keep pace with him as they ducked and dodged in vain, trying to avoid the sweeping arcs of water, but given that he was a good six inches taller than her and she felt like a human Popsicle, it wasn't easy. In fact the only part of her that didn't feel like an icicle was her hand, which was wrapped in the warmth of his—a surprisingly tingly warmth that felt suspiciously like a…sizzle? Nah. Couldn't be.

They were nearing the end of the lawn, the door to Constant Cravings a mere ten yards away, when she lost her footing on the wet grass. She cried out, involuntarily tightening her grip on

Evan's hand in an attempt to stay upright. But her feet flew out from under her and she went down with a bone-jarring thud, landing flat on her back on the soggy lawn. Before she could catch her breath, a heavy weight landed on top of her and what little air remained in her lungs *whooshed* out.

She looked up and found herself staring into Evan's wet face and startled eyes, which hovered only inches above her own. For several stunned seconds it felt as if her heart had halted along with her breath as she became aware of his body pressing down on hers. It had been a long time since she'd felt a man's weight on top of her. And... *Oh, my.* It was...nice.

"Jesus, Lacey..." He pushed himself up on his arms, but his lower body remained plastered against hers. His gaze scanned her face. "Are you all right?"

No, I don't think I am. And I think it's all your fault. She shifted beneath him, then froze at the slide of her drenched body against the hard form above her, the drag of her pelvis across his. His eyes widened slightly at the movement and then he went perfectly still. Well, not quite perfectly still. No, there seemed to be one part of him that was, um, rising to the occasion. In the most fascinating way.

Holy cow. Wasn't ice-cold water supposed to have a shriveling effect on men? Well, either Evan was carrying around a zucchini in his pants or that shriveling theory had just been shot all to hell.

A muscle ticked in his jaw and he shifted off her, leaving her pressing her lips together to contain the protest that rose in her throat.

"Are you okay?" he asked again.

She managed to nod, then struggled to sit up. Evan lightly clasped her shoulders and the warmth of his palms heated her skin even through her wet shirt. Staring into his eyes, she had to swallow twice to locate her voice. "I'm—"

Splat. A blast of cold sprinkler water hit her squarely on the cheek. The sprinkler continued its arc and swished water across

Evan's forehead. A ferocious frown bunched his face while droplets dripped off his nose and chin, and in spite of her discomfort, Lacey coughed to disguise the giggle that bubbled into her throat.

"I'm fine," she managed to say. "Cold and wet, but fine."

"Good." He stood, then held out his hands to help her. "Let's get out of here before we need to build a raft and paddle out." Even as he said the words, arc after relentless arc of water pelted them.

Lacey gripped his hands, but when she stood, a sharp pain in her ankle made her cry out. "Yee-ouch," she said with a gasp, hopping on her other foot. "Damn. I think I twisted my ankle."

"It hurts?"

Relieved that the odd sexual current she'd felt was now gone, she shot him a glare, one that most likely lost some of its potency due to the sopping wet hair sticking to her face as if glued to her skin. "Yes, it hurts. That would be why I yelled 'ouch.'"

She'd expected him to offer her a hand, perhaps wrap an arm around her to help her walk, but instead he dipped his knees and before she knew what was happening, he'd swung her up into his arms and was striding toward Constant Cravings.

"Wh…what are you doing?"

"I would think that's obvious," he said, his tone the only dry thing about him. "I'm carrying you the rest of the way."

"I can walk," she felt compelled to say, even as her hand curved around his wet neck. "Or at least hobble."

"Uh-huh. At a rate that will get us away from these sprinklers sometime next week." He stepped onto the sidewalk, out of the sprinklers' range, then headed toward the green-and-white striped awning over Constant Cravings' door.

"Pretty impressive for a guy who sits behind a desk all day," she said.

"I don't sit behind a desk *all* the time."

"Still, I'm not exactly a flyweight."

"You're…" His voice trailed off and his gaze skimmed down her form. A muscle ticked in his jaw, then his eyes raised back to hers. "Fine. Not heavy." Water from his hair and face dripped onto her chest as he stopped in front of the shop's glass door. "Where's the key?"

"In my purse." She bit her lower lip. "Which I dropped when I fell."

"I don't suppose you picked it up again?"

"Well, I would have if someone hadn't turned all he-man and scooped me up like a sack of potatoes and stomped off with me."

"Well, excu-u-u-use me for trying to help. Next time I'll leave you flat on your back on the cold, wet grass."

A fissure of shame shivered through her. "Point taken. You're right, and I'm sorry. I appreciate the help."

His eyebrows raised, then narrowed with suspicion. "Did you hit your head when you fell?"

"Ha-ha. No. But I'm woman enough to admit when I'm wrong and apologize."

"Apology accepted. And I didn't *stomp*."

"If you say so."

"Now about your purse…" He turned and she followed his gaze. Her purse sat like an oversized lump on the soaking-wet no-man's land where they'd fallen.

A moan escaped her. "I think I'm in mourning. That bag was brand new. And suede."

"Mourn later. Right now I need to get the bag, which means I need to put you down." He gently lowered her legs, sliding her thighs down his torso. He felt hard and strong and muscular and a sensation akin to standing too close to a brush fire whipped through her. When she sucked in a hard breath, he paused in the act of slipping his arm from around her legs and looked at her.

"Did I hurt you?"

His compelling gaze seemed to pin her in place. And his voice…it sounded deep and slightly husky. As if he'd just awakened—after a night spent indulging in no-holds-barred sex. His warm breath brushed over her cold lips and she realized with a jolt how close his mouth was to hers. A mouth that somehow managed to look both soft and firm at the same time.

At that instant she underwent some sort of surreal out of body experience where, as if from a distance, she saw herself lean forward and kiss him. She blinked and the image—or mirage or whatever it was—disappeared like a puff of smoke blown away by the wind, leaving a trail of heated awareness in its wake.

"Lacey, did I hurt you?"

The unmistakable note of concern in his voice yanked her back. Not trusting her own voice she simply shook her head.

"Brace your hand against the wall and keep your weight off your injured ankle." After she'd done so and gained her balance, he gently released her.

"You okay to stand like that for a minute while I get your purse, or do you need to sit down?"

"I'm fine," she said, not at all sure she was, in a way that had nothing to do with her throbbing ankle and everything to do with the way he'd felt pressed against her. And the way his wet dress shirt clung to his body—his obviously *very nice* body—as if it were painted on. "Go." *Now. Quick. Before I reach out and grab you. And run my hands over your chest and abs to see if they're really as incredible as they look. Then peek down your pants to see if what I felt on the lawn lives up to its promise—*

"Ack!" When the horrified sound escaped her, he hesitated. She waved her hand at him, hoping the motion didn't look as frantic as it felt. "I'm fine. Really. Go."

He gave a nod, then headed briskly back into the water-spewing arena. Her gaze zeroed in on his wide back, then cruised down to his butt—all perfectly outlined in his sopping clothes.

Whew. No doubt about it, Evan Sawyer had hit some sort of genetic lottery. Still, Madame Karma had been certifiable to suggest he was Mr. Right.

But, wow.

Unfortunately, "wow" was the exact opposite of how she should be reacting to him.

So…what the heck was she going to do about it?

4

EVAN STRODE TOWARD Lacey's purse, grateful for the blasts of cold water pelting him. Because he sure as hell needed cooling off.

What in God's name was wrong with him?

A humorless sound escaped him. Stupid question. He knew damn well what was wrong. The problem was that he could still feel the imprint of her on his body. Could still see the awareness dawning in her eyes as she lay beneath him. Still recall the erotic sensation of her wet body sliding against his. Still smell the subtle scent that had risen from her damp skin—a mismatched combination of sugar and flowers that logically should not have been appealing or sexy. Yet it was. Shockingly so.

As was his reaction to her. He couldn't recall the last time he'd gotten so turned on so fast. He'd looked down at her, into those wide eyes, seen those moist, full, parted lips, and he'd gone from zero to rock hard in a heartbeat. A physical reaction she'd clearly noticed. One he'd been helpless to stop. And was now equally helpless to explain.

Oh, sure, she was attractive—but why *her?* She was so completely not his type it was laughable. Why did it have to be her—the one woman who irritated him beyond belief—who had his damn libido clenched into a wad?

His jaw tightened. Damn it, this entire mess was that crazy fortune-teller's fault. Ever since she'd read his cards earlier today he hadn't been able to stop thinking about her words. Which was insane because he didn't put any credence into things like psychic abilities. The fact that Madame Karma had hit so eerily close to home on what she'd said about his past and present was simply a case of clever word manipulation. The things she'd told him could apply to ninety-nine percent of the population. After all, show him a person who, by the age of thirty-two, hadn't endured some hardships, heartaches and bumps in the road, and he'd show you a person who'd spent the last three decades living in a sterile room.

And then, what she'd said about his future… He blew out a quick breath filled with disbelief. A bunch of nonsense about his "aura" and about his "soul mate" being right under his nose.

In the form of Lacey Perkins.

The same weird sensation gripped his insides now as when she'd first uttered her bizarre prediction. Probably indigestion. He shouldn't have eaten that spicy sausage hero, especially on the heels of his visit to Madame Karma's table.

He'd wasted no time telling the woman that she couldn't be more wrong, but she'd stared at him with those unnerving dark eyes of hers and had insisted, stating that both his aura and the cards plainly indicated that Lacey Perkins was Ms. Right.

What a boatload of crap.

He reached the purse, bent down to retrieve it—a move that resulted in another bull's-eye-like sprinkler blast to his ass—and with a grunt straightened and tucked the soaking wet bundle under his arm. Turning, he started navigating his way back toward Constant Cravings. Where Lacey awaited him. Standing beneath the awning, illuminated by the silvery glow of the full moon. Looking so damn sexy and hot he was surprised smoke wasn't rising from her.

The fact that he was having these outlandish sexual thoughts about her was obviously nothing more than the power of suggestion. Madame Karma had suggested, very mistakenly, that in spite of his knowledge otherwise, he and Lacey were compatible in every way—mentally, emotionally and sexually. And now that the stupid seed had been planted, it had, against his will, taken root. Sort of like the way a person got a song stuck in their head.

Damn it, he hated when that happened. Sometimes it took days to exorcise the melody. Last time it had happened, the song had been "The Itsy Bitsy Spider," which he'd sung a couple of dozen times, much to the delight of his next-door neighbors' four-year-old son, who'd "helped" him wash his car. Unfortunately it had taken more than a week to clear the words from his brain.

Good God. What if it took that long to empty his mind of these crazy thoughts about Lacey? Thoughts about slowly peeling the wet clothes off that outrageously curvy body. Thoughts about tasting that full, pouty mouth, which had been only inches away from his. Although, if he were to be *completely* honest, he'd thought about peeling off her clothes long before tonight. If he were to be completely honest, he'd entertained those thoughts the instant she'd asked him if he'd like a Slow Glide into Pleasure. Fortunately, up until now, he'd been able to shove those thoughts aside. Most of the time. But now?

His gaze fastened on her, on the sight of her clothes clinging to her like a second skin, and the impact nearly knocked him off his feet—in a way that had nothing to do with the slippery grass. Holy crap. If he managed to get away from her without putting his hands—and mouth—on her it was going to be a freaking miracle.

Yet surely the only reason he was losing his mind was because she was *wet*. There was just something irrationally sexy and fantasy-inducing about a wet woman. Once she was dry, he'd be fine. Absolutely. Probably.

Hopefully.

After one last sprinkler blast to his back, he joined her beneath the awning and held out her soggy purse.

"Thanks," she murmured.

As soon as she'd unlocked the door, he scooped her up into his arms, absolutely not noticing how soft and incredible she felt pressed against him.

"It's really not necessary for you carry me," she said, but her protest sounded somewhat half-hearted. In fact, her voice sounded kinda breathy. And husky. And sexy as hell.

Once again his brain—which was very emphatically instructing him not to look at her—and his eyeballs—which were in full ogling mode—disagreed with each other, and the eyeballs won. He looked down, saw those huge eyes, those full lips, that mass of wet curly hair, and *whammo*. It was like he'd been clocked by a brick.

With an effort he roused himself from the stupor she'd somehow put him in and entered the store, pushing the door closed behind them with his foot.

"It might not be necessary to carry you, but I lugged you this far, so a few more feet won't kill me." Hmm. Not necessarily true as having her wet curves pressed against him really was killing him. He cleared his throat. "Let's see what's going on with your ankle. Then we can argue about whether or not you can walk without assistance."

He headed for the nearest chair, an overstuffed leather sofa set along the wall near the door, but she shook her head, spraying him with droplets of water. "Not there. I don't want to ruin my vintage sofa. The counter is fine."

He did as she requested and set her down on the glossy countertop next to the cash register. "Where are the lights?"

"Next to the door, right-hand side."

He made his way back to the door, then flicked the switch, flooding the room with light. Blinking against the brightness, he walked back to the cash register. Lacey had removed her shoe and hiked up her pant leg. With her leg stuck straight out, she slowly rotated her ankle.

His gaze zeroed in on the wet skin of her leg. Her very shapely, wet leg. That slowly circling ankle was lulling him into a trance…round and round. Damn, even her feet, with their fire-engine-red polished toes, were sexy.

He forced his gaze away from her bare leg, but found no relief when his errant eyeballs roamed upward. Her soaking wet white shirt covered her about as effectively as cellophane. Any question he might have harbored regarding what sort of bras she favored was answered right then and there—lacey and flimsy. He could see the shadows of her erect nipples through the material. What felt like a gallon of blood gushed from his already addled brain straight to his groin.

Two seconds ago he'd been cold. Now he felt as if steam could pump from his pores.

Enough. He was a grown man for cryin' out loud, not some horny frat boy. He gave himself a sharp mental shake and forced his gaze from her distracting and oh so tempting nipples.

"How does it feel?" he asked. *Hard and aching,* his inner voice chimed in, answering his own question. He silently told the pesky voice to shut the hell up.

"It barely hurts. Look." She waggled her bare foot. "It's not even swollen. I think the worst injury was to my pride. At least I can be thankful I wasn't wearing a skirt when I fell ass over backward."

"Right." Because then he would have seen her ass. Encased in… *What sort of panties does she wear? Something lacy and flimsy to match that bra? Or maybe she doesn't even wear panties—*

"Are you okay, Evan?"

Hell, no. "Heck, yes."

"You sure? You look…flushed."

Good God. "It's the lighting in here. And the exertion of, um, carrying you."

Her eyes narrowed. "You insinuating I'm fat?"

He latched on to the speck of annoyance like a lifeline. Anything to diffuse the lust raging through him. "Why do women always ask questions like that?"

"Why do men always make statements that can be interpreted as that?"

"I wasn't insinuating anything. And you're not fat. You're…"

"I'm what?"

Gorgeous. Sexy. Making my heart pound so hard it's going to crack my ribs. "Looking for compliments, Lacey?"

Her eyebrows rose. "A compliment? From you? Hardly. I'd be stunned into silence if one passed your lips."

"Well, if that's the only way to shut you up, I'll play. You're…curvy."

A snorting sound escaped her and her lips twitched. "Gee, thanks. You entice many women with smooth lines like that?"

"I meant it as a compliment," he said through clenched teeth, not sure if he was more irritated at her for being amused or at himself for sounding like a jackass.

"Oh. Uh, thanks. I think." She glanced down at her bare foot. "I probably should put some ice on my ankle."

"Ice. Right. Good idea. Something icy cold is just what I, I mean you, need."

She wrapped her arms around herself. "Although how I'm going to stand having ice on me I don't know. I'm already freezing." As if to prove her words, her teeth chattered.

When it looked as if she meant to get down from the counter, he said, "Stay put. I'll get the ice. But first, why don't you let me have a look?"

The instant he spoke the words he regretted them. Looking at her ankle would mean moving closer to her. Touching her. And those were the last things he wanted. Really.

But this time it was his brain and his feet that disagreed because seconds later he stood in front of her. His gaze flicked down to her ankle. "May I?"

She set her palms on the counter and leaned forward, a position that afforded him a heart-pounding view of her generous cleavage. "I wouldn't have thought you the sort of guy who'd be polite enough to ask before you touched."

"I guess there's a lot you don't know about me. Now, are you going to let me take a look, or are we just going to remain here and freeze?" Freeze? Definitely an impossibility as far as he was concerned. The way she was looking at him, with those big caramel-colored eyes, made him feel as if fire were about to spew from his scalp.

Keeping her gaze steady on his, she raised her foot and rested it against his belly, a move that had him sucking in a quick breath. There was no missing the challenge in her eyes. "By all means. Look all you want."

He lightly grasped her ankle and gently prodded her soft, damp skin. And told his raging libido to behave.

"What does a property manager know about ankles?" she asked.

"I put in some time as a camp counselor and a few summers as a lifeguard. It's been a while, but I remember the basics." He gently rotated her ankle. "Does that hurt?"

"No."

He felt the weight of her stare as he continued to manipulate her ankle. Her very shapely ankle. That he really needed to let go of. Now.

But instead of doing so, he looked up. And found her staring at him. In a very distracting way. His fingers stilled. Her tongue peeked out, a flick of pink that tensed his every muscle.

"Well?" she whispered.

"Well what?"

"What's the verdict?"

I'm guilty of extreme lust by reason of temporary insanity.

When he remained silent, she prompted, "My ankle?"

Her words brought him back with a jolt. Good God, maybe he really was insane. "It's fine," he said, ignoring his brain's command to release her. Instead his thumbs lightly massaged her instep. "No need to call in a surgical team."

"That's…um…" Her foot flexed in his hand. "Oooh. Good. Really good." Her eyes drifted closed and a long sigh escaped her, a sigh that ended on a husky moan that shifted his libido into overdrive. "Soooo good." After another deep moan, her eyes slid slowly open and his fingers stilled at the unmistakable arousal he saw.

"Evan…I think we should take off our clothes."

5
_____

LACEY'S BREATH CAUGHT at the fire that flared in Evan's eyes at her words. There was no mistaking that heated glitter for anything other than what it was.

Arousal.

Pure lust swamped her, an unstoppable wave of the very sexual longing she'd been desperately trying to hold back since the moment he'd clasped her hand for their ill-fated dash across the lawn. No doubt about it, Evan Sawyer had everything female in her standing at attention and saluting.

And she'd been doing a damn good job of controlling her libido, if she said so herself, especially given the incredible way he'd felt lying on top of her. The delicious press of his body against hers when he'd carried her. The warm strength of his hands massaging her ankle and foot. Why, she deserved an Academy Award for managing to retain her air of aloofness.

But now, now that he was looking at her like this—as if she were a bowl of cream and he was a very large, very hungry cat—her resolve to stay indifferent was dissolving at an alarming rate.

"Take off our clothes?" he repeated in a husky rasp that instantly brought to mind naked entwined bodies and rumpled sheets. "But Lacey…we haven't even kissed yet."

The sound of her name whispered from those gorgeous lips shot heated tingles straight to her womb. Surely the reason she opened her mouth was to inform him that she'd merely meant they should put on something dry, but any words she might have spoken turned into a shocked gasp of pleasure when he raised her foot and pressed his lips to her inner ankle.

Fire sizzled through her. Holy cow. His mouth looked positively sinful pressed against her. And felt positively sinful, too. His teeth lightly grazed her skin, and before her mind could process all the jolts of pleasure shooting up her calf, he lowered her ankle and stepped between her legs. Tunneling his hands into her wet hair, he slowly lowered his head. Anticipation pumped through her, and she parted her lips.

His mouth settled on hers and Lacey felt as if everything inside her melted. Good God, the man knew how to kiss. He tasted warm and delicious and the sensation of his tongue exploring her mouth pulsed heat to her every nerve ending. She ran her hands up his chest, over his broad shoulders, then skimmed her fingers through the thick wet silk of his hair. All thoughts of time and place evaporated in a haze of lust. Her every heartbeat seemed to reverberate with the word *more*. Taste more. Touch more. Feel more.

Want more. Need more.

Too soon, much too soon, he raised his head. A groan of protest rose in her throat and she forced her eyes open. Evan was staring at her as if he'd never seen her before. His hair was rumpled from her impatient fingers and he was breathing hard.

She had to swallow to find her voice. "Wow."

He blinked several times, as if coming out of a trance. She knew exactly how he felt. After clearing his throat, he said, "Yeah. Wow."

"What the heck *was* that?"

"You mean besides amazing? I'm not sure." He leaned forward and nuzzled the sensitive skin behind her ear with his warm lips. "I think we should do it again to find out."

His tongue lightly flicked her earlobe and she actually felt her eyes glaze over. Okay, this guy's effect on her just wasn't *right*. One kiss and one tiny tongue flick shouldn't make her feel as if she were a rocket about to explode into orbit. A fissure of common sense worked its way through the fog of desire surrounding her and she clapped her hands against his chest, then gently pushed him back.

"Not so fast, bucko." She needed to think for a minute or two. Bracing her hands on the counter, she slid down until her feet touched the floor then eased from his grasp—and immediately missed the warmth of his strong hands on her skin. But because he was so very tempting, it was essential she put some space between them, at least until her head quit spinning. After an experimental shake of her ankle, which didn't produce any pain, she took several steps away from him.

"I think we should concentrate on doing what we came here to do." And she'd make sure they did—as soon as she remembered what the heck it was.

"You mean calling for roadside assistance?"

"Exactly." Hey, she would have remembered. Eventually. As soon as her raging hormones had quit buzzing.

"*I* wasn't the one who suggested we take off our clothes."

Annoyance threaded through her at his smug tone, thankfully dissipating a bit more of the sensual fog that had caught her so unawares. "I *meant* I wanted to get out of these wet clothes," she informed him, proud of the cool disdain in her voice. "I'm cold and uncomfortable." Or at least she'd been cold a few minutes ago. Now she was just uncomfortable. "Aren't you?"

"Cold? No. Actually, I'm the exact opposite of cold—all your fault, by the way. And do you really think getting naked is going to make us more comfortable?"

"I didn't mean for us to be naked." *Liar!* her conscience shouted. Especially given the preview his wet clothing provided—muscular chest, toned abs, slim hips, long legs. Her gaze settled on his groin. His clinging pants proved he was as affected by that kiss as she. And he was clearly *still* affected— as was she. A rumble of admiring approval rose in her throat and she quickly swallowed it.

"That's what usually happens when you take off your clothes."

His voice jerked her back and she yanked her gaze upward. "Huh?"

"You get naked when you take off your clothes."

"Okay. Sounds good to me." She mentally thumped herself on the forehead. "I mean we should change into dry clothes."

"That would be nice, but I'm afraid I don't carry around a spare outfit."

"Neither do I. But it just so happens that I have a spare set of clothes for each of us at my disposal." She nodded toward the front window. "Courtesy of my mannequins."

He turned his head toward the window, then slowly turned back to her. "You can't be serious."

"Why not? You have another suggestion? Other than staying in these sopping clothes and catching pneumonia?"

"Personally, I preferred the 'get naked' suggestion."

"There was no 'get naked' suggestion."

"No? Well, I'd be happy to make one." He erased the distance between them in one step. The fire in his eyes made her feel as if someone had poured a vat of warm honey over her body. Her breath caught when he reached out and lightly clasped her hands, entwining their fingers. "Wanna get naked?"

"I do—" The truth shot from her mouth like a speeding bullet, appalling her. Good grief, she sounded like a desperate, horny, Valentine's Day–dateless nympho. And hey, maybe she *was* one, but she needed to recall that this was Mr. Thorn-in-her-side, and that he didn't need to know. Hadn't she embarrassed herself enough already?

"—not," she added, coughing twice for good measure. "I do *not* want to get naked. What I *do* want is to call roadside assistance. Then I want to change into dry clothing. Then I want a cup of coffee. And a cookie. Then I want to drive home. And forget this evening ever happened." *Good luck with that last bit,* her inner voice sneered, to which she issued her inner voice a stern mental *shut up.*

He studied her for several long seconds, and she found herself holding her breath, a part of her desperately wanting him to just yank her against him and stun her with another hypnotic kiss. Instead, he gave a tight nod, then released her hands and stepped back.

"Good idea," he said. "Is your roadside assistance American Car Association?"

"Yes. Isn't everyone's?"

"Probably. That's who I use. How about I make the call while you, um, change your clothes."

"Deal. Then I'll put on the coffee."

"Deal."

After nodding toward the counter where he'd sat her, she said, "The phone's on the back wall." She watched him turn and walk toward the counter, then forced herself to head to the front window so as not to stand there and gawk at his very fine butt.

Now that she wasn't plastered against Evan, the chill of her wet clothes penetrated through to her skin. With quick efficiency she stripped the female mannequin of her dress, making a mental note to arrive at the store extra early in the morning so she could re-dress her props. If Mr. Thorn-in-her-side freaked over a display featuring fully dressed mannequins, he'd throw an absolute conniption over naked ones.

Although…for a guy she'd thought to be completely uptight, he'd clearly been more than willing to get naked with her—

Stop it, Lacey, she commanded herself. Do *not* think of him naked. In fact, don't think of him *at all.* Sadly that proved difficult, especially while she stripped her male mannequin. Holding the two sets of clothes, she stepped from the window. Her gaze instantly found Evan and saw him hanging up the phone.

"The Car Association said they'd have someone here in about an hour, hour and a half. I told them to come here, to the store, so we don't have to wait outside."

"Great." She held out the robe and matching boxers. "Here you go. Dry clothes."

He crossed his arms over his chest. "I am not putting on that ridiculous robe."

She took immediate umbrage. "It's not ridiculous. It's *romantic*—something you obviously know nothing about."

"I know plenty about romantic, and let me tell you straight up, that robe ain't it. No self-respecting guy would wear that. It's got pink hearts on it, for cryin' out loud."

"Uh-huh. And what do you know about fashion? You who I've never seen wear anything other than an uptight suit and tie?"

"I know enough not to wear that." He jabbed his index finger toward the bundle she held. "And you had your chance to see me wearing a hell of a lot less than my uptight suit and tie, so don't blame me."

"Has anyone ever told you you're very arrogant?"

"Has anyone ever told you you're extremely annoying?"

"I'm suddenly remembering all the reasons I don't like you." She stomped over to the counter and slapped down the robe and boxers. "If you want to stay in your wet clothes and catch a chill while your skin grows pruney, be my guest. I'm going into the back room to change."

With that, she marched toward the rear of the store, head held high. Just before she slammed the door behind her, she heard him call out, "I am *not* going to wear that goofy robe!"

6

EVAN COULDN'T BELIEVE he was wearing the goofy robe.

He looked down at himself and grimaced at the sight of his bare legs and feet beneath the robe's hem. Good God. If Paul saw him wearing this getup, his friend would laugh himself into a seizure. Actually, *anyone* who saw him wearing this would laugh.

Why the hell couldn't Lacey have dressed her stupid mannequin in something a normal guy would wear? Like maybe shorts and a polo shirt? He had to grudgingly admit that the goofy robe was a huge improvement over his cold, wet, sticky clothes, which had started to chafe, but still. And as long as he already felt like an ass, he figured what the hell and had donned the matching boxers—but only because his own boxer briefs had been so damn wet and uncomfortable.

Well, he'd just keep the freakin' robe belted shut and pretend he was wearing his own clothes. Pretend he was home in his own apartment. Pretend he was with anyone other than Lacey.

Lacey. Whose skin felt like satin and tasted like sugar-sprinkled flowers. Lacey, whose potent kiss had fired through his system like a shot of straight whiskey burning its way down to an empty stomach. Lacey, who was right now walking toward him from the back of the store, her hourglass curves encased in the mannequin's skimpy red dress in a way that literally knocked the air from his lungs.

Jesus. The woman not only knew how to kiss, she knew how to move. Her hips undulated with a slow, sexy, mesmerizing roll that made him feel like one of those cartoon characters whose eyeballs *boinged* out on springs. He'd never seen her wear anything other than her work outfit of black pants and white top. If he had a vote, he'd cast it in favor of her wearing that dress every damn day. It made her look incredible. And downright edible. The bright cherry-red perfectly set off her creamy skin and contrasted with the mass of damp, glossy midnight curls falling just shy of her shoulders. She looked like the perfect embodiment of his every fantasy.

She headed behind the counter and reached for a coffeepot. Her gaze flicked over him and her lips twitched. "Decided not to grow pruney, I see."

"Don't you dare laugh."

"I won't laugh if you won't." She grimaced, then tugged on the short hem of the dress while performing some sort of all-over shimmy that had him stirring against the satin boxers. "This dress doesn't exactly fit. My mannequin is a few sizes smaller than me. Thank God the material is stretchy."

Yeah. God definitely needed to be thanked for the way that dress fit her. "Looks good to me. Perfect, in fact."

Surprise flickered in her eyes. "Another compliment? I'm stunned. But in keeping with this apparent détente, I'll offer a compliment in return. That robe has never looked so good."

The unmistakable appreciation in her eyes told him she wasn't kidding, and his pulse rate kicked up another couple of notches. Apparently some women didn't mind men dressed in goofy robes decorated with pink hearts. Go figure. "Thank you. So…truce?"

"Truce." Her smile flashed. "At least until the auto service people arrive. Then all bets are off. You want regular or decaf?"

"Regular. I don't want to fall asleep on the drive home. Need help?"

"Thanks, but I think I can handle a pot of coffee."

In an effort to concentrate on something other than her, he turned his attention to the eclectic mix of collages and photographs decorating the walls while she ground fresh beans, filling the air with the rich scent of coffee. How had she made a mismatched collection work together so well? The collages featured themes as varied as desserts and classic movies, and the photographs displayed everything from flowers to skyscrapers. The effect was vivid and eye-catching. Just as she was. And it occurred to him that the store was a perfect reflection of her.

"Those are from my mother's garden," she said when he paused in front of a whitewashed framed photo depicting a crystal vase overflowing with puffy pale pink blooms.

"I've seen these flowers before. What are they?"

"Peonies. I gave my mom that plant for Mother's Day several years ago. They're my favorite flower and my favorite scent."

Ah. Finally a name to put to the subtle floral fragrance that clung to her skin. "Did you take this picture?"

"Yes. I had a lot of wall space to cover in here and couldn't afford anything fancy, so I grabbed my trusty camera and voilà— instant artwork. I also made all the collages."

His eyebrows shot up in surprise. "They're really good."

"Thanks. Making them is very relaxing. I put on some music, enjoy a glass of wine and let my imagination flow."

He pointed toward a turquoise-framed collage of beach scenes on the wall behind her. "That's what I find relaxing. Being near the beach."

"Hey, we might want to videotape this moment because it appears we actually agree on something. I call the beach my tranquil place. The sound of the ocean, the salty breezes, the sand between my toes…" She breathed out a sigh. "Someday I hope to buy a home right on the beach."

"Same here. Where I can sit on my balcony and enjoy the view of the ocean with my morning coffee."

"And my after-dinner coffee." Her smile bloomed, creasing those sexy dimples into her cheeks and any relaxation he'd achieved over the last few minutes was shot to hell. "If I had a balcony that overlooked the ocean, I'd stay out there all day. Every day. I'd probably want to sleep out there."

"Again we agree," he murmured, instantly imagining her curled against him as they lay beneath the stars, surrounded by the gentle crash of waves washing on the shore.

"Wow. Two agreements in a row. Who'da thought?"

"Not me." Yet it was becoming clearer with each passing minute that there was more to this woman than just killer curves, a defiant attitude and a propensity to annoy him. He nodded toward another collage, this one of puppies, and he couldn't help but grin. "This one's great. You have a dog?"

She shook her head. "Had one growing up. A golden Lab named Lucky. I'd love to have one now, but there's a No Pets rule in my apartment building."

He approached the counter and watched her fill two thick ceramic mugs with fresh brew. "My dog's part golden Lab, at least I think she is. Based on her size, I think the other part is St. Bernard."

She looked up from her pouring. "You have a dog?"

"A big, sloppy, lovable four-year-old who drowns everyone she meets with wet kisses."

"You somehow don't strike me as the big, sloppy dog type."

"Guess I'm just full of surprises."

Their eyes met. "I guess so," she said softly. "What's your dog's name?"

"Sasha. I adopted her six months ago when I went with Paul to a shelter just north of L.A. because *he* wanted to adopt a dog. Sasha and I took one look at each other and it was love at first sight. Only problem is the language barrier."

"Sorry?"

"The family who used to own Sasha only spoke Russian. Dog doesn't understand a word of English."

She stared at him for several seconds, then laughed. "You're kidding."

"I kid you not. And my Russian doesn't go much beyond *caviar* and *vodka*."

She shook her head and chuckled. "I've never heard of such a thing."

"Me, neither. So if you happen to know any handy Russian commands such as *sit, heel, stay* or *don't eat my flip-flops,* let me know."

She snickered. "Sasha eats your flip-flops?"

"*Eats* probably isn't the right way to describe it. It's more like she gnaws them to death. But just my flip-flops. Luckily she doesn't seem to like dress shoes or sneakers."

"Who takes care of her when you're at work?"

"I have a dog walker. On nights when I work extra late, like tonight, my neighbor checks in on her."

She slid the mugs across the counter. "Why don't you take those to a table while I get the cookies?"

He picked up the cups, then crossed the room to set them on a small, round, glass-top table situated between two comfy-looking chairs. She joined him seconds later, setting down a plate containing two oversized cookies. She sat in the chair opposite him and although he tried, he couldn't help but notice how her short skirt scooted even higher on her thighs when she sat.

With an effort he pulled his gaze from the long expanse of silky leg and focused on the red and pink frosted lip-shaped cookies. "Are these the cookies you mentioned earlier today?" he asked. "The ones you call Bite Me?"

"They are." Handing him a napkin, she invited, "Help yourself."

Given how delectable her thighs looked, a cookie wasn't even close to what he wanted to bite. But since she'd only offered a cookie—for now—he accepted. The first bite had his eyes glazing over.

"Wow. That is one outrageously good cookie."

"Thank you. It took a lot of trial and error to perfect the recipe."

"Mission accomplished. You know a cookie's outstanding when you can actually feel your arteries harden."

She laughed. "If I could only figure out a way to keep the texture and flavor yet make them calorie free, I'd be a zillion-aire. At least for you, being a guy and all, desserts don't take up permanent residence on your hips. I wish someone would invent a home liposuction kit. Something that could be hooked up to your vacuum cleaner. Or your car battery."

"Wouldn't work for you. Your car battery's dead."

"Ha, ha."

He took a sip of coffee and closed his eyes in appreciation. She not only knew how to kiss and move, she baked the World's Greatest Cookies and brewed the World's Best Coffee. Damn. That was a pretty lethal combination. Why the hell didn't he like her? He knew he had reasons. Lots of them. But damned if he could remember what they were. Better get her talking again—surely she'd say something that would jog his memory.

"Since I told you all about my language-challenged relationship with Sasha, now it's your turn."

"My turn for what?"

"To tell me something about you I don't know."

She leaned back in her chair and studied him over the rim of her steaming mug. "What do you want to know?"

Everything. The realization hit him squarely between the eyes, catching him off guard, yet it was undeniable. Keeping his tone light, he said, "Anything. Why don't you tell me about your family? Any more at home like you?"

She shook her head. "I have one sister, Meg, but we look nothing alike and are so completely different in every way, people who know us both can't believe we're actually related."

"Different how?"

"Meg was the gorgeous, popular, outgoing cheerleader with straight blond hair. I wore glasses, had braces, was self-conscious, shy and a total klutz. And I was stuck with this." She grabbed a handful of her curly hair and gave it a gentle tug. "When we were growing up, Meg wasn't exactly sensitive or sympathetic to my less than spectacular appearance. We're close now, but as kids, it was tough. To this day she still calls me Dimples just to piss me off."

His gaze dipped to the sexy creases that flanked her gorgeous mouth. "Seems to be a perfect nickname—you have a great pair."

"Thanks. Except when Meg foisted the name on me I was a toddler, and she was referring to the dimples on my butt. Thank goodness I ended up with them on my face so I didn't have to spend my life explaining what the name really meant."

He chuckled, then asked, "What's your nickname for her?"

"Prom Queen. I think she must hold some world record for attending proms." She took another sip of coffee and a wistful expression filled her eyes. "When we were growing up, I would have given anything to look like her. To be like her. But now…now I wouldn't trade places with her for any amount."

"Why's that?"

She hesitated, as if debating whether or not to tell him, then said, "She's been married for six years and things aren't going well. Unfortunately, Meg's husband Dan is a carbon copy of our dad—financially successful but emotionally unavailable. She has a beautiful home, two terrific kids, every material possession she could ever hope for, but Dan's first, second and third priorities are his career. Meg and the kids are a distant fourth."

"That's too bad."

"It is. They separated once, three years ago, but after going to counseling they reconciled. Yet nothing's changed. I give her credit for not wanting to give up on her marriage, but under all the material things she just seems so…lonely. Just like our mom was."

"Your parents divorced?"

She shook her head. "My dad died when I was in high school. I'd lived with him my entire life, yet I barely knew him. He was always working or on a business trip, always too busy to play or go to the mall or come to school events. He never took time to enjoy life, to enjoy his wife or daughters. For a man who had such a strong drive to succeed, he couldn't see that he failed at the things that were most important. His family. His marriage." She looked down at her hands and when he followed her gaze, he saw how her fingers were clamped tightly together.

Reaching out, he laid his hand over hers. "I'm sorry, Lacey," he said quietly. "I know how much it hurts to lose a parent. I lost my mom five years ago. Cancer."

She looked up, her eyes full of sympathy. And something else. Surprise and confusion, as if she were seeing him for the first time—the exact way he knew he'd looked at her only moments earlier. "I'm so sorry, Evan."

"Me, too. She was a great lady and a terrific mom. Like you, I wasn't exactly a standout in school. I was the pudgy kid who always got teased, the nerd who sucked at sports and always got picked last in gym class."

Her eyebrows shot up. "You're kidding."

"I'm not. I kept trying at sports, but it was hopeless. Still, my mom always encouraged me, always cheered me on, even when I kicked the winning goal in soccer for the opposing team."

Her eyes widened. "I did the exact same thing. In fourth grade. I wanted to die. Instead my mom took me out for ice cream to celebrate that I'd scored my first goal."

"My mom took me for pizza." He smiled and squeezed her hand. Looking down, he saw the way his fingers were curled around hers. And liked the way it looked. Raising his gaze back to hers, he said, "Half an hour ago I wouldn't have believed it, but it seems we have a few things in common."

She nodded slowly, as if she couldn't quite believe it, either. "Seems so. What about your dad?"

"He died in a car crash when I was a baby. I don't remember him at all. It was always just me and my mom."

Her gaze searched his. "So you're alone."

Those softly spoken words resonated deep inside him. They weren't true—he had lots of friends, good neighbors, work colleagues, even some distant cousins who lived in Florida. But that wasn't what she meant and he knew it. She meant immediate family.

"I'm alone," he agreed. Because in spite of his friends and neighbors and colleagues, he indeed felt very alone. And had for a quite some time.

Until tonight.

He didn't feel alone here, in this coffee shop, talking to her. In fact, he felt…good. Really good. The evening, which had started out so disastrously with broken cars and cell phones, insane sprinklers and a ridiculous robe, had definitely taken an unexpected and—he had to admit—not unpleasant turn.

"No girlfriend?"

Her voice jerked him back. "No one steady. If there was, that kiss wouldn't have happened. I know you think I'm a pain in the ass and maybe I am, but I'm not a cheater."

A hint of rose blossomed on her cheeks. "Believe it or not, I haven't thought of you being a pain in the ass for at least five minutes."

"That makes two of us. And sets a new record. Wanna go for ten minutes?"

Her smile flashed. "Think we can make it?"

"I'm game."

"Okay. So tell me why you don't have a steady girlfriend. I mean, even though you're a pest, you should be able to get at least a first date just on the basis of your looks."

"Uh, thanks. I think. And I date. But lately…" He shrugged. "I've grown tired of the games. Which is why Sasha is working out so well. She's always happy to see me, doesn't mind me hogging the remote, never complains if I leave my clothes on the floor and she doesn't speak English."

Lacey laughed. "If you could just cure her of the flip-flop eating—"

"Gnawing to death," he corrected with a grin.

"She'd be perfect," they said in unison.

Their laughter slowly died and Evan became aware— painfully aware—of how close they sat. How romantic and intimate this setting was. How alone they were. How soft and smooth her hand felt beneath his. He brushed the pad of his thumb over the velvety soft skin of her fingers and the desire he'd successfully held in check shot to the surface.

Did she feel it, too? This sexually charged tension that suddenly seemed to crackle in the air between them? Based on her quick intake of breath and the heat kindling in her eyes, he was certain she did. But before he acted on it, there was something he wanted, needed, to know.

"What about you?" he asked. "Boyfriend?"

"No. At the risk of repeating your words verbatim, if there were, that kiss wouldn't have happened. I know you think I'm a pain in the ass and maybe I am, but I'm not a cheater."

"At the risk of repeating *your* words, you should be able to get at least a first date just on the basis of your looks."

"Actually, it feels as if I've had a first date with half the single guys in L.A. I've been through my share of bad relationships. But I figure you've got to go through the bad ones to get to a good one, and I must be due for a good one if for no other reason than the law of averages. But the men I meet somehow always turn out to be like my dad and brother-in-law—all work, no play, success at any cost. I call them soulless clones. Like you, I'm tired of games. At this point in my life, I'm not looking to impress a whole bunch of different guys. I'd rather impress the same guy over and over again."

"Shouldn't be too difficult. You're pretty impressive. Especially in that dress."

"Uh-huh. You're just saying that because you want another cookie."

"I wouldn't say no if you offered."

He knew his tone clearly implied he was talking about more than cookies, and for several seconds they simply stared at each other. Evan could almost hear her internally debating how, or even if, she should respond to his words. Would she play it safe? Or take a risk?

"Another cookie, coming right up," she murmured, then slowly rose. He watched her walk toward the counter, the rear view of her making him draw in several deep, careful breaths. When she reached the counter, she kept her back to him. Rising on her toes and bending forward—a move that nearly stopped his heart—she reached into the glass display case. Then she turned around and leaned her hips on the counter. The smoky look in her eyes arrowed a jolt of fire straight to his groin.

"Here it is," she said, waggling the cookie, her voice as smoky as her eyes. "Bite Me."

With him wearing the robe and her in that dress, offering him a cookie, it was as if the widow display had come to life, just as he'd fantasized earlier today. He didn't hesitate, but he had to force himself to stand slowly and cross to her with measured steps. He stopped when less than two feet separated them and planted his palms on the counter, caging her in.

"That's an offer I can't refuse." He leaned forward and lightly grazed his teeth down the side of her neck.

She moaned and tilted her head to the side, an invitation he immediately took advantage of, nipping his way up to her earlobe.

"Nice," he murmured against her fragrant skin. "But I think you should rename your cookie Kiss Me."

She let out a long, pleasure-filled sigh. "Okeydokey."

"You're very agreeable all of a sudden."

"I get that way when a sexy man is nibbling on my neck. Don't say I didn't warn you."

"Noted." He pressed his lips to the spot where her pulse throbbed. "But surely you don't think that's going to scare me off."

"I sure as hell hope not."

She turned her face toward him and with a growl he covered her mouth with his. Any thoughts he might have entertained that the sparks flying during their earlier kiss had been a fluke were instantly erased. He felt as if his circuits had been hooked up to a nuclear reactor and someone had flipped the switch.

He leaned into her, pressing his hardness against all that gorgeous, feminine softness and everything faded away except her. The way she felt in his arms—all curves and warmth. The taste of her in his mouth—cookies and frosting. The scent of her filling his head—sugar and peonies. With a deep groan, he ran his hands down her back, pressing her closer, kissing her deeper, his tongue exploring the satin of her mouth while he filled his palms with the round fullness of her bottom.

She squirmed against him, and his erection jerked, vibrating a ragged moan of pure desire in his throat. He couldn't recall ever wanting a woman this badly. A desperation he didn't recognize had him firmly in its grip, and apparently whatever insanity had come over him afflicted her as well because her hands were suddenly all over him. Inside his robe, coasting up his back then down to his ass, pulling him tighter against her.

A red, steamy haze of lust engulfed him and he lifted her onto the counter. She gasped an approving sound against his mouth and spread her legs. Evan stepped between her splayed thighs and trailed his lips across her throat while his hands tugged down the stretchy neckline of her dress. Her breasts sprang free, and he filled his hands with their warm fullness, teasing her already hard nipples between his fingers. His mouth cruised lower, circling the aroused peak with his tongue, then drawing the tight bud into his mouth.

"Evan…" She uttered his name in a passion-filled, husky groan and arched her back. She jerked the robe off his shoulders then ran her hands over his chest, down his back, setting bonfires on every inch of skin she touched.

His hands skimmed downward, over her incredible curves, to her silky smooth thighs, then under her dress. Where he encountered nothing but bare skin.

"No underwear," he growled, the discovery spiking the fever raging through him and he pushed the stretchy material up to her waist. Dipped his hand between her splayed thighs. Found her wet and hot.

She gasped as he slid two fingers into her silky heat. "Didn't think I'd, *ahhhh,* need it."

"You don't. Believe me, I'm not complaining."

Panting, she tugged his boxers over his hips, freeing his

erection, then stroked her fingers down its length. He sucked in a hissing breath and thrust into her hand.

"Condom," she said, leaning forward to nip his neck.

"In my wallet. On the other side of the room. Damn it."

"My purse. It's closer."

While he continued to stroke her, she reached behind her and dragged her wet purse forward. Something clattered to the floor. They ignored it. Muttering an impatient sound, she dumped her purse upside down, spilling an assortment of feminine stuff on the counter. He spied the condom and rolled on the protection as quickly as his unsteady fingers allowed. Then she wrapped her legs around his waist and he entered her in a single, deep thrust.

Their mutual groan filled the room. Her wet heat gripped him, and he withdrew nearly all the way, then sank deep again, experiencing the slow glide into pleasure he'd wanted since the moment he'd stepped into her store. Again, and again, the erotic pull of her body rendered him oblivious to everything except the intense pleasure. Her fingers dug into his back, and he gritted his teeth against the overwhelming need to come. When she threw back her head and gasped, he let himself go, thrusting deep, his orgasm rocketing through him.

When the shuddering ended, he tipped back his head and struggled to regain his breath. She dropped her forehead limply against his heaving chest, her ragged breaths pelting his skin.

A beeping sound broke through his postcoital fog, and he raised his head. And frowned. That beep was familiar.

"Is that a beeper?" Lacey asked, lifting her head. She looked as dazed and glazed as he felt.

Beeper. That noise was his business beeper going off. Reality returned with a jarring thump that felt like an anvil falling on his head. Jesus. What the hell was he doing? He'd just had sex with a tenant. He *never* had sex with tenants—it was one of his hard-and-fast rules. But one look at Lacey in that dress had morphed his hard-and-fast rule into a bout of hard-and-fast sex.

He stepped back and raked his hands through his hair. "My business beeper."

She stared at him for several seconds. "Business? At this hour? On a weekend?"

"It's my boss. He's in London this week. It's the afternoon there now. Doesn't matter that it's a weekend—he works seven days a week."

She didn't reply, but based on the chill that filmed over her expression it was clear that she'd just filed him under the category of soulless clone. Without a word she handed him a wad of paper napkins, then slid off the counter.

"Listen," she said, adjusting her dress while he pulled up the silk boxers, "I'm not sure what came over me, but what just happened between us…that isn't normal behavior for me."

"Believe it or not, it's not for me, either."

"Things just got…out of hand." She looked at him and he barely suppressed a groan. With her tumbled hair and moist, parted lips, she looked like living, breathing sin. "I'm pleading temporary insanity."

"That makes two of us."

"This isn't going to happen again."

He knew he should agree, but the words stuck in his throat, refusing to be uttered.

"In fact," she continued, "we need to forget it happened *this* time."

Before he could reply, a knock sounded and he swiveled his head toward the door. A man wearing a tan jacket proclaiming he was from the American Car Association tapped on the glass.

His interlude with Lacey was officially over.

And it occurred to Evan that maybe he really *was* cursed.

7

AT TEN O'CLOCK Tuesday evening, Lacey locked the door to Constant Cravings and headed across the courtyard. Sales had been unusually sluggish Sunday, Monday and today, and she'd spent the bulk of her time baking to fill cookie platter orders. Not good, as that had left her with too much time to think, and her mind had remained firmly focused on the one thing she desperately wanted *not* to think of.

Evan Sawyer.

Okay, the *two* things she desperately wanted not to think of—Evan Sawyer, and that bout of mind-blowing sex with Evan Sawyer.

You'd think the fact that she hadn't seen him since they'd parted company late Saturday night—technically Sunday morning—would have been enough for "out of sight, out of mind" to kick in. But no. Instead, she'd thought of him about every three seconds or so. Sometimes more frequently. The feel of his hands and mouth on her, the sensation of him buried deep inside her, the deliciously potent taste of his kiss, his skin pressed against hers, all seemed to be tattooed onto her senses. They'd all given her libido a jolt equal to a nuclear blast. Three days later and she was *still* hot and bothered.

Yet more than hot and bothered. He'd not only turned her on, he'd surprised her. And disarmed her. With his revelations about his family and his non-English-speaking dog. He'd been amusing and intelligent and, well, *likable*. Extremely so. Unsettlingly so.

She hadn't expected to see him on Sunday, but when he hadn't come into the shop yesterday or today, it was clear he'd taken her "we need to forget it happened" words to heart and was ignoring both her and the explosive attraction that had flared between them.

Which was for the best. Definitely. Still, despite that he was only doing what she'd asked, if she were brutally honest, she had to admit his complete and total brush-off unreasonably pricked her feminine ego and, damn it, annoyed her. Clearly he hadn't found her as amusing, intelligent and disarming as she'd found him. And the fact that she was annoyed *really* annoyed her. So why couldn't she write him off and stop thinking about him?

Well, she'd almost succeeded today—had gotten to the point where he'd only invaded her thoughts every six seconds or so—when she'd checked her e-mail during a quick break. And discovered a message from him. Just seeing his name in Constant Cravings' in-box had set her heart aflutter, a fact that thoroughly irritated her. After clicking open the note, she'd read his brief message: Would appreciate it if you'd stop by my office before going home tonight. Doesn't matter what time— I'll be working late. Evan.

The impersonal tone and complete lack of details had only served to fuel her mind with questions that had plagued her for the remainder of the day. Why did he want to see her? Had he been thinking about her? Did he want a repeat performance? Did he want to find out if making love would be as explosive the second time around?

Not that it mattered if he wanted that or not. Because she didn't. No way. Absolutely not.

Okay, damn it, she did want that. Desperately. Wanted to feel his body pressed against hers, thrusting into hers. Taste his drugging kiss. Run her hands over all those lovely muscles. Discover if the powerful sparks had been real or just a figment of her imagination.

But giving in to that temptation…definitely not a good idea. Just because he'd been intelligent and amusing didn't mean he was her type. Still, it wasn't as if she had to *marry* the guy.

Nothing wrong with just having him put out this damn fire he'd started. No, nothing *wrong* with that, but she wasn't convinced it was smart, either.

Drawing a bracing breath, she adopted her best aloof manner and entered the west section of the building, then took the elevator to the fifth floor, where the property management offices were located. After a quick mental pep talk to remain calm, cool and collected, she knocked on the oak door bearing a brass plate engraved with Evan's name. Several seconds later the door opened, and calm, cool and collected melted into a puddle at her feet.

She'd been prepared to see him wearing his usual prim dress shirt, proper suit, boring tie and perfect hair. But "prim, proper and boring" wasn't the Evan who answered the door. No, this Evan sported rumpled hair and a stubble-darkened jaw that lent him a dark and slightly dangerous air. The suit and tie had been replaced with a black T-shirt that made her fingers itch to test the breadth of his shoulders, and a pair of jeans that, based on the fascinating set of fade patterns, were old favorites. He looked rumpled and casual and sexy and utterly delicious and, damn it, he wasn't supposed to!

"We need to talk," he said, opening the door wider.

His abrupt words jerked her from her stupor. Not even so much as a hello. Arrogant jerk. Had she really wasted three days fantasizing about him? Actually, she was glad for his abruptness as it effectively cooled any flames he'd lit.

She lifted her chin and sailed into the office. After putting a safe distance between them, she turned to face him. Crossing her arms over her chest, she watched him close the door, refusing to acknowledge that the rear view was a good as the front view. And that she knew exactly how great his ass felt beneath her palms. Then he turned and leaned his shoulders against the door and regarded her with an unreadable expression.

When the silence stretched into what she considered the uncomfortable zone, she said, "You wanted to talk? I'm listening."

He studied her for several more seconds, his eyebrows

drawn into a frown, then asked in a very serious voice, "How are you, Lacey?"

She blinked. "Uh, fine. You?"

"I'm…not sure. The past few days have been…strange. I was wondering if you'd experienced anything unusual since we last saw each other."

Yeah—I can't stop thinking about you. But then an odd tingle shivered down her spine as she mentally flicked through the weird series of mini-disasters that had occurred over the past three days. "A few things, I guess," she admitted.

"Like what?"

"A flat tire—"

"Me, too."

Another odd tingle shivered down her spine. "My dishwasher broke."

"My refrigerator died."

"Some kid must have put a red crayon in the dryer at my apartment complex's laundry room, and I ruined an entire load of clothes."

"The dry cleaner lost all my suits and dress shirts."

"Sales have been off at the store."

"Two clients decided not to renew their leases."

Lacey slowly set her purse on the floor. "Let's see…the timer on my stove quit and I burned two batches of cookies. The heel broke off my favorite pair of sandals at the supermarket and I fell into a display of oranges, knocking a bunch of them down on me. I locked myself out of my apartment, dropped my mail in a mud puddle and…" *had several highly erotic dreams about you* "…had a couple of weird dreams. You?"

"My microwave suffered some sort of hiccup and spewed leftover *moo shu* pork all over my kitchen. Sasha suddenly decided that she liked the taste of leather and chewed up every pair of shoes that I own. I locked myself out of my house, and my neighbor who has my spare key naturally wasn't home. Sasha also gnawed a couple holes in my mail."

Stunned, she stepped back several paces and leaned her hips against his desk. "Okay, that's bizarre."

"Yes, it is," he agreed.

She attempted a laugh. "At least you didn't have any weird dreams."

"Oh, I had dreams. But I don't think *weird* is the right word to describe them."

"What is?"

His gaze, which had remained steady on hers up until now, cruised slowly down to her feet then back up again. "Erotic."

She suddenly felt as if she stood in a ring of fire. Before she could think up a reply, he pushed off from the door and walked slowly toward her. "Wanna guess who was prominently featured in my *X*-rated dreams, Lacey?"

She had to swallow to find her voice. "Carmen Electra?"

He made a sound like a game show buzzer. "Wrong answer." He didn't stop walking until less than an arm's length separated them. Lacey curled her fingers over the edge of his desk to keep from giving in to the overwhelming temptation to touch him.

"You," he said, his eyes filled with a heat that all but singed her. "You were the woman in my dreams."

Even though her better judgment told her to shut up, curiosity got the better of her and she couldn't stop herself from asking, "Did any of your dreams involve a nineteenth-century pirate ship?"

He nodded slowly. "I was the captain."

Her heart began to pound in slow, hard beats. "You kidnapped me from my ancestral home."

"Because you belonged to me."

A heated flush engulfed her. "You cut off my gown. With your knife."

"You liked it."

"I had nothing else to wear."

"We both liked that."

"You made love to me," she whispered.

"Every chance I could."

"Every chance you could," she agreed. Another wave of heat swamped her as images from her dreams flashed through her mind. Of Evan over her, under her, deep inside her, his hands and mouth everywhere…relentless…

His gaze searched hers. "Maybe the other stuff could be explained away by coincidence, but the fact that we had the same dream? That just convinces me that my idea is sound."

"What idea?" she asked, hoping it had something to do with making that dream come true. Every cell in her body wanted to reach out and grab him, but she was afraid that once she touched him she wouldn't be able to stop. Was that why he hadn't touched her? Was he afraid of what would happen if he did? Was he suffering from the same "should I, shouldn't I?" dilemma as she?

Instead of telling her his idea, he said, "I paid Madame Karma a visit today."

She couldn't hide her surprise. "You did? Why?"

"I wanted to talk to her about my sudden run of bad luck. She didn't seem the least bit surprised, and told me it was because I was fighting fate. She predicted that you'd suffered a similar series of unfortunate events. Based on what you've told me, she was right."

"Did she have any suggestions?"

"As a matter of fact she did. She told me the only way to fix my cursed karma was to stop fighting fate. And the only way to do that was to spend time with you—which would also fix your karma problem. So that's my idea. That we spend some time together. Worst-case scenario is we won't be any worse off than we are now. Best-case scenario is we'll undo our karma curse and our lives will return to normal."

"I thought you didn't believe in any of that karma or fate stuff. Called it a bunch of nonsense."

"I *didn't* believe in it, and I'm not sure I do now. But there's no denying the oddball things that have happened to both of us since Saturday, and I'm at a loss to explain them. Frankly, I'm exhausted from this spate of bad luck and am willing to try just about anything—no matter how off-the-wall it sounds—to end it."

"Including spending time with me?"

"Yes."

"Well, that's certainly not the most romantic offer I've ever received."

Instead of looking abashed, he appeared amused, which she found highly irritating. "Do you *want* a romantic offer?"

"Certainly not. You're not at all my type."

He folded his arms over his chest and shot her a quizzical look. "Not that I'm arguing that point, because, to be blunt, you're not my type, either, but what is it about me that you find…unacceptable?"

Lacey studied him for several long seconds, debating how honest to be with him, then decided what the hell? No point in sugar-coating anything. He'd been blunt with her, and it wasn't as if she were trying to impress him.

"I've always avoided getting involved with soulless clones. I see them every day. They come into Constant Cravings at the crack of dawn for their caffeine fixes, already talking business on their cell phones, tapping on their laptops, completely consumed with their work, never taking a moment of downtime. I see them sitting in the courtyard at lunch, hunched over reports, never so much as looking up to enjoy the sunshine." She shrugged. "You're one of them."

He didn't say anything for nearly half a minute, but she could tell by his frown that he was considering her words. Finally he cleared his throat. "There's nothing wrong with having goals and working hard. In trying to succeed."

"I agree. But I think there *is* something wrong when all your time and energy is devoted to your career and every other aspect of your life becomes just going through the motions. When success is measured only in terms of getting ahead profession-ally. When people and relationships and participating in *life* cease to matter."

"And you think I'm one of these soulless clones?"

"Yes."

"That's pretty harsh."

"Did you want me to lie?"

"No. But I think you're wrong."

"Really? I'll prove I'm right. Close your eyes. And no peeking." After he'd complied, she asked, "What's depicted in the painting on the wall behind your desk?"

A frown bunched between his eyebrows. "There's a painting on the wall behind my desk?"

"Oh, brother. You're worse than I thought."

He opened his eyes and looked at the wall behind her. "That's not fair. My office was redone during the renovations."

"Uh-huh. And when was it finished?"

"Three weeks ago."

"Three weeks is a long time not to notice something that's right under your nose, or in this case, hanging right over your head. I rest my case."

"Give me another chance."

She blew out a sigh and closed *her* eyes. "Fine. What color are my eyes?"

Without hesitation he said, "Golden-brown. Like caramel. With little flecks of gold. The irises are surrounded by a dark ring that looks like melted chocolate."

Lacey's lids popped open and she found him looking at her intently. "You seem surprised," he said.

"I am. Stunned actually. I didn't think—"

"I'd noticed? Believe me, I've noticed. Maybe I'm not the soulless clone you think I am."

"Maybe not. But you're still a rigid rule follower. And way too prim and proper for me."

"You think I'm rigid? Prim? Proper?"

"Yes, I do."

"You say that to a man with whom you shared wild sex against a coffee-house counter?"

"One bout of wild sex that we both agreed was the result of temporary insanity isn't enough to change my opinion."

"I see. So then you say that to a pirate who used a knife to cut off the dozens of tiny buttons running down the front of your gown?" He reached out and traced a single fingertip down the front of her shirt, slowly circling each button, halting her breath…and hardening her nipples. "A pirate who made love to you until you were too exhausted to move?"

She had to swallow twice to find her voice. "That was just a dream."

"And a helluva good one."

"Can't argue with that."

"Your assertion that I'm too proper…you realize it challenges me to prove you wrong."

His words, spoken in that husky voice, the way he was looking at her, as if he wanted to devour her, ignited fire in her veins. She could feel her pulse throbbing everywhere. In her temples. At the base of her throat. Between her legs.

"Well, even if my assertion is incorrect, that still doesn't mean us spending time together is a good idea. After all, you said I wasn't your type."

"I think it's probably more accurate to say that based on the wrong way we've rubbed each other since almost the minute we met, I wouldn't have believed us compatible in any way. But there was nothing wrong with the way we rubbed each other Saturday night." As if to prove his point, he stepped forward and lightly brushed his pelvis against hers, shooting sparks to her every nerve ending.

"Uh, no," she murmured. "There was nothing wrong with that."

He studied her for several heartbeats, his blue eyes breathing fire. "Since we've both said we're tired of games, I'll throw out the unvarnished truth—I know you said we needed to forget what happened between us Saturday night. And believe me, I've tried. But I can't. I've tried to stay away from you, but I simply don't want to. I haven't been able to stop thinking about you, even when I managed to fall asleep. And there is nothing prim or proper about the things I want to do to you."

A dark thrill she couldn't name rippled through Lacey. And based on his honesty, she couldn't give him anything other than the same consideration in return. "I could waste a lot of time repeating everything you just said or I could sum it up in five words: that makes two of us." She slid her palms up his chest and over his shoulders to link her fingers at his nape. "And I'm tired of wasting time. Here's my unvarnished truth—I've been dying to get my hands on you again."

With a groan, he pulled her against him. "Me, too. My hands, my mouth…all of me on all of you."

"That sounds perfect. And, um, now would be fine with me." She settled herself more firmly against him and a combination of impatience and anticipation sizzled through her at the intimate press of his erection against her belly. *"Right now."*

8

Lacey's words reverberated through Evan's mind, snapping the thin thread he'd managed to retain on his control. Desperate to taste her, his mouth came down on hers, demanding and insistent, and her lips parted, dragging a groan of relief from his throat. Finally…*finally,* she was in his arms again.

Clearly, whatever had gripped them Saturday night wasn't a fluke. She was as impatient to touch him as he was to touch her because she yanked his T-shirt from his jeans and coasted her hands up his back. Pleasure shuddered through him, but it wasn't enough. He needed them skin to skin.

"Hold on," he ground out. Her arms tightened around him, and cupping his hands around her buttocks, he lifted her. "Wanna see if a desk works just as well as a counter?"

"God, yes."

He stepped between her legs, spreading them wide, and rolled his hips against her. She wrapped her legs around his waist, and he leaned forward to press his lips against the base of her throat.

"You smell so damn good," he muttered against her fragrant skin while his fingers made quick work of the buttons on her shirt. He ran his tongue down the side of her neck in a long, slow lick, absorbing the shudder that ran through her. "Taste so damn good. Like sugar and flowers."

She tipped back her head, affording him better access to her soft skin. When he'd flicked the last shirt button free, he skimmed his hands inside the white cotton and filled his palms with her lace-covered breasts. He kissed his way down her chest and circled his tongue around her already hard nipple, then drew the peak into his mouth.

Gasping, she slapped her hands on the desk and arched her back, offering more of herself, an invitation he instantly accepted. The rational part of his mind commanded that he not rush this time, that he savor her, but between his own raging need and her impatience, his body wasn't listening. He skimmed her shirt down her arms then dropped the garment to the floor. Seconds later her bra joined her shirt, baring her generous breasts to his avid gaze.

"Beautiful," he said, his voice a husky rasp, watching her eyes darken with arousal as he rolled her tight nipples between his fingers.

"No fair," she murmured, reaching for his shirt. "You have on more clothes than I do." She tugged his shirt upward and seconds later, it topped the growing pile on the floor.

She ran her hands over his chest, then down his abdomen. His muscles jumped with jolts of pleasure everywhere she touched him, and with a groan he kissed her again, feeling like a starving man who'd just been given a feast.

Forcing himself not to rush, he flicked open the button on her black pants, then slowly lowered the zipper. When he slipped his hand inside her panties, they both groaned.

"You're already wet." His fingers glided over her slick flesh, and the musky scent of her arousal filled his head, tightening his groin. He circled her opening, then slipped two fingers inside her. "And so damn hot."

She gasped and threw back her head. "I've been this way. Hot and aroused. Since Saturday night. All your fault."

"Hot and aroused…glad to find out it wasn't just me."

"*Really* glad to find out it wasn't just me." She leaned farther back and pressed herself against his hand while his fingers slowly pumped in her wet heat. "I'm not going to last very long if you keep that up."

He eased a third finger inside her and leaned forward to tease a plump nipple with the tip of his tongue. "Good. Let's see how fast you can come."

She came fast. And hard. Throwing her head back and pulsing around his fingers while her body arched and quivered and her long, guttural groan of pleasure filled the room.

He slipped his fingers from her body, and still breathing hard, she raised her head and looked at him through glittering eyes. "Wow. Thanks."

"My pleasure."

"More mine." She reached out and trailed her fingers over the bulge in his jeans. "Looking forward to returning the favor."

"That makes two of us." Stepping back, he lifted each of her feet and slipped off her shoes. "Raise your hips." After she complied, he slipped her pants and panties down her legs where they joined the rest of the clothes on the floor.

"I have a condom in my purse."

"I have one in my back pocket."

She opened the button on his jeans with one hand while reaching behind him with the other. The whisper of his zipper opening tightened his muscles in anticipation. "Condom in your back pocket, huh?" she said, drawing her hand forward and wiggling the packet between her fingers. "Pretty sure of yourself."

"More hopeful than sure. But I figured I'd better keep protection close by. I knew if I got my hands on you again, all bets would be off."

"I like your hands on me."

"Again, that makes two of...us." The last word ended on a hiss of pleasure as her hands slipped beneath the waistband of his boxer briefs. He toed off his sneakers, yanked off his socks, then held his breath while she slid his underwear and jeans down his legs. He kicked both garments aside with his foot.

"Oh, my," she purred, touching the base of his straining penis with a single fingertip and dragging it slowly upward. "You've managed to change my opinion about you being prim and proper, but *rigid* is obviously still a problem."

"You've no one to blame but, ahhhh, yourself." The erotic sight and feel of her fingers surrounding him, cupping him, gently squeezing him was driving him insane. "You have no idea how incredible that feels."

Her lips curved upward in a lazy, sexy smile. "Bet I do—thanks to you."

"I don't know how much more I can take." He watched a drop of pearly fluid bead on the head of his penis, a drop she captured with her fingertip and slowly spread over the sensitive head. "I'm done," he ground out, reaching for the condom.

He quickly sheathed himself, then settled his hands on her thighs and urged them wider apart. Lacey wrapped her legs around his waist, and grasping her hips, he lifted her over his erection and then slowly lowered her.

Once he was buried to the hilt, he settled her back on the desk and rolled his hips. A hum of approval rumbled in her throat, and he withdrew nearly all the way from her body then sank deep again, the slick pull killing him with pleasure. Again, another long, slow thrust, then another, faster, harder. He fought the need to come roaring up his spine, knowing he couldn't hold it off much longer. The instant she cried out and he felt her tighten around him, he let himself go. His orgasm exploded through him, shudders racking his body. When they subsided, he hauled her against him and she buried her face in the spot where his neck and shoulder met.

"You've certainly given me something new to think about every time I sit at this desk," he managed to say.

"Good," she said, her warm breath caressing his skin. "Listen, except for Saturday night, it's been a while since I've done that, so I've gotta ask—and I want the unvarnished truth. Was that as incredible as I think it was?"

"I think so. But I think we should do it again. Just to make sure."

Her huff of laughter blew against his jaw. "Good thing I brought a condom, too."

"*Very* good thing," he agreed, dipping his chin to brush his mouth over hers. "And maybe we can actually make it to a bed, or at least a sofa at some point."

She smiled. "There you go, being all prim and proper again."

He skimmed a fingertip down one of those sexy dimples. "You said it's been a while. How long?"

"Since I've had sex? Other than Saturday night, a few months. Since a man made me feel like that? Umm, I don't know. I don't think any man has ever made me feel like that." She ran her tongue over his bottom lip. "You're...potent."

"That makes two of us," he said, echoing the earlier sentiment. He lightly ran his hands up and down her smooth back. "You know, I think I've figured out how we can spend our time while we un-curse ourselves."

She looped her arms around his neck, leaned back and smiled. "Is that an invitation to have yet another bout of wild sex?"

"Another bout or two or twelve or twelve dozen."

"Twelve dozen? We're gonna need a lot more condoms."

"Got plenty at my place." He cupped her face between his hands and tried to name the warm feeling spreading through him. He wasn't quite sure, but it felt suspiciously like...happiness. "Wanna come home with me?"

The invitation surprised him since it broke his own rule of not bringing women to his house. But he couldn't deny he wanted her there. In his home. In his bed. Her serious eyes searched his and he wished he knew what she was thinking. Then her lips twitched. "You have a desk there?"

He nodded. "And a hot tub. And a nice big bed."

"Sounds good to me."

A smile lifted his lips. "That makes two of us."

9

On a Friday evening one month after that first night spent with Evan, Lacey locked the door to Constant Cravings and headed across the Fairfax courtyard. She'd arranged to take the weekend off, and anticipation curled through her at the getaway she and Evan had planned. He needed to be in San Francisco next week for business and had invited her to drive up with him two days early so they could enjoy the weekend there. Lacey planned to fly home Sunday night while Evan remained.

As she made her way across the courtyard, she realized that next week would be the first time in a month that they wouldn't be together. And she further realized that she was going to miss him—more than she ever thought she could miss a person.

She continuously marveled at how things could change so drastically in a matter of only a few weeks, and pinched herself at least twice a day to make sure this relationship with Evan was real and not some figment of her imagination.

She'd spent the first week of her time with him convinced that their attraction was nothing more than sex, a firecracker of lust that would quickly burn out after a few sparks. Simply a case of wildly aroused libidos colliding.

But the exact opposite had occurred, and as that week rolled into another and another, she realized this was not just sex. Every moment spent with him was a revelation, showing another aspect of his personality, stripping away another layer of the soulless clone she'd mistakenly believed him to be.

Given their explosive first encounter in her shop, she'd fully expected to enjoy spending time with him in bed—where she'd quickly learned that there was *nothing* prim or proper about him—but this…this was different. She'd enjoyed good sex before. Had even experienced what she'd thought, at the time, to be stupendous sex. But making love with Evan was like the opening of a new dimension. He engaged not only her body, but her mind and spirit as well, touching her on every level in a way no other man ever had.

Every day she realized something new about him, and she'd yet to learn anything she hadn't liked. What was there not to like about a man who was kind to his neighbors, adopted a zany stray dog and, as she'd discovered, had single-handedly arranged for GreenSpace Property Management to make a sizable contribution to the local children's hospital? He loved surprises—both giving and receiving them—and had greatly appreciated her efforts when she'd baked him a batch of bed-shaped cookies, which she'd dubbed Take Me to Bed. He'd loved the sweet treats, and she'd loved the way he'd done just that—taken her to bed. Again and again and again. He equally enjoyed the ice-cream-cone cookies she'd baked him last week called Lick Me—as had she when he'd taken the command literally.

In spite of his claim that he hadn't excelled at team sports as a kid, she discovered during excursions to the beach and a local park that they shared of a love of swimming and jogging and that he built a mean sand castle. She also learned that he couldn't toss a Frisbee to save his life, although the latter could have been blamed on the Sasha-chewed holes in the plastic disk. Clearly *Frisbee* translated into "chew toy" in Russian.

He taught her the strategy of playing strip blackjack—better than strip poker, he claimed, because you got naked faster. Lacey had ended up naked first and been declared the loser, but as far as she was concerned, the way he'd run his hands and tongue over her body had made her the winner. In return, she'd taught him the many erotic ways that frosting could be used—none of which appeared in any cookbook.

She also discovered they had a lot in common. A shared love of trying new foods. Action films. Murder mysteries. Crossword puzzles. A dislike of lima beans. They discussed current events, pop culture, religion and politics. They agreed on some issues, disagreed on others, but regardless of whether their views were similar or not, she found their discussions and debates exhilarating. There wasn't a single subject he shied away from talking about, and unlike previous men she'd dated, Evan really *listened*.

The biggest surprise of all, however, was the fact that the man she'd thought for so many months to be a soulless clone had proven heart-meltingly romantic. He'd surprised her with a late-night champagne and chocolate picnic in his hot tub. Burnt a CD of her favorite songs. Slipped her sexy, handwritten, one-line notes when he came into Constant Cravings in the morning for his coffee. Called during the day to see how she was doing. Little things that he said were his way to show that he could stop and smell the roses—because, he'd admitted, she was right. He hadn't been taking time to do that. All his time and attention had been devoted to work and his career. But, as he'd explained last night, that was because he hadn't met anyone who'd inspired him to make a change. Until now.

Last night… She made her away into the building, pushed the up button on the elevator and her eyes slid closed. Last night had been…perfect. She'd prepared dinner at her place, an Italian feast of antipasto and lasagna, setting the mood with candlelight and Evan's favorite red wine. He'd arrived with his arms filled with dozens of pale pink peonies. *You must have bought every peony in California,* she'd said, delighted at the sweet gesture. He'd looked at her through serious blue eyes, then said, *You're worth it.* And that was the instant that it clicked into place in her mind.

She was in love with him.

Yes, he was a rule follower, but he was also a man of integrity, something that had been sadly lacking and too easily compromised in many of the other men she'd dated. And, yes, he still thought her window displays were too risqué for Fairfax, but, as in other matters where their opinions had differed, they'd agreed to disagree.

"And to think, without Madame Karma, we might have just gone on thinking the worst of each other," she murmured to herself as the elevator doors slid open. Indeed, during the past month, not only had their streaks of bad luck ended, but some of the previous disasters had corrected themselves. Sasha no longer chewed on shoes—except for flip-flops—and the dry cleaner had recovered Evan's clothes. The timer on Lacey's stove had been miraculously "cured," and she found a pair of the exact sandals that had broken—on sale. As crazy as she'd thought it a month ago, she now believed Madame's prediction. Evan was Mr. Right.

She stepped inside the elevator and pushed the button for the fifth floor. Yes, Evan was Mr. Right, but did he feel the same way about her? Last night, when she'd realized she loved him, the urge to tell him had nearly overwhelmed her. But she'd held back, afraid that it was too soon. Afraid that the *L* word would catapult him into masculine panic and cast a pall over what had so far been magical and perfect.

But, after thinking about little else all day today, she'd decided to tell him, and what could be a more perfect time than during their romantic getaway to San Francisco? They'd spent the past month telling each other the unvarnished truth, and she didn't want to start playing games now. She loved him. She wanted him to know. And hopefully, he would tell her he felt the same way. And if he didn't, well…she'd cross that bridge if she came to it. He cared, she knew he did. It was obvious in everything he said and did. But did his feelings run as deeply as hers? She didn't know, but with her heart on the line, she needed to find out.

The elevator door pinged open, and she strode down the corridor to his office, her pulse quickening at the mere thought of seeing him. A happy laugh bubbled in her throat and she gave her arm another quick pinch. Yup—this was real. Real and fabulous.

Evan's door was open, and she was halfway across the room

before she realized he was on the phone. When she noticed, she paused. "Yes, I understand," he said into the receiver, his eyebrows bunched into a frown. "I'll take care of it."

Just then he looked up. His frown disappeared and their gazes locked. Something warm and intimate passed between them, and Lacey's insides turned to syrup, as they seemed to every time he looked at her. With his gaze steady on hers, he ended his call, then rose and walked toward her. He didn't stop when he reached her. Instead he just lifted her up, then kept walking, his eyes burning with intensity, not halting until she was pressed against the wall.

His mouth descended on hers in a hot, hungry, demanding kiss that dragged a groan of want from her. She vaguely heard him push the door shut. But then all thought drained from her mind when he pressed his erection against her.

"I missed you," he whispered against her lips.

"I missed you, too."

"So that makes two of us."

"That makes two of us," she agreed. "Show me." Her words ending on a groan when his hands plunged beneath her shirt and found her nipples. "Show me how much you missed me."

And suddenly his hands, his mouth, were everywhere. As if he didn't just want her, but *craved* her and couldn't have her fast enough. Which was fine by her since she felt as if she'd explode if she didn't feel his skin against hers.

Impatient fingers yanked at buttons while lips nipped and tongues tasted. With clothing hastily removed or simply shoved aside, he rolled on protection, then lifted her, impaling her on his erection. Lacey wrapped her legs tightly around his hips and held on, absorbing every hard, fast thrust. Her orgasm screamed through her, mindless throbs of pleasure that tore a cry from her throat. He thrust a final time, then she felt him shudder against her.

Feeling deliciously limp, Lacey's legs slid down. Planting her feet and locking her knees, she leaned against the wall. "Wow," she managed between ragged breaths. "I guess you *did* miss me."

He cradled her face between his hands and gazed at her with an expression she couldn't decipher. "I did." Something flickered in his eyes. "We need to talk."

Uh-oh. Her postcoital euphoria evaporated. In her experience, nothing good ever followed "we need to talk." Especially when those words were said in such a serious voice. And accompanied by such a serious expression.

"Bad day?" she asked, hoping that whatever was wrong was merely business related, but the way he was looking at her gave her the sinking feeling it was more than that.

"Bad day," he agreed in a tired voice.

She watched him adjust his clothing while she scooped up her pants and underwear from the floor and slipped them on. When they were both put back together, he said, "When you arrived, that call I was on, it was from Greg Mathers, my boss."

The wave of relief that swamped Lacey loosened her knees and she rested her shoulders against the wall. Clearly whatever was wrong was business related. Nothing to do with them.

"What did he say?"

"There's something he's insisted I take care of. Immediately."

Realization dawned. "I see. So we have to postpone leaving for San Francisco?"

"This has nothing to do with our trip to San Francisco, Lacey. It has to do with you. You and Constant Cravings." He waved a hand toward his desk. "Would you like to sit down?"

Her instincts immediately went on red alert, at both his words and his suddenly businesslike demeanor and tone. "No, thanks, I prefer to stand."

He nodded, then drew what appeared to be a bracing breath. "Greg made a visit to Fairfax last week, to evaluate the retail and office spaces. We've since had several meetings, and after careful consideration, it's been decided that Fairfax won't be offering you a lease renewal after Constant Cravings' lease expires three months from now."

For several long seconds she could only stare at him in shock.

Then she said, slowly, in a voice that sounded as if it came from far away, "You're *evicting* me?"

"No, we're simply not offering you another lease."

A plethora of feelings bombarded her, all fighting for attention—disbelief, confusion, hurt, anger—but anger was the one that broke through first. Fighting to keep her voice calm, she asked, "Can you please explain why?"

"After his site visit, Greg doesn't feel the store is a good match for the complex."

"A *good match?*" She pushed off the wall and clenched her hands. "What the hell does that mean?"

"It means he doesn't like the image you've projected with your sexy window displays and product names."

"So he's *evicting* me?"

"Not offering you a new lease is *not* the same as evicting you." He dragged a hand through his hair, an impatient gesture matched by his tone and the flicker in his eyes. "This has been an issue since you came here, Lacey."

"Not for me. But obviously for you and Greg Mathers. He has no grounds not to offer me another lease."

"He doesn't need any. And even if he did, as far as he's concerned, the sexy nature of your window displays violates your lease agreement."

"Those window displays have generated a lot of income," she fumed.

"No one is arguing that. But the bottom line is he wants something in that space that is more in keeping with the image he and the investors want Fairfax to project."

She stared at him, frozen with an incomprehensible mixture of disbelief, anger, and numbness. "So that's it? All my hard work, all my dreams, all my time and energy dedicated to making my store something special, something different, is all gone?" She huffed out a short, bitter breath, then narrowed her eyes. "You seem very calm. I take it you agree with this decision?"

He said nothing for several long seconds, during which time

Lacey's heart pounded, each beat feeling as if it broke off another piece. Finally he said, "I can't deny that I see Greg's point. I tried to tell you, many times, to tone it down, yet you refused to listen. But I did try to talk him out of this."

Anger exploded in her. "Well, that was damn big of you."

It was clear he was getting angry, too. "Listen, I can't deny that I think Constant Cravings would fare better in a different location."

She felt as if he'd shot her. "I see. And you obviously told Greg that. Thanks for the support."

"I supported you—"

"Sure as hell doesn't seem like it, seeing as how I've been evicted."

His eyes flashed. "For the last time, you weren't evicted."

"Right. I just won't have a store three months from now. Well, consider your job done. Your boss wanted you to tell me and you have." She reached down and grabbed her purse, which had slid to the floor when he'd carried her to the wall. "Nice timing, by the way, getting in a last quickie before imparting your news."

His face darkened, and he reached her in two steps, then grasped her shoulders. "That had nothing to do with it."

She jerked away from him and retreated several paces. "Of course not. The sex was personal. What you told me was just business."

Relief relaxed his tense expression. "Exactly."

He moved toward her, but she backed up and held out her hand to stop him. "Don't touch me. The last time you touched me was just that—the last time."

He halted as if he'd hit a wall, then dragged his hands down his face. "Lacey, I understand you're upset—"

"*Upset* is an understatement."

"I can see that. But we have the entire weekend to discuss this."

"There's nothing to discuss. Your boss wants me out, you

agree with him and you've given me the boot—without so much as the courtesy to talk about the situation with me. Even if there was nothing more than business between us, that would 'upset' me. Given our personal relationship, it not only upsets me, it really hurts." Her voice quavered on the last word and she pressed her lips together, hard, fighting to hold back the tidal wave of emotion bearing down on her.

"I didn't mean to hurt you. You must know that."

"I'm afraid I don't. My first impression of you was that you were one of the soulless clones who only thought about business. I wish I'd listened to that first impression. As for this weekend? Not going to happen. We're through."

"Lacey…" He raked his hands through his hair. "You don't mean that. You can't just walk away like this."

She raised her chin and looked into his eyes. "I mean it. And, yes, I can just walk away."

Turning on her heel, she strode to the door, opened it, then left without a backward glance.

She forced herself to concentrate on her anger, on the deep sense of betrayal she felt, until she made it home. But the instant her apartment door was closed and locked behind her, a wrenching sob broke free. She sank to the floor and listened to her heart shatter.

10

EVAN SPENT THE WEEK IN San Francisco trying to convince himself that the gut-wrenching sense of loss clenching his insides was relief—or bad seafood—but by the time Friday rolled around he couldn't lie to himself any longer.

He'd done his job, followed the rules. And lost Lacey.

Lacey, who made him laugh. Who could turn him on with a mere look. Who could talk about any topic under the sun. Who could make the most mundane activity interesting and fun. Who appealed to both his body and mind in a way no other woman ever had. Whose wicked sense of fun and "stop and smell the roses" personality had prodded him to take a good, long look at himself and at the way he was living his life. And when he'd done so, he hadn't particularly liked what he'd seen.

While he didn't think he'd turned into one of the soulless clones she'd described, he'd absolutely been headed in that direction. Thanks to her, he'd reversed that trend. And he had never been as happy as during the month they'd been together. She was the first woman he'd known in a very long time whom he enjoyed as much out of bed as in bed. He'd thought he'd been in love a couple of times, but what he'd felt for those other women paled to insignificance when compared to the feelings Lacey inspired.

He'd known he was a goner the first time he'd seen her with Sasha. Watching a laughing, carefree Lacey splash in the surf with his zany dog, getting covered with salt water and sand, it had hit him like a sucker punch to the heart. He loved her. Loved her sense of fun, her lively personality, her intelligence. The way she cared for her store and customers. If he had to describe her in one word, it would be *vivid*. She made everything around her more colorful, more alive. Including him.

He'd debated whether or not to confess he loved her, not wanting to scare her off given the short amount of time they'd dated. He'd finally decided to tell her during their weekend in San Francisco. But then Greg had called, and all hell had broken loose.

He couldn't deny that on some level he agreed with Greg. Constant Cravings, with its sensual window displays and products, definitely bucked the image of the other stores in the Fairfax complex, a fact that had been a bone of contention between him and Lacey from the moment she'd opened her doors.

But he also didn't like Greg's assessment and subsequent decision. When his boss had initially told him he wanted Constant Cravings out of Fairfax, Evan had tried to dissuade him, presenting him with facts and figures to prove the store was performing well. He'd also promised to talk to Lacey about toning down the displays, figuring that if she knew her lease renewal was at risk, she'd finally listen.

But Greg didn't want any part of it. Bottom line for Greg was that his nephew wanted to open a Java Heaven—a coffee franchise quickly catching up to Starbucks in terms of popularity—in Fairfax. When Evan had protested that the complex was large enough to support two coffee places, Greg had flatly refused to listen. He simply didn't want the competition Lacey's shop would have offered. So Evan had been given no choice but to tell her.

And that had been that.

And now he felt as if there was a hollow space in his chest where his heart used to beat.

Over the past week he'd picked up the phone dozens of times to call her, but had resisted. He wanted to talk to her, but decided it was best to do so face-to-face. The fact that she hadn't called him didn't bode well, but he couldn't let that stop him. He intended to go to Constant Cravings tomorrow and camp out on the doorstep if necessary until she'd talk to him.

Weary beyond belief, he pulled his car into his dark driveway, then entered his house. Leaving his laptop and briefcase in the foyer, he headed toward the kitchen. After twisting the top off a Heineken, he walked into the den. He'd just plopped into his favorite chair when the phone rang. His heart jumped with hope that it might be Lacey, but a glance at his caller I.D. indicated it was Paul.

He lifted the receiver. "What's up?"

"So what's the deal with Constant Cravings?"

His fingers tightened on the receiver. He hadn't spoken to Paul all week. He hadn't wanted to talk about Lacey, and he knew his friend would ask about her, as he always did. "What are you talking about?"

"The fact that it is no more, as if you didn't know. I go out of town for a couple of days and come back to find my favorite coffee place closed down. Damn, I'm totally addicted to those cookies. So where'd Lacey go? And why didn't you give me a heads-up?"

Evan's every muscle tensed. "What do you mean 'closed down'?"

Something in his voice must have clued Paul in because his friend said slowly, "You didn't know?"

"No. Tell me."

"I drove by my office on my way home from the airport to pick up some papers. Since Constant Cravings is usually open late on Friday nights, I decided to get a coffee. When I got there, the place was dark. No mannequins in the windows. Nothing. Just a note on the door saying that the store was permanently closed at this location."

Evan squeezed his eyes shut, then blew out a heavy sigh. "Damn."

"How come you didn't know about this? What the hell is going on?"

He rubbed at the throbbing in his temple. "We broke up." He gave Paul an abbreviated version of the previous Friday night's events.

"So, she didn't have to leave for three months, but she packed up and closed shop in less than a week?" Paul whistled through his teeth. "Wow. That is one seriously pissed off woman."

Right. And clearly not one who would be receptive to seeing him.

"So what do you intend to do about it?" Paul asked.

"Do?" A humorless sound pushed past his lips. "She's made it pretty clear she's done with me."

"Are you done with her?"

No. And the truth, the vehemence behind that single word in his head had him sitting up. No, damn it, he wasn't done with her. Would never be done with her. "Not by a long shot."

Paul's chuckle drifted through the receiver. "Atta' boy. You were silent for so long I was worried. You know she's the best thing that ever happened to you, and that's not a sentence I'd say to you lightly."

"I know—on both counts."

"So…what are you going to do about it?"

"I'll let you know as soon as I figure it out."

EXACTLY THREE WEEKS TO THE day after she'd last spoken to Evan, Lacey sat in her apartment, listlessly channel surfing. She'd spent the day as she had all the previous days since closing the store—scouting for a new location to lease so Constant Cravings could rise from the ashes like the proverbial phoenix. Unfortunately, she hadn't liked most of the places she'd seen. And the ones she had liked charged outrageous rent. Damn it, Fairfax had been perfect. If only—

She sliced off the useless thought, as she did dozens of times each day. There was no point dwelling on what-ifs.

Right. Just as there was no point in dwelling on thoughts of Evan. But no matter how many times she told herself that, it didn't work. He filled every corner of her mind. Even after three weeks, her heart still felt…gone. How the hell long did it take to forget someone? Why couldn't the brain and the heart come with a reset button? She didn't know, but had the sinking fear that she'd never forget him. That her heart would never recover.

Well, she'd found a possible place today, and while it wasn't perfect, it was acceptable. Barely. She couldn't afford to remain out of business for months—that would eat up all her savings. She'd go out looking again tomorrow and hope something better turned up. Otherwise she'd have to settle for the one she'd seen today.

In the meantime there was reality TV and the extra cookies from the last party platter she'd made for the grand opening of a new hair salon. She looked down at the hair dryer-shaped cookie she'd dubbed Blow Job and, as happened at least one hundred times every day, an image of Evan rose in her mind, an image so vivid it was as if she could feel him. Taste him. And, right on cue, hot tears pooled in her eyes. Damn it, she needed to bake a batch of cookies in the form of a bright red *stop* sign— and then do it. Stop thinking about him. If only that were possible.

Her doorbell rang, indicating her Chinese food had arrived. She glanced down at herself and sighed. Hopefully she wouldn't scare off the poor delivery guy. She was wearing the black satin robe with the pink hearts she'd loaned Evan from her mannequin. Probably it would be better if she burned the damn garment. Certainly it would be smarter for her not to wear it, but she couldn't seem to help herself. Paired with stand-on-end hair and no makeup, she looked like she should have crime-scene tape wrapped around her.

After grabbing some money from her wallet, she schlumped to the door and opened it. And stared. At Evan. At least she thought it was Evan. She blinked twice, and he was still there, so it had to be him and not some mirage born of her lovesick imagination.

He wore one of his perfect suits with a perfect shirt and

perfect tie. His hair was perfectly smoothed and he held a perfectly beautiful single pale pink peony. He looked…perfect.

"Hi," he said.

Her heart seemed to stall in her chest. She opened her mouth, meaning to say hello, but then she noticed the bag he held in his other hand. A bag bearing the name of her takeout place. "You're not the Chinese food guy."

"True. He arrived at the same time I did. I offered to deliver your meal." He held out the bag. "Here you go."

"Uh, thanks."

His gaze drifted over her robe and a muscle tensed in his jaw. Damn it, she'd fantasized countless times of this exact scenario—him coming to her door—but in her version she was always wearing a killer dress and sporting glossy curls. And of all the things to have him catch her wearing! Ack! This damn robe made it appear as if she'd been moping around pining for him. Which she had, but *he* didn't have to know that.

"Is this a bad time?" he asked.

"A bad time for what?"

"I was hoping we could talk."

She raised her eyebrows. "I thought we said everything that needed saying."

"I thought of a couple of more things." His frowning gaze shifted to look over her shoulder into her apartment and his jaw tightened. "Is someone with you?"

For a split second she was tempted to lie and say yes, but damn it, as much as it galled her to admit it, she wanted to hear what he had to say. "I'm alone."

His gaze shifted back to hers. "Me, too." Holding out the flower he said, "I hope they're still your favorite."

To her chagrin, her throat slammed shut, so she merely nodded. Reaching out, she took the fragrant bloom. Her fingers brushed his and heat shot up her arm. Just that whisper of a touch had felt so good. She cleared her throat. "C'mon in."

He followed her into the kitchen and remained silent while

she set the food bag on the counter, then put the flower in a bud vase, keeping her back to him while she attempted to regain her composure. When she finished, she turned to face him and leaned her hips against the counter.

He stood about eight feet away, regarding her with a thoughtful expression. "How have you been, Lacey?"

Awful. Terrible. Miserable. And it's all your fault. "Fine. You?"

"Awful. Terrible. Miserable."

She blinked. Did he read minds? Before she could decide, he continued, "I assume you're looking for a new location for Constant Cravings."

She jerked her head in a nod. "Yes."

"Find anything yet?"

"I have a possibility. Have you rented my space at Fairfax?"

"It's been leased, yes. To a Java Heaven. Managed by Greg Mathers's nephew."

Realization dawned and a spurt of fresh anger rushed through her. "I see. I bet that's not a coincidence."

"No, it's not."

"In that case, I'm glad I'm not there any longer."

"That makes two of us."

"Yes, you made it very plain you were glad I wasn't there any longer. Is that all you have to say? Because my dinner is getting cold."

He shook his head. "When I said 'that makes two of us' I meant that I'm glad *I'm* not there any longer."

She frowned. "What do you mean?"

"I mean I resigned. Gave my two-week notice the Monday after I returned from San Francisco. As of an hour ago, I no longer work for GreenSpace Property Management and I'm no longer the property manager for Fairfax."

It took her a good ten seconds to find her voice. "I don't understand. Why would you resign?"

"Because I decided that I didn't like the way Greg Mathers

did business. I didn't like the way he treated you or the store you worked so hard to build. While he was perfectly within his rights not to renew your lease, I think it sucked that he didn't. He wanted that space for his nephew and now he has it. I just didn't want to be a part of it any longer."

Lacey could scarcely believe her ears. "So you don't have a job?"

"Oh, no, I have a job. You are looking at the new property manager for Bryant Properties."

"How did you manage that?"

"I've known Bill Bryant for many years and he's a good man. Has told me a number of times to let him know if I was ever interested in making a change. When I decided to leave GreenSpace, I called him."

"I…I don't know what to say."

"How about congratulations?"

"Congratulations."

His lips curved upward in a slow smile that stole her breath. "Thanks." He walked toward her and reached into his suit jacket. He pulled out an envelope and handed it to her. "For you."

"What is it?"

"There's one way to find out."

Lacey slid her finger beneath the flap and withdrew several sheets of folded paper. She read the first few lines, then looked up at him in amazement.

"This is a lease agreement."

"It is, and my first official deal in my new job. Bryant owns a building complex similar to Fairfax, but I think you'll find after I show you the place that it's a much better fit for Constant Cravings. The stores are more eclectic, and it's located closer to the city."

She shook her head. "I can't afford anything closer to the city."

"Read the terms. I think you can."

She looked back down at the papers and continued reading. Stunned, she raised her gaze back to his. "There must be some mistake. I've checked out lease space in this general area, and the rents were much higher than this figure."

"It's no mistake. That's one of the perks of being the manager—I can offer incentives."

"I...I can't believe you've done this. Left your job. Made me this incredible offer. I'm...speechless."

"Then just listen." He reached out and gently clasped her shoulders. "Nothing's been right since you walked out of my office, Lacey. *Nothing.* I tried to convince myself that what we had was over, that it didn't matter you were gone, but I couldn't. Nothing matters more. And what we had...for me, it's not over. These weeks without you have been hell. I know I hurt you, and I'm sorry." He studied her through very serious eyes. "I love you, Lacey. I want you back. Madame Karma hit it right on the nose. You're Ms. Right. You're The One."

The dam holding back the tears she'd fought against all day burst, and with a sob, she threw her arms around his neck, as much to touch him as to have something solid to hold on to so she didn't slither to the ground.

"I lied when I said I was fine," she sobbed against his neck. "I've been completely miserable."

"I guess I shouldn't say 'good,' but, well, good."

"I can't believe you've done all this."

"Believe it. And please, please stop crying. You're killing me."

She raised her head and framed his face between her trembling hands. "I love you. So much."

He yanked her against him and kissed her in that toe-curling way that left her breathless. "Say it again," he demanded against her lips.

"I love you."

She felt his smile, then he leaned back. Cupping her face, he brushed at the tears wetting her cheeks. "God, I've missed you."

"Me, too." A profound sense of happiness filled all the spaces that less than half an hour ago had been so depressingly empty.

She pressed herself against him, enjoying the low groan that rumbled in his throat as their bodies met.

His hands skimmed down her back to curve over her buttocks and he pulled her tighter against him. "Listen, now that we've made up verbally," he said, his eyes hot on hers, "I'm thinking we should continue with the time-honored tradition of makeup sex. And then talk about our future."

She kissed him, then leaned back and smiled. "That makes two of us."

TOGETHER AGAIN?
Jill Shalvis

1

Pragmatic and practical, Chloe Cooper didn't believe in letting fate have its way. Nope, in her opinion, people made their own destiny, thank you very much.

That knowledge was the driving force behind her entire life, including putting herself through college and running her own accounting firm. Things were good for her, because she'd made them so through sheer will.

Sure, there was the occasional hiccup, like right now, for example. She sat outside, at a table surrounded by the evening's jovial festivities. The Fairfax building complex was holding a Valentine's Day celebration. The southern California evening was February mild, warm and lovely. Perfect for the commercialized holiday, if one went for that sort of thing—which Chloe didn't.

She also didn't go for palm readers—which explained her discomfort in finding her hand presently being held by Isabelle Girard, a fortune-teller hired to entertain the party goers with their individual fortunes.

Uh-huh. Being her own boss had benefits. It meant she could leave whenever she wanted, which she'd just done. Upon coming out of her office and down into the courtyard, Chloe had tried to sneak past the table, so she could instead head directly for what she'd come outside for in the first place—refreshments. But apparently The Legendary Madame Karma, as she called herself, had eyes in the back of her head.

"Sit," she'd commanded, pointing a long, bony finger at the chair in front of her table.

Chloe had never done well with confrontation, so she'd sat. One thing about the faux winters here in L.A., she got away with light skirts and sweaters at work. No gloves required, not when the air hovered near seventy-five degrees.

Madame Karma took Chloe's hand, while Chloe squirmed. She'd chewed her thumbnail to the quick, she hadn't painted her nails and she'd forgotten to put lotion on her dry skin this morning. She also had several paper cuts, the hazard of her job as an accountant. Not exactly a pampered hand, or a pretty one, and she resisted the urge to shove it beneath the table so it wouldn't have to bear any closer scrutiny.

"Pay attention," Madame Karma admonished.

Right. Pay close attention because this was so important. *Much* more important than, say, heading directly to the coffee shop where she'd planned to buy her goodies.

Madame Karma dipped her head over Chloe's palm, studying it intensely. "Hmm," she said ominously.

Chloe resisted the urge to roll her eyes. Instead she pressed her tongue firmly against her cheek because here it came, the doom and gloom. "I know. I have a short lifeline, right? Or wait, let me guess. I'm going to have three kids someday?"

"No," Madame Karma said. "And yes." She lifted her head, her startlingly red hair blowing around her head in the light evening breeze. From far away came a flash of lightning, a weak one, but Chloe still jumped.

Creepy. "Well, that clears that up, thanks." Chloe started to stand but Madame Karma didn't let go of her hand. "Uh…my hand?"

With a fierce frown, the older woman tugged on said append-age until Chloe reluctantly sat once more. "No, you do not have a short lifeline," Madame Karma clarified, bending again over Chloe's palm. "And yes, you're going to have three kids."

Chloe had been biting her tongue but a snort escaped. Madame Karma's head snapped up, her brow knitted tight as the breeze turned into a wind. Around them there were a few squeals of surprise from the other party goers, but the fortune-teller only had eyes for Chloe. "You don't believe?"

"I'm sorry." Chloe tried a smile. "I'm sure you're very nice, but—"

"Nice has nothing to do with it. Your destiny is on a very clear path, young woman, and I suggest you take it much more seriously than you have."

Chloe glanced across the spacious courtyard of the Fairfax complex. Behind the graying clouds, the sun had just gone down for the count, but instead of looking gloomy, the outdoor area was lit with sparkling festive lights. She could easily see through the coffee shop window to the display cases strewn with cookies, cakes and pies, and her stomach growled. "Okay. Yes, you're right. I'll take it seriously. Let's hear it." Because the sooner she did, the sooner she was out of there.

Madame Karma was quiet a moment, studying Chloe in a way that might have made her feel bad if she hadn't been on a hell-bent cookie mission. "I have a prediction for you."

Hopefully that she had cookies in her near future. Lots of cookies. Despite Chloe's good intentions, her eyes strayed again to Constant Cravings, the coffee shop, which undoubtedly had the best cookies Chloe had ever tasted.

"True love is going to walk into your life," the fortune-teller said instead. "Tonight."

Chloe's eyes snapped back to the woman, and, she couldn't help it, she burst into laughter.

Madame Karma's eyes seemed to penetrate her. Again the wind whipped through the courtyard. "You find that funny?"

"I'm sorry." Chloe swallowed hard. "It's…well, it's just silly."

"What? *Love?*"

"No." Chloe shoved back the strands of hair loosened from her ponytail by the wind and shivered. Was the temperature dropping? "It's the fact that you can tell me, with a straight face, that love is about to walk into my life. I mean, I'm just picturing love walking, that's all, and…" She let out a small laugh.

Madame Karma straightened her bony shoulders as the wind increased again. A few sequins fell off her colorful costume, drifting through the swirling air around her. "Are you doubting my talents, or mocking your own ability to find love?" she asked, not unkindly.

Um…both? Chloe was nothing if not sensible, and maybe occasionally hard-headed. Okay, a lot hard-headed. But having her feet firmly on the ground at all times guaranteed a bit of both at times.

The thing was, she didn't believe in love at first sight.

Oh, in theory, it was a nice concept. And she'd certainly gone after that concept in her youth. Hadn't she kissed a bunch of frogs, just waiting for her prince?

Only he'd never actually appeared.

Or maybe it was that he'd never stuck around.

Not that she needed to share *that* with Madame Karma, who sat there staring at Chloe as though she were a specimen under a microscope. "Your true love *is* about to walk into your life," the woman insisted. "You can't change your destiny by being in denial."

"You seriously expect me to believe that some guy is going to walk into this party, seek me out and be the love of my life?"

"I didn't say anything about seeking you out," Madame Karma replied. "I've been doing this for six decades now. I say only what I absolutely mean, and I mean what I say. In fact, you'll seek him out."

Chloe laughed again, but Madame Karma didn't even produce a smile. The woman could have no idea how amusing that was. Chloe liked to see things in their place, all nicely totaled and balanced. It was what made accounting such a perfect profession—the numbers always obeyed.

Love, on the other hand, wasn't nice and neat, and it certainly didn't balance worth a damn. She knew that firsthand. She would never willingly seek out love. "I'm sorry. It just all sounds utterly ridiculous to me."

"Fine." Madame Karma leaned forward over the table. "But that is your fate—whether you think it's ridiculous or not."

"I didn't mean to insult you—"

"Oh, you didn't. But I'd watch your back if I were you." Madame's eyes were dark and serious, made all the more intimidating by the way the wind continued to whip her hair around her head, with more sequins flying off to parts unknown. "Because, Chloe Cooper, your karma is heading south for the winter."

"What? You don't seriously believe—"

"Yes, I do," Madame Karma said with a grim smile. "It's what happens when people laugh at their fortune. Their karma takes a vacation to the Bahamas. Your love life? Consider it *cursed*."

"Oka-a-a-ay." Chloe didn't believe in cursed love lives any more than she did in karma taking vacations. If she wanted a lover, she could get one, thank you very much.

Probably.

Maybe.

Okay, who knew for sure? But that was beside the point. So she'd been a little busy, and maybe she'd ignored certain aspects of her world. *Like her love life.* But since graduating college six years ago, she'd been working her tail off, building up her bookkeeping business, spending long days and nights with numbers as her closest company, because security and stability were extremely important to her.

She would not apologize for that.

So she didn't have a valentine this year. She refused to associate that with her so-called cursed love life. She'd simply forgotten to put a man on her to-do list.

Had she had a valentine last year?

Sad to say, she couldn't even remember. Jeez, that couldn't be a good sign, and for a second, for a blink really, she almost wished she believed in all this destiny talk, because bumping into the love of her life right now might be nice.

Madame Karma stood to her barely five foot height, signaling that their little meeting was over. That's when Chloe saw the small discreet jar with a sign indicating the fee for a "reading."

She just threatened me with bad karma and now I have the privilege of paying her for it, she thought.

"Since you don't believe in what I do," Madame Karma said, "what I said can't possibly be a threat."

Chloe blinked. She'd swear the woman had just read her mind—if she believed in that hooey. "Fine," she said and slapped her pockets for the bills she'd put in there—her cookie money, damn it—then stuffed them in the jar. Not messing around, she pushed away from the table, her gaze shifting to Constant Cravings.

She *really* needed some sugar. Near the coffee shop was the huge fountain marking the center of the courtyard. It shot streams of water into the air, spritzing the myriad colorful flowers lining the walkways. The wrought-iron benches were filled with people, some nibbling on food, some going after their valentine.

She stalked directly to the coffee shop. The owner and Chloe were friends, and as soon as she entered, Lacey smiled and greeted her. Knowing she could buy on account if she had to—which she now did have to, thanks to Madame Karma—Chloe ordered several scrumptious-looking cookies.

There. That would help dispel the odd quivering in her belly, which she knew damn well was hunger and not, definitely not, a niggling sense of discomfort.

As soon as she stepped outside with her bag, Chloe dug into the first cookie, moaning out loud when the peanut butter-chocolate treat melted in her mouth. The wind still whipped around, which she had to admit was slightly comforting, because for a few minutes, she'd almost believed Madame Karma had somehow been creating the wind.

The air felt sticky. Close. A storm was definitely brewing. She swiped a hand over her damp forehead and began to work on her second cookie.

There was a good turnout; many of the party goers were from the various businesses in the Fairfield complex. People milled about the flower-lined walkways, checking out the craft stalls or enjoying the art galleries and other novelty shops. Many carried shopping bags bearing the Fairfield logo, evidence that this party wasn't just for fun, it encouraged business.

Chloe counted many of these businesses as her customers, which pleased her. Life was good, she reminded herself. With or without a valentine—

Her gaze snagged on the entrance.

A man was walking into the open courtyard from the street, his sunglasses dangling in his fingers, his stride easy and loose. A man, just like any of a hundred before him, though none of the other men milling around had stopped her heart. None of them had sent her reeling, the years falling away on the light wind.

It couldn't be.

But it was. A blast from her past in the form of one tall, dark and way too gorgeous man. He was broader now, but still leanly muscled like the basketball player he'd once been. His hair was longer than she remembered, still dark as sin, curling around his collar.

Ian McCall, her first kiss, her first real boyfriend.

Her first everything....

2
_____

THE CROWD SEEMED TO SWELL and grow, and for a second, Chloe lost sight of him.

No!

Weaving through the crowds, she gripped both her bag of cookies and her sanity in a tight fist.

Where was he? Had the decorative lights played tricks on her? Had she simply dreamed him up?

It was entirely possible, given the hours she'd been keeping, which were pretty much 24/7. Nothing she could do about that. Mid-February was right about the time people tended to begin their pretax panic. She'd been deluged, without much time for sleeping.

That was it, she decided. She was simply sleep-deprived, nothing more. Today especially, as it was nearing seven o'clock and she'd begun work at seven that morning.

Twelve hours. No wonder she was seeing things. Anyone would be.

Suddenly the throng of people parted and she let out a low breath because there he was—in the center of the courtyard now, near the band, beneath the myriad white lights strung around a makeshift dance floor.

He had his back to her, shoulders straight, long legs taking him closer to the people dancing. He wore a simple black polo shirt untucked over faded black jeans that looked like beloved old friends, well worn and fitted to his undeniably hot body.

A body that she could, with some authority, say that, once upon a time at least, had looked just as good without any clothes at all.

True love is going to walk into your life.

It almost weakened her knees, how accurate Madame Karma had been. If she'd used past tense, that is.

Because once upon a time, when Chloe had been young and giddy and very, very naive, Ian McCall, with his dreamy green eyes and naughty smile, had been the love of her life.

Had been.

As in past tense.

As in a very long time ago. Ten years. Now she was no longer young and giddy, and she was certainly no longer very, very naive.

So why did just the sight of him grab her by the throat, by each and every erogenous zone…*by the heart?*

Stuffing another cookie in her mouth—clearly she needed the sugar fortification even more now—she began to make her way toward him. A group of women, their hands full of bags, all laughing and talking and making as much noise as a gaggle of hens, got in her way.

"Damn it." She pushed her way through. "Excuse me— *Excuse me,*" she said with growing impatience as she craned her neck every which way… Unbelievable.

She'd lost him again.

What was he doing here, anyway? They'd gone to high school together in Burbank Hills, and they'd been best friends, which had turned into something more. He'd been an absentminded but sweet and sexy basketball star, and she'd been his English tutor. He'd taught her hoops and she'd taught him Shakespeare. He'd shown her how to loosen up and she'd kept him on task, whether that task had been an English paper or kissing her senseless….

But then he'd gone off to NYU for the art history program, and she'd gone to Cal State Northridge for the accounting program, and they'd lost touch.

Well, except for that next year when he'd come home for the holidays and she'd run into him at her mother's New Year's Eve party….

Oh, yeah, that had been a night for the memories. Back then, it'd been six months since they'd been together, and it'd felt like six years. They'd caught their first glimpse of each other—

Ohmigod, she thought, as he reappeared, still near the dance floor. On that New Year's Eve all those years ago she'd caught her first glimpse of him, after their separation, over her mother's makeshift dance floor.

Just like now….

Destiny?

Or just crazy coincidence?

A picture of Madame Karma appeared in her head, the older woman waggling an I-told-you-so finger.

No. No, this wasn't fate, it was just a wild chance meeting—

There. He was still there. She caught a flash of his head, above most of the others, and the sunglasses he now had on top of it. Slowly, as if feeling the pull from her own shocked gaze, he turned to face her.

And from across the twenty-five yards of grass filled with people, with the band playing, and with the laughter and the deepening night sky lit up by the bright, cheerful lights, their eyes met. It seemed like a silly cliché, but Chloe would have bet her last dollar that time actually stopped.

Or maybe that was just her heart—which, in any case, immediately kicked back into gear with a heavy, fast beat that felt as if it came from her throat.

And he was the cause. She knew it.

And then just that fast, the crowd and the night closed in and swallowed him whole.

Gone.

She didn't know how or why, but Ian was here. She dumped her bag in a trash bin—quite a sacrifice—and cut across the dance floor, the fastest way to get to where she'd last seen him.

She strode across the grass and walkway, plowing into a block wall of dancers playfully executing a half-drunken version of the Macarena. She got caught up in them for a moment, with one particularly eager idiot from the framing shop not letting her pass until she'd stopped and gone through a whole verse.

With a forced smile, she rushed through the motions, thinking she had not consumed enough alcohol for this. Finally she got around them and waved goodbye, walking backward two steps before she again plowed into someone.

A someone with a rock-hard chest. "Sorry," she said, turning, looking up—

Her mouth fell open, because that hadn't been just any rock-hard chest. "Ohmigod," she said in an unintentionally breathless voice as his hands came up to steady her.

With his big, strong hands on her arms, and those warm, warm eyes locked on hers, it was like being catapulted back in time, so that she couldn't help sounding like Marilyn Monroe there for a second.

She'd never been one to use her femininity purposely. In fact, she'd been a tomboy all her life, which her own athletic frame had made natural, and had only recently become more comfortable in dresses and makeup and all things associated with being female.

Secretly she was glad, because it meant she was wearing her flowing, flowery skirt, pretty and flattering. She just wished she didn't sound as if she needed him to give her an orgasm. "My God, Ian. It's amazing to see you. What are you doing here?"

"I'm sorry." He spoke in the same low, slightly husky voice that had always turned her on so much. But something stopped her cold, and that was the fact that he also sounded like he was addressing a perfect stranger.

"Ian, it's me. Chloe. Chloe Cooper."

"Chloe." He frowned, his expression serious, and also now carefully, completely blank. "I don't— I think you're confusing me with someone else."

No way. But all the warmth had left his gaze, and now she couldn't even be sure…had she imagined the initial recognition in his eyes? The air in her lungs deflated, along with any ego or pride she might have had, which, granted had, been slim to begin with.

He didn't recognize her.

Embarrassed, she laughed a little. "High school. Junior and senior year…" She trailed off when he shook his head. Oh, God, he really didn't remember her. "I'm sorry. I— Never mind." Heart beating uncomfortably fast, she moved around him. Wow. She had no idea what had just happened, but it had been truly awkward. Definitely past time to get back up to her office, where she could put both this and Madame Karma's silly predictions and subsequent curse right out of her head.

Damn, she wished she'd kept that bag of cookies, she thought as she walked away.

What else could she do?

But then…then something made her glance back. Maybe it'd been his scent, some mixture of soap and deodorant and all man, a scent that was so damn familiar she wanted to pinch herself and wake up.

Maybe it'd been the undeniable certainty that she *wasn't* wrong.

Or maybe…maybe it was something much, much simpler. Such as the scar beneath his ear.

She remembered that Ian had a scar like that, too, from when he'd taken a flying header out of his dad's truck the day he'd turned sixteen and had wrapped the vehicle around a telephone pole while attempting to find a good song on the radio and drive at the same time.

A scar that she'd once pressed her mouth to and kissed. He'd loved it when she'd done that, and in return, she'd loved the sound of his harshly indrawn breath from just feeling her lips on him.

Why didn't he remember her? There had to be an explanation, she decided, and turned back. "Ian—"

He hadn't moved, but seemed to stand frozen to the spot, looking at her. "I'm not Ian."

His identical twin then. Only Ian hadn't had a brother. In fact, after his dad had died in their senior year, he'd had nobody. She pointed to his scar. "You got that in your car accident, remember?"

"No." Lifting a hand, he covered the scar. "You're mistaken. You're confusing me with someone else."

"So you're not Ian McCall."

"You're confusing me with someone else, that's all." He looked around him, at the party, the people, the pleasant chaos. "And I'm sorry, but I really need to get back to my...date."

Okay, he wasn't who she'd thought, and he also wasn't available. She got it. But being this close made her body ache, which was a ridiculous phenomenon all in itself that she would worry about later. For now, she just couldn't stop staring, just couldn't get over the fact that she was wrong, that this man wasn't Ian.

As she stood there somewhat in shock, the music changed, quickened, and there was a surge toward the dance floor. A group of people shifted behind the Ian-imposter, nudging him into her so that their bodies brushed.

Hers reacted immediately, as in nipples hardening, thighs tingling, the whole deal. And the bottom line was that her body recognized this man's body.

Again she was bumped, and she nudged up close. "I'm sorry," she whispered, putting her hands up to his chest to brace herself because it was getting extremely crowded around them.

And because she couldn't help herself.

His hands went to her waist to steady them both, and in what undoubtedly was more of her overactive, sugar-induced imagination, he gently squeezed her hips, regret flashing in his eyes.

Regret, and...something. But it was gone so fast she couldn't be sure she hadn't made that up as well.

True love is going to walk into your life.

The words wouldn't leave her brain. She'd laughed them off, but deep down she felt uneasy about the slight, very slight, possibility that she really did believe.

A fact she'd deny to her dying day, because even if this man *was* Ian, her once-upon-a-time teenage love, he couldn't possibly be the love of her life now, all these years later.

That, she definitely did not believe. "I just can't get over it," she murmured. "You look so much like—"

"They say we all have a twin out there."

"Yeah." The music slowed again, and the lights dimmed. All around them people drifted into pairs as the slow dance began.

The two of them stood there, awkwardly staring at each other, not moving except for the constant bumping of the crowd.

"I should—" he started.

"Yeah. Me, too."

He nodded. "Because I need to find…"

His date. Right.

And she should go upstairs.

Any moment now.

But neither of them moved. She, for one, didn't want to, and she'd like to think he didn't, either.

And then somehow they'd shifted even closer, her body flush against his again, as they sort of somehow fell into the rhythm of the music.

"I really need to go…" he started.

But he didn't go. His face was almost fierce with intent as he looked at her, same as when he'd been in the middle of a basketball game, or about to kiss her… And unable to resist, she melted into him. She couldn't help herself, he felt that good, that unbearably familiar.

Did he feel it?

She closed her eyes to let her body absorb the pleasure. It was as if time really had stopped, as if everything had stopped except this, and, helpless to the odd pull, she opened her eyes again and tipped her head up to say something, *anything*.

But she was interrupted by a startling flash of lightning, followed by an almost immediate crack of thunder that had her jerking nearly right out of her skin.

In reaction, he spread his fingers on her back and slid his hand up and down in a gesture that felt incredibly protective. Comforting.

And yet somehow so sexual she nearly purred.

And then the storm, which had been slowly moving in, finally arriving in all its glory. Around them, everyone gave a collective gasp and scattered off the dance floor, just as it began to rain.

The next thing Chloe knew, she was standing there, surrounded by the moving crowd and yet somehow utterly alone as the first drop of cool rain hit her heated face.

Ian was gone.

And she couldn't help but wonder…if true love had just walked into her life, then the second part of her fortune couldn't be far behind. Which meant her karma was about to go south for the winter.

3

CHLOE MOVED OFF THE dance floor, through the grass to the concrete pathway just as the sky let loose. Although let loose in Los Angeles meant that the ground was dotted with big, fat drops so few and far between that they didn't even run together or dispel any of the dust.

In fact, the drops felt good, so good she made sure not to stand beneath the protection of the awnings as she searched the crowd.

It was a well-dressed group as always, but then again, this was Baxter Hills, a wealthy suburb of Los Angeles, and the Fairfax complex had status. People always dressed well here, and behaved themselves, to boot.

Nowhere did she see those buttery soft jeans and polo shirt…

But she knew one thing—she had *not* dreamed him up.

No. She simply knew herself better than that. She wasn't prone to fantasies or daydreams. He was out there, somewhere. She'd had her hands on him, she'd felt the warmth of him, the flesh and hard sinew, the beat of his heart. She'd looked directly into his eyes and, no matter what he'd said, her body had recognized his.

And his had recognized hers as well.

As to why he refused to admit to being Ian, she had no idea. She hated that, and wouldn't, couldn't, accept it. It had been him, all six feet of him, just as she remembered.

She remembered everything. The fact that he could lose his wallet while it was still in his hand, or that he could make a backward, left-handed layup while looking sexy as hell, a feat she'd always rewarded with a kiss.

Did he remember any of those things? Going on tiptoes, she scanned the throng of people. He couldn't have vanished into thin air.

And yet he had.

The rain continued to cool her skin, which would have felt great if she'd been able to relax and enjoy it. She loved a good storm, loved the smell of the rain on the grass and flowers, loved the way everything looked when the clouds eventually moved on, leaving beads of water covering the landscape.

But tonight she couldn't concentrate on any of that. She couldn't concentrate on anything but finding Ian.

Finally, she gave up walking in circles and told herself it was over. He was gone. She could go home, or she could go upstairs and work some more, losing herself in the numbers. After all, numbers never let her down. Numbers never disappointed her, or hurt her.

Or vanished into thin air.

And even better, at the end of the day, numbers always fell into place. No strings, no worries for another day.

Couldn't ask for more in life than that. Or so she told herself. And if a little niggling doubt crept into her thoughts, a little voice that said maybe there was more to life than that—far more, and if she'd open up her mind and heart to it, she'd find out for herself—she filed it away into the same distant spot where she'd tucked away Madame Karma's doom and gloom.

She didn't have time for fantasies.

The Fairfax building was shaped like a big U, and her office was on the fourth floor at the bottom left corner of that U. Normally she took the stairs, considering it her daily exercise, thereby giving her an excuse at lunch to indulge her love affair with junk food. But since she'd already walked up and down those four flights today, she gave herself a break and took the elevator.

On her floor, she got off, passed the potted plants lining the hallway outside the chiropractor's suite, and then the cute little

African statues outside the antiquities importer and auction house, and then finally, arrived at her own business at the end of the hallway.

She unlocked her office door and flipped on the lights. She had enough time to take in her reception area, her large, organized desk with the computer and adding machine on it, just before the lights surged, then went out.

With a frown, she backed to the wall again and reached for the switch, hitting it off and then on.

Nothing.

She'd lost power.

Karma going south for the winter…

From the large window to the right of her desk came a flashing strobe of lightning, followed almost immediately by a cracking boom of thunder that made her jump again. "Relax," she told herself, the voice of reason. "The power's out because of the storm. That's all."

She waited a moment, thinking the lights would come right back on, because this was L.A. People didn't lose power in L.A.

But the electricity remained off. No comforting hum from her computer, just an eerie, strained silence in which all she could hear was her own breathing.

Well, damn. What was a workaholic to do when stressed if she couldn't work?

Not to be thwarted, she made her way to her desk, which she could have found blindfolded. After digging into the top drawer, she pulled out her handy-dandy hit-an-intruder-over-the-head-with-it flashlight, which she used to guide her as she lit several candles around the perimeter of her desk.

By candlelight, she opened her laptop and blessed the fact that she was anal enough to have the battery fully charged. Telling herself to forget the events of the evening—including both Madame Karma and the phantom Ian McCall—she got to work.

After a little while she realized she was way too warm, courtesy of no air conditioning. She slipped out of her light sweater, leaving her in just a skirt and a flimsy tank top. Then she twisted her ponytail on top of her head and secured it there with two pencils from her drawer.

She was nothing if not resourceful.

And then she bent back over her keyboard. But only a moment later, her head came up again.

Had she heard something?

Head cocked, she stared into the darkness and waited…then laughed at herself and went back to her numbers.

Thud.

Okay, that was something. She stood up and pushed her chair back. The noise hadn't come from her office, but one of the others on this floor. She moved to her door and pulled it open, then peered into the utterly black hallway.

Thud.

It didn't come from the chiropractor's office, but the antiquities and auction office. Odd because that office was closed. Steve and Al Adams, the two brothers who ran it, were overseas this week, which she knew because they were clients of hers.

And yet she'd heard what she'd heard. Contrary to the oddities of the night, she was not going crazy. Needing to prove it, she went back for her flashlight, then let herself out into the main hall. She knocked on her neighbor's door, knowing she wouldn't get an answer. "Hello? Steve? Al? Anyone?"

Nothing but another unmistakable *thud.*

Oh, boy. Just last month Steve had somehow left a window open in there. They'd ended up with a sparrow flying around the ceiling tiles until Al had managed to chase it out with a broom.

Thinking of all the damage a wild bird could do before the guys got back on Monday, Chloe once again trudged back to her office, this time for the spare key the brothers had left her. She quickly retraced her steps and opened up the auction house and swallowed into the utter blackness. "Here, birdy, birdy," she said, and waved her flashlight around. "Come out, come out, wherever you are."

This office was much larger than hers, and contained a huge

front room, designed to display various valuable and exotic antiques from around the world, which were sold at private and invitation-only auctions.

She didn't know the Adams's well. Steve and Al were both private, quiet guys who kept to themselves. They paid her on time and that's pretty much all that mattered.

They'd just had a large auction before they left so the place was empty. Anything they hadn't sold was locked safely away in storage somewhere.

Beyond the reception area was a conference room, where the auctions were held, and then two private offices, and also a large storage/cleaning/research room.

Chloe stood in that inky blackness, which was relieved only by her own small beam of light. Nothing looked out of the ordinary, and now, thankfully, she didn't hear a thing—

Thud.

Damn. She considered pretending she hadn't heard it. The sound had come from the offices in the back, and with a sigh, she headed in that direction. "Dear batteries, please don't die…"

Holding her breath, she turned to the first door, the auction room. It was empty, and very, very silent. So was Steve's office. But Al's…locked.

She looked down at the key in her hand, shrugged, and tried it. It worked, and she slowly turned the handle, the hair on the back of her neck rising when she heard a soft scuttle and then nothing.

Silence.

"Okay, bird," she said out loud to make herself feel better. "Or squirrel."

Nothing except that disconcerting sweat-inducing silence. Because she was suddenly claustrophobic, she moved around the desk to the window and looked out. She could see down to the courtyard and realized the other two wings of the building had not lost power. "Nice move, karma." With a sigh, she faced the dark room. "Hey, you know what, birdy? You just go ahead and stay. I'm fine with that."

And now she was talking to herself. Perfect. She headed to the door, then nearly killed herself when she fell over two ajar drawers. From her new position on the floor, she kicked the first one closed, but the second was jammed so she stood up and then pushed it.

Nothing.

Fine. She pulled it open to fix it. It was caught on files, filled with...bank statements?

Odd. She did the Adams's banking, and this couldn't be right. She hadn't seen these statements. Pulling out a file, she flicked her light over it, and her stomach began to sink as she realized these were recordings for banking accounts she knew nothing about, all fat with money.

"Damn," she said to the still unseen bird. "I hate it when they turn out to be crooked—" She broke off at a sound. And not just any sound, but a footstep.

A heavy footstep.

Nothing, nothing at all, like a bird or squirrel.

Oh, boy. Yeah, definitely she'd overstayed her welcome, but before she could hightail it to the door, she was yanked back against a strong, hard chest.

A squeak escaped her. That was all she got out as a big, warm hand came down over mouth and a muscled arm encircled her belly, rendering her immobile.

Her flashlight hit the floor, and she was hauled up against a large man. Panic gripped her. With his hand over her mouth, she was unable to move, unable to scream, and she could only think of one thing. Madame Karma really had cursed her.

She wouldn't take this with just a whimper. No way. She'd read *Self-Defense For Dummies*—she knew what to do. One kick to the nads and this sucker would drop like a stone.

Please drop like a stone.

She twisted to the side and thrust up her knee as hard as she could. An *oomph* escaped him, and then a concise, single-worded oath that singed her hair back and struck terror to her heart.

Because she'd missed and caught him in the thigh. Not

enough to incapacitate him or loosen his hold on her. But when he sagged back against the desk, she used their momentum to shove hard. They both crashed to the floor. Gasping for breath, she scrambled to crawl away, thinking *door.*

Get.

To.

The.

Door—

He grabbed her ankle and tugged hard, and she flew back against him.

"Hold still," he grated out.

Hell if she would do that, and she kicked him as hard as she could.

"Ow, goddammit!"

The next thing she felt was the slap of cold metal on her wrist, and the sound of something clicking into place. She tugged her hand but she couldn't move it.

Oh, God, he'd handcuffed her to him!

Then she was hauled to her feet, whipped around and pressed to a wall, held there by that hard body.

Then there was a narrow beam of light in her face.

"You," said that voice, the voice that was unbearably familiar because it belonged to the man who claimed not to be her first lover, the guy who'd vanished on her tonight after a near miss with an erotic slow dance…the tough, sexy, edgy Ian McCall.

And either he was extremely happy to see her, or he had a gun in his pants.

4

IAN MCCALL HELD Chloe Cooper against that wall and sighed to himself in the dark office. Hell. How had he managed to get himself in *this* predicament?

Simple. He'd gotten sloppy.

Well, not sloppy, never sloppy. *Overcome.* As in overcome with memories, thanks to the blast from the past that felt like a one-two punch to the solar plexus.

He'd let Chloe Cooper get into his head.

And against his body.

He'd been shocked to see her tonight outside in that courtyard, looking sweet and sexy and like hopes and dreams revisited. But if he'd been shocked to see one of his greatest memories, he'd been even more shocked to find her snooping inside the auction house he'd been casing.

"Ian." She was fighting him, fighting the handcuffs. *"What's going on?"*

He'd like to know the answer to that question himself. With all his heart he'd like to know. Not wanting to give himself away, he said nothing, but she was struggling. Unfortunately for him, the way he had her pressed between the plaster and his body, the only thing she was really doing was making his eyes cross with lust.

And it wasn't just his eyes. It actually wasn't his eyes at all, since he couldn't see a damn thing and had lost his penlight in the scuffle.

But he didn't need to see. Not with her ass pressed into his crotch, and the arm he'd wrapped around her now trapped between her breasts and the wall. He could feel her nipples pressing into his forearm, two hardened peaks that were making him sweat.

And she was still wriggling. Wriggling and squirming, rocking and rolling all those glorious curves against him. He tried not to notice, he really did, but he'd have to be dead not to be affected.

Then there were the memories assaulting him, pummeling him, reminding him how much she'd once meant to him, which was to say everything. Once upon a time, in her arms, he'd felt as if he could do anything. He'd been stupid enough to leave her behind when he'd gone off to find himself, but he'd never been too stupid to know what a great thing he'd lost.

It was driving him crazy now.

She was driving him crazy, and if she didn't stop wriggling— "Hold still," he ground out.

Of course she didn't, she continued to fight him with everything she had, and then some.

"I know it's you!" she cried. *"Why are we handcuffed?"*

Another most excellent question, which begged yet another, which was…just who didn't he trust, her…or him?

"Just tell me why you won't admit it's you!"

Yes. Why didn't he just admit it was him? Simple. Acknowledging their connection would jeopardize his case, not to mention his equilibrium.

Chloe. After all these years. Soft, beautiful, giving, passionate, wonderful Chloe. His first lover, keeper of his heart and, truthfully…

His biggest mistake.

God, he'd been so lost at eighteen, so sure he'd needed to leave town to make something of himself. And not just leave town, but go all the way across the country.

That's what came of growing up in an unhappy household.

But he'd learned a lot since then—such as, happiness came from within, not from a job or a location.

He'd been happy enough in New York, and after college had been recruited by the FBI as a stolen-antiquity specialist. But he'd been happier when he'd come back to Los Angeles.

He could smell her, some intoxicating scent, and he wanted to bury his face in her hair like a homecoming, because God, this was Chloe. He'd been with women since her, and he'd even had a connection with some of those women, but nothing like he'd had with her.

Hell, even tonight, when he'd seen her across the grass and courtyard, he'd felt the pull of her, had been helpless against it. Now, here, being this close felt more essential than breathing.

And that was a problem, a big one.

"Say something!" she demanded, *still* wriggling like crazy. "Goddamnit, say something, *anything!*"

He'd been trying to restrain her before she made him a eunuch but something in her voice stopped him cold. He was scaring her. Torn between losing his cover and the need to make sure he didn't give her a heart attack, he leaned over her and pressed his forehead to the wall, squeezing his eyes shut, his mind whirling. "I'll tell you what's going on, but you have to be still and quiet. Okay?"

She was breathing like a misused race horse, her soft warm exhales brushing his jaw.

"Okay?" he repeated, his hands gentle on her.

Still panting, he felt her nod. A strand of her hair caught on the day-old growth on his jaw and stubbornly clung. Another stray piece of silk stabbed him in the eyes.

Torture.

He waited a moment to make sure she was really going to behave because she'd nearly kicked his balls into next week, and, as he was particularly fond of all his parts, he didn't want a repeat.

She didn't move.

He'd thought that's what he wanted but it turned out, no. Because now everything that had been moving before was still, giving him a much better grip on her.

And with the grip he had, combined with the blackness al
around them, every little thing was magnified.

Intensified.

She was everything he remembered, everything that got int
his dreams sometimes late at night: smart, gorgeous and tena
cious as hell. God, he'd be so happy to see her, his first lover
the girl who'd once completely stolen his heart. Happy, excep
for two reasons.

One, he was deep into this stolen antiquities case. And two
as the accountant for his suspect, Chloe had some serious ex
plaining to do. "I'm going to try to find my flashlight," he said

"It's in your pants."

No, what was in his pants was a hard-on to rival all hard-on
"Actually…"

She'd been holding herself rigid, but now she gave nev
meaning to the phrase *still as stone,* and he grimaced. "It's o
the floor. Bend with me to reach for it." Without waiting for he
to protest or decide to try to unman him again, he hunkered an
forced her down with him. He had his free hand on her belly
which he could feel quivering. His other hand—attached to her
by the wrist—reached out to feel around the floor. Bent as the
were, with her practically in his lap, the position became unin
tentionally erotic.

Or maybe not so unintentionally.

He couldn't seem to help himself. Feeling like a pervert, h
gritted his teeth and felt around for the light, finally grabbing it
When he straightened, she did as well, and this time, she turned
facing him within the tight circle of his body and the wall now
at her back.

He held up the light, and she drew a steadying breath. "It'
you. I know it."

Damn it. He lowered the light to their sides. He had to be
careful here, very careful. When he'd taken this case, he'd had
no idea that she was involved in any way. When he'd first seen
her name, he'd hoped it'd been another Chloe Cooper.

"I know it's you," she said softly in the dark. "Say it's you or I'm going to—"

He felt the shift of her weight and knew she was going to try to kick him again. To avoid that he sandwiched her between the wall and his body, chest to chest this time, thighs to thighs...and unfortunately, everything in between.

At that, all professionalism packed up and left him. He needed to back away, needed to put some space between them, but that was damn hard when all he wanted to do was grab her close, kiss her blind and push up into her body.

Yeah, that was professional at its finest. He struggled to get it together and, lacking that ability, simply tried to locate some working brain cells.

"Ian—" Accompanying her soft plea, her free hand came up, sinking into his hair, tugging his head down, and then...oh, God, and then...she kissed him.

And it was like coming home.

Yeah, way to back away there, champ. But she was kissing him, letting out a soft little sexy-as-hell murmur from deep in her throat, her body moving against his, her hands clutching at him, all lush and warm and needy female.

Ah, God, it was good. So good he was already trembling, his breath trapped in his throat the way all his blood was now trapped behind his button fly.

Get it together.

He didn't. Well, except to better line up their lips. Not his smartest decision, but his brain was truly no longer in control. The feel of her lips sent waves of heat and hunger and a barely repressed longing he hadn't realized he still felt, all of it colliding within him, surprising him with its force so that he shook with it. "Wait," he gasped.

She didn't. Of course she didn't. Instead she nibbled first one corner of his mouth and then the other, while inside him the heat burst into flame. *Stop,* he ordered himself, but that was far more difficult then he'd imagined, and he kept kissing her for another minute, lightly, softly now, trying like hell to let them both down easy. "We have to stop," he whispered.

Her answer to that was to run the tip of her tongue along his lower lip.

Unable to control himself, he sucked it right into his mouth. Oh, yeah. God. This was crazy.

Crazy.

She was driving him right out of his mind with that heart-stopping mouth of hers, and he let out a dark, shockingly needy sound that would have destroyed him if he hadn't sensed she felt the same way. He told himself to back away, but he didn't.

He wasn't sure what kind of fool that made him, but then she cupped his face and took that sweet tongue of hers on a tour of his and that was it, he was one, two, three, down for the count. Helplessly drowning in her and not caring, he went to band his arms around her, but came up against the barrier of his own handcuffs.

Shit.

How he'd nearly forgotten was beyond him. He slipped his free hand around her, low on her spine, so that he could haul her up against him. His other hand, the one linked to hers, he drew up over her head, against the wall, holding it there as he let the kiss take him.

And take him it did. At her back, his fingers closed over the material of her thin top, fisting in it so that he felt bare skin.

Heated, smooth, bare skin.

Once upon a time he'd known how every inch of her tasted, and she'd tasted like heaven. He had no doubt that hadn't changed, and his mouth watered just thinking about putting his mouth on her.

Everywhere.

"You kiss the same," she murmured against his mouth. "It *is* you…." Her lips slid along his jaw. "The whole palm-reading thing threw me off balance, but deep down, I knew…"

Palm reading? He had no idea what she was talking about, but he turned his head to capture her mouth again, deepening the kiss, and when he'd drowned in her, when they'd drowned in each other, she pulled back.

"Say it," she whispered intensely, breathlessly, completely and one hundred percent undoing him. *"Say it."*

Sunk, he pressed his forehead to hers.

"Ian," she urged.

Hell. His heart was thumping against hers and he was sucking in air like a beached fish. "Yes. It's me." Goddammit.

"I knew it!" She let out a low laugh. "God. Why didn't you tell me?"

"I'm sorry." And he was. He really was one big sorry son-of-a-bitch.

"And why are we handcuffed together? Are you a cop?"

"FBI agent."

"So you thought what, that I was breaking and entering?"

The story. He needed to remember his story. Not easy when he had her in his arms, his engines still revving. "I was here—"

"Because of the party?"

That worked. "Yes. The party." He could feel her looking at him, clearly absorbing his hesitation.

"You were on a date," she said.

Right. Only what kind of slime would be on a date and yet kiss another woman? "Uh…yeah. A date."

"She left you?"

Yes, if "she" was his very male partner. And if by *left,* she meant Danny taking Ian's car home because of a nasty case of the Shouldn't-Have-Had-That-Whole-Pizza.

Up until that point he and Danny had been narrowing in on their antiquities/fencing case, the one that had taken up the past six months of their lives. The case involved an entire ring of thieves involved in selling stolen antiques, apparently led by two: Steve and Al Adams, partners in the antiquities auction house that they stood in at this very moment.

Up until last night, everything had been quiet, mostly just research and endless tailing on his and Danny's part, but then last night they'd discovered the two dead bodies in Al's garage—the informants who'd led Ian and Danny to the antiquities business in the first place. Yeah, things were ratcheting up. "I'm here alone now."

"Oh, Ian."

God, she bought it. She bought that he'd been on a date and then dumped, and he felt like crap.

Her fingers were gentle on his jaw. "I can give you a ride home."

Lower than crap.

"So why are you up here?" she asked. "In the antiquities office, when it's closed? Handcuffing me?"

Good question. And a valid one. "I came up here to see you again."

Or investigate you.

Pick one.

"Oh." Confusion clouded her voice as she tugged lightly on the handcuffs. "I still don't understand why you didn't tell me."

Ah, hell. Hurt had replaced her fear, and while he was glad she was no longer afraid, hurting her was pretty much the last thing he wanted to do.

Too bad he didn't always get to do what he wanted.

He had to tell her some of the truth. "I didn't tell you because I can't be seen here tonight."

"What do you mean? People saw you downstairs."

"Doubtful. I blended in. No one can know," he repeated, lifting her face to his in the dark. "No one. Do you understand?"

His question hit a brick wall of silence.

In fact, she was silent for so long he nearly checked for a pulse, except that he could still feel her heart thundering against his.

"You're looking at me funny," she said very quietly. "Am I in trouble, Ian?"

He touched her hair and fought with himself against pressing his face into the sweet spot of her neck. Yeah, she was in trouble.

And so was he.

5

"IAN?" CHLOE WHISPERED IN the dark. She was still touching him, one hand on his face, the other linked to his by the handcuffs.

Handcuffs.

She was handcuffed to Ian McCall, which, she reminded herself, wasn't the oddest thing that had happened.

Not when she thought about that kiss they'd just shared.

That explosive kiss. Explosive and wildly passionate and hotter than anything she'd experienced since...well, since him. "I don't understand," she said. "Who are you watching? What's going on in here that requires an FBI agent?"

He pressed his forehead to hers and answered her question with one of his own. "Chloe, why were you in here tonight?"

"I heard a noise."

"You have a key?"

"I do their books, and when they're out of town, I keep an eye on things."

"So you're close friends with them?"

She went still from the very inside. Still and cold. "Why does this suddenly feel like an interrogation?"

He didn't answer that, either, and she slid her hand down his taut arm to grab the flashlight, which she lifted to see his face.

He didn't flinch but looked right at her from those once dreamy eyes, which now held more than a hint of the hunger she'd just experienced.

And something else, something that made alarms go off in her head, even more than the handcuffs.

Worry. "Ian. You're scaring me. What's going on?"

"Let's just get out of here," he said, turning away.

Oh, no. She wasn't going anywhere without answers. So she pulled him back, unfortunately dropping the flashlight to do so.

It hit hard, and, given that the light flickered and went out, it also broke.

"Two for two," he murmured.

His low, slightly gruff voice, disembodied in the dark, seemed to ruffle something within her.

Or maybe the kiss had done that.

Or just his close proximity. Who knew? All she knew was she couldn't take a breath without him knowing, and vice versa. Granted they were handcuffed, but they could have made more room between them. Neither of them had. Even after all this time, even after their awkward meeting and more awkward second meeting up here, something still shimmered between them.

It was undeniable. It could have been the dark, or the past, or simply the fact that it'd been far too long since she'd been held or touched by a man.

No, that didn't compute. It wasn't being touched by a man that had taken over common sense.

It was being touched by *him*.

"Let's get out of here," he said again. "We'll talk then."

All right, she was game for that, and she rattled the handcuffs. "Key?"

He shifted his weight and she guessed he was searching his pockets, a suspicion confirmed when she heard him patting himself down with growing agitation. "Ian?"

"Yeah. Hold on."

More rustling, accompanied by a roughly uttered, "Ah, hell."

"What?"

"Just a second."

Okay. But the longer she stood there listening to him fumble around in his pockets, the more she knew. "Let me guess."

"Don't."

"You lost your keys."

"I did not lose them."

"Uh-huh." She felt like laughing. How that was possible was beyond her. "Then, where are they?"

"Obviously, they're in the last place I had them."

"So you're still absentminded," she said, and let go of the laugh in her throat.

"Yeah. And you're still a smart-ass." He said this utterly without annoyance.

In fact, it sounded pretty darn affectionate.

A flash of lightning lit the room in a blue-white glow, followed by a heart-pounding boom of thunder. In that split second, her gaze locked with his.

Not all of that flash of electricity came from the storm—not even close. Nope, most of it came from the combustible, explosive, chemical-like attraction between the two of them, and quite frankly, after all this time, it shocked her. "Can you still do that layup?" she whispered.

"If I say yes, are you going to kiss me again?" He let out a rough breath. "No. Don't answer that. Look, the handcuff key is a small one, all by itself. It must have dropped from my pocket in the shuffle. We need another flashlight."

"I have a spare in my office."

"Let's go."

She wanted to know why it was such a bad idea to kiss him. She wanted to know a whole helluva lot of things, like why he was really here and why every time she took a step forward, he took one back.

She moved toward the door, forgetting that one of the drawers was still open. She'd have fallen flat on her face if he hadn't encircled her waist with an arm and hauled her back against him.

"Careful," he said in her ear, his voice low and thrillingly gravelly.

She could have told him that the only thing in danger was her heart, but they shuffled their way out of the antiquities office together, which meant lots of banging into each other to keep their balance in the dark.

Chloe had never been so aware of a man in her life. "Here," she said when they finally got down the hallway to her office. She opened the door. Candlelight still flickered on the walls, relieving the darkness they'd had in the hallway and the auction house.

She glanced at Ian standing at her side, letting her gaze drift over his wavy hair, his furrowed eyebrows indicating he was deep in thought as he took in her office.

He caught her staring. "What?" he asked.

"I just can't believe that it's you. You've changed, Ian."

"Grown up, I hope."

Yes, and developed a razor sharpness that suggested he was no longer all fun and games. His face was tanned, more rugged now than baby smooth, and carved in classic lines that were admittedly drool-worthy.

He'd definitely changed. Where he'd once been lanky and lean to the point of being too thin, he'd bulked up some, all corded muscle and sinew wrapped in an undeniable masculinity. There was something else, too, something about him that suggested a will to walk into danger, a readiness to face whatever came his way. She grabbed her spare flashlight out of a drawer, watching as he leaned over her desk and blew out her candles.

"Fire hazard," he said, and when he'd blown out the last one, plunging them back into darkness, she gripped the flashlight but didn't turn it on.

Truth was, she liked being in the dark with him. She didn't know what that said about her, but ever since he'd appeared at the party outside, she'd felt more alive than she had in a long time.

"Let's go get the key," he said, taking the flashlight, heating her skin everywhere they touched. Oblivious to that fact, he led her back to the antiquities office.

Together, they hunkered down by the desk searching, and Chloe stared into his profile.

He hadn't shaved today, and maybe not yesterday either, but the intriguing growth on his jaw made her fingers itch. He had laugh lines around his eyes and bracketing his mouth, a mouth she happened to know curved with slow, wicked intent, making his amusement contagious.

Also, he smelled...wonderful. Knee-weakeningly wonderful, which didn't seem fair since she probably smelled of fear and stress—not wonderful at all.

His hair was still lush and unruly, and as thick as ever, and she couldn't help it, she reached up and brushed a lock from his forehead.

Lifting his head, his gaze met hers, full of heat and a testosterone that oozed trouble. "Chloe." His voice held warning and that sexy hunger as he looked into her eyes, his utterly unfathomable.

"What?" she whispered.

He just shook his head. "Nothing."

But she knew it was something. She knew it with every bone in her body. "No key?"

"No. We'll have to get one from my place."

His place. That probably shouldn't have given her a shiver of thrill. "Okay."

They made their way out of the office and to the stairs, which they took in silence, close but not touching except for where they were linked by the cuffs. She had so many questions she didn't know where to start, and she wished she knew him better, like she used to, so she could press him for answers.

"Where's your car parked?" he asked.

And it hit her. They were going to go through the outdoor party to the lot, and all the way to his place—wherever that was—handcuffed. She knew this. She should have been upset by this. Furious.

Instead, a frisson of arousal went through her. "Back parking lot."

They stepped out of the building into the courtyard, and it was as startling as if they'd walked onto another planet. In one blink they went from utter darkness, back into the festive lights, music and sounds of laughter and people conversing.

The rain had stopped. The temperature had dropped quite a bit, making her wish for her sweater, which she'd left upstairs.

Had it been only a few minutes ago that she'd been down here herself, standing on the dance floor, laughing over Madame Karma's predictions?

True love is going to walk into your life.

She squirmed a little at that thought, and glanced at Ian over her shoulder.

He was holding her handcuffed hand in his so that they didn't draw any attention to themselves.

Your karma has gone south for the winter.

So which was he, Madame Karma's first prediction, or the second?

And why did she suddenly believe what the fortune-teller had said at all? "Are you sure your date—"

"Gone," he said with certainty.

Who would ditch him? And why? She couldn't imagine… But looking into his tense face, she knew she was missing more of his story, and that made her nervous. Still, she led him through the throng of people, past the dance floor where only a short time ago she'd stood next to him, thinking about gobbling him up from head to toe.

She was still thinking about it.

They left the courtyard out the back of the building, and into the parking lot.

At her car, he waited until she unlocked the door, then pulled it open for her. She stood in the V of the opened door, and he stood just behind her, his free hand on the roof of the car, the other linked to her, surrounding her. His body heat seeped into her, through her, and she closed her eyes to savor every second, because she knew that when she took him home and they were unlocked from each other, he was going to vanish again.

Maybe for good this time.

Unable to stand the thought, she turned to face him. Cupped his jaw.

"Chloe—"

In answer, she kissed him, kissed him until his hand left the top of the car and came down to her waist.

When she opened her eyes, his held surprise and that intoxicating heat that made her knees wobble. "I just wanted to do that one more time," she whispered.

He stood there a moment, and then, when he opened his mouth to say something, it began to rain again. He nudged her aside so he could slide into the car, moving slowly across the passenger seat to allow her the time to keep up with him.

They drove in silence except for Ian's giving her directions to his condo complex. When she'd parked and turned to him, he was already looking at her.

"Ready?" he asked.

Yes. Yes, she was. The real question was, what was she ready for?

The rain topped its earlier show, coming down in thick sheets. They ran up the path to Ian's front door, where he quickly slapped his pockets for his keys while they got soaked. Finally, he dropped his head and swore.

"Let me guess," she yelled over the sound of the rain hitting the roof. "You misplaced your house keys, too?"

He looked at her, the irony and a good amount of wry amusement in his eyes. She could do nothing but laugh.

He joined her, until the sky lit up with a strobing bolt of lightning, followed by a booming clap of thunder that made her squeak.

"The back!" He led, and by the time they ran around the building and through a gate, they were both a soggy mess. Chloe could barely see through her streaming hair. Shoving it back, she looked at Ian, who was also trying to see, and laughed.

His eyes laughed, too.

It was true. His eyes laughed, which brought another silly smile to her face, because suddenly she felt like a kid.

No, scratch that. Not a kid. A teenager.

A rather horny one.

"Sorry," he said, reaching up into a potted plant, and then the next thing she knew she was standing in his kitchen. He had hardwood floors and pale green walls with gorgeous trim, and like a real guy, dishes piled in the sink, a fact that made her want to smile as she dripped all over his pretty floor.

Ian dripped, too. Water ran down his temples, in his face, making his dark eyelashes inky-black and spiky.

He was looking at her, slowly taking in her wet clothes, including her thin tank and gauzy skirt that had to be clinging to her like a second skin.

And his smile slowly faded.

So did hers.

His was replaced by a heat that singed her every erogenous zone, of which she apparently had a lot more than she remembered.

Lifting the hand that was connected to hers, he pulled, and she found herself in his arms, staring at his mouth as he slowly lowered it to hers.

"Stop me," he whispered. "Stop me now, Chloe, because I can't seem to do it."

Instead she lifted her free hand to his chest, gliding it up around his neck, cupping his nape to tug his head down to hers.

6

AH, HELL, IAN HAD TIME TO think as Chloe's soft lips touched his. The kiss, *her* kiss, felt better than anything had in a damn long time.

He'd been working around the clock, neglecting pleasure for so long that it whipped through his veins, demanding more, more, *more.*

Never mind that he shouldn't.

They shouldn't. She was a possible suspect, a definite witness, and hell, he couldn't take his hands off her.

With Chloe, he had no resistance, not when her curvy body had shrink-wrapped itself to his, not when she'd slid her warm, sweet tongue inside his mouth….

At this rate, he wouldn't survive if they stopped. "Chloe…" His fingers sank into her hair, gently tugging her head back so he could look into her eyes, but instead he pressed his mouth to her bared throat and made his way along her wet skin, to her jaw, her ear.

She let out a shaky exhale and held on. "Ian…why were you really in that office?"

He'd expected the questions. What he hadn't expected was to be so completely blindsided by needing her that his guard was down. Down, hell. It was flat-out gone.

"For a case, I'm guessing. Right?"

He sank his teeth lightly into her earlobe, then soothed the spot with his tongue.

"Ian." Her voice was wobbly, her free hand clutching at him, as if she was having trouble standing. The handcuffs clanked, reminding him again of their presence. They were a tool of his job, not a sex toy. He'd never really been into bondage. Yet he couldn't have begun to explain how unbearably erotic it felt to be handcuffed to her.

"Are they in trouble?" she asked. "The guys?"

It took a moment to get past the sexual haze and be able to talk. "Guys?"

"Steve and Al? I do their books."

Against her deliciously wet, warm skin, he sighed.

And she went still. "I suppose you probably already know that." Lifting her head, she stared at him. "Talk to me, Ian."

He knew the regret was all over his face. "I—"

"Can't." Her worried smile broke his heart. "Or you'd have to kill me, right?" She lifted their handcuffed wrists. "Key?"

"Yeah." He backed her to the countertop and opened a drawer at her hip.

"Um…" She rocked her hips to his, making his eyes cross with lust.

"Chloe," he said on a low breath. "You're killing me."

"It's like we were never apart. Do you remember?"

He looked into her eyes. "Everything."

"Our first time…?"

Especially that. He'd driven them through the Angeles Crest forest, to an overlook where they could see the lights of sprawling Los Angeles far beneath them.

Neither of them had noticed the view. Instead they'd ravaged each other in the front seat of his truck, and then the bed of his truck, stretched on a blanket beneath a sky littered with a million stars…. "I remember."

He'd had plenty of sex since then, some really good sex, but looking into her eyes now, he knew the truth—nothing had ever quite lived up to his time with her.

No one had ever come close to touching his heart the way she had.

How to explain that to her, much less to himself, he hadn't a clue.

"Today, it was like you appeared out of thin air." She leaned in close as he searched the drawer. She brushed a wet strand of hair from his temple, letting her fingers linger on him.

His gaze locked on hers as his fingers closed over the key.

She smiled and somehow the simple gesture warmed him. "You grew into your skin quite nicely, Ian McCall."

"Not nearly as well as you…" Straightening, he ran his fingers over her bare shoulders, playing with the spaghetti strap of her very wet tank. "You're wet."

Her eyes widened, maybe wondering if the double entendre had been intentional, which actually it hadn't, but now he could think of nothing else.

"So are you," she whispered, running her free hand over his shirt, then under. Her fingers brushed his nipple, and he actually dropped the key.

The pulse at the base of her neck was racing. She wasn't breathing all that steadily either, but then again, neither was he.

Neither of them bent for the key.

Send her home, his brain ordered. He had to, before he did something stupid.

She was still touching his chest, sliding her hand back and forth over him, lingering. "Chloe—"

She shivered.

He could see her white lace bra—it was playing peekaboo with the wet cotton of her tank, blowing his mind. So were her nipples, pebbled to two hard points, clearly outlined and defined, making his mouth water. "You're beautiful, Chloe," he breathed. "So damned beautiful." His finger slid beneath one of her straps, and then, *oops, look at that,* it fell to her elbow.

Stop, he told himself. *Seriously, stop.*

But then Chloe lifted their joined hands and slipped the other strap off…and then the top slid down so that it was just barely, oh, God, *barely* covering the very tips of her breasts. "Chloe—"

"That's my name," she said in a soft, whispery voice that

reminded him of long, achingly deep, toe-curling sex. She tugged on the hem of his shirt, leaving him no choice but to lift up his arms and let her pull his shirt all the way off.

No choice at all.

Now his shirt hung between them, caught on the handcuffs. And then she was working on the button fly of his jeans, and he was trying to find the zipper on her skirt, but their hands were getting tangled up. Breathless with anticipation and with a hunger so all-consuming neither of them could talk and make any sense, they fell back against the counter, mouths fused, bodies still damp from the rain and practically steaming they were so heated up.

Unable to get her skirt off, he bunched the light, gauzy material in his fingers. She broke off the kiss to drag hot, wet openmouthed kisses down his throat and over his chest.

He found her panties.

She got his buttons undone.

Being with her like this felt like a homecoming in ways he couldn't really wrap his brain around, except that stopping was no longer an option—

And then he heard something that snapped him out of it like nothing else could have.

"What?" she murmured, her mouth on his pec.

"I thought I heard something—" His brain had gone hazy. "I heard—" She sank her teeth into him and his knees nearly buckled. "Hold on—"

She slid a hand into his pants. "I am."

His head came up as he realized two things at once. One, he *loved* feeling her hands on him again. Two, someone was in the house with them. And he was standing here with his hand down the back of her panties, more than half-undressed himself, still handcuffed to her, and shockingly, frustratingly helpless. "Be very quiet," he said in her ear. "I'm going to—"

That's when the lights went out.

7

CHLOE GASPED AT THE sudden, unexpected darkness. "The storm?"

"No."

That was when she realized Ian had gone taut with tension, and not the good kind of tension.

"Someone's in the house," he said quietly, without inflection. "They just cut the power."

"Ohmigod." Since he was so calm, she panicked for the both of them, clutching at him, feeling all one hundred and eighty pounds of him quiver with a dangerous edge. "Are you sure?"

Instead of answering, he reached for something, came up against the restraints of the handcuffs, and swore beneath his breath.

"*What are we going to do?*"

"Not we." His voice was low, a barely there sound against her ear. "Me. You're going to—"

"We're handcuffed! There is no just you!"

He pushed her behind him, where she concentrated on breathing. Not easy. Only a moment ago she'd been breathless for an entirely different reason, and now with the adrenaline flying through her, she felt dizzy, light-headed and sick.

She heard another drawer open and then caught the glint of something—

A knife. He'd grabbed a knife.

Oh, God. Her hands were on his back, smooth and sleek and shirtless.

Defenseless.

Not defenseless, she reminded herself. He was trained; he knew what to do.

She hoped.

He moved, and without any choice she followed, thankful at least that they were on familiar territory for him because she couldn't see a damn thing.

God, she was tired of the dark. After tonight she wanted never to be in the dark again.

"Careful," he said, craning his neck to speak softly to her. "Stay behind me."

Which she'd be glad to do, except that left him even more defenseless because he had one hand twisted behind his back, attached to her.

Oh, God.

He flattened them against a hard surface. Given the icy-cold steel that hit her bare shoulders, she realized it was the refrigerator. She bit back her gasp, and with her free hand attempted to right her tank top. But it was twisted around her and not cooperating—

"Stop."

Yes, she understood he wanted her to stop fiddling around, but hell if she'd be chased around the house by a burglar while half-naked.

"Shh," he added, as if she'd dare say a word, and he brought their joined hands to her belly, maybe as comfort, but more likely to hold her in place so she didn't give them away.

She heard a light squeak and caught the vague outline of the double kitchen doors opening, which had her heart launching into her throat.

Ian's hand tightened on her stomach. Definite warning.

But she wasn't going anywhere, she was paralyzed in fear.

A shadow stepped into the kitchen, crouched low, holding something that looked like a—

Oh, God, a gun.

Then Ian stepped into the middle of the room—dragging her with him—and executed some amazing sort of roundhouse kick that sent the intruder flying. It would have sent her flying too, just from Ian's momentum, but he grabbed her and they both fell to the floor.

Ian immediately rolled toward the intruder, but what exactly he did after that, Chloe couldn't be sure, she couldn't see, she was too busy trying to keep out of Ian's way while attached at the wrist.

"Got him," he said grimly.

She came up to her knees. She realized Ian was on his as well, at her side. *"Who is he?"* she whispered.

"No idea." He was holding the guy down with his free hand. With his other he tried to reach into his pocket and instead came up against the cuffs. "Damn it. My cell phone. It's in my pocket. Can you—"

She slid her fingers into his pocket. Only a few minutes ago she'd been in his pants for an entirely different reason.

"Call 9-1-1," he said.

Sitting back on her heels she did just that, thinking of how just a short time ago her plans for this evening had been a few cookies and more work. Well, the evening had veered just about as far from her plans as it possibly could have.

CHLOE SAT IN A cold, hard metal chair at the police station sipping the water Ian had brought her before he'd gone to talk with a group of police officers.

Each of whom repeatedly kept glancing over at her.

Ian's intruder had been ID'd from his driver's license, but once the police had arrived and had shone their flashlights on them all, Chloe hadn't needed to see the guy's ID because she'd recognized him.

He was one of Steve and Al's employees, and at the sight of him and the gun he might have used on them, she instantly realized two things. One, this case of Ian's was apparently far more dangerous than she could have imagined. And two, given the clench in her heart every time she so much as looked at Ian, she'd fallen for him all over again.

Which actually brought her to a third problem—did he think she was connected to his case?

Was she…good God…a *suspect?*

She shivered wildly, and almost before she'd finished, he was there, wrapping his own zippered hoodie sweatshirt around her shoulders. "Almost done," he promised in a low voice, giving her arms a quick squeeze.

She hugged herself tightly and didn't look at him. Looking at him screwed with her head because she couldn't seem to reconcile the man she'd played tonsil hockey with, with the FBI agent with secrets.

"Chloe?" he asked. "You okay?"

Taking a deep breath, she bit the bullet and asked, "Am I a suspect in something, Ian?"

"McCall," one of the men called out, gesturing with his chin for Ian to join them.

She just looked at him, wanting, *needing,* an answer.

His eyes held regret. "Give me a minute, I'll be right back."

It didn't escape her that he was avoiding her question.

"Chloe. I will, I promise."

"I think I'll just go home, and—"

"You can't."

Oh, yeah, he was definitely bad for her mental health. "Why not?"

He grimaced, and scrubbed a hand over his face. "Because there are questions."

"Theirs? Or yours?" She could see his colleagues waving him over, and she shut her eyes. "So. I am a suspect. Do you kiss all your suspects like you kissed me?"

"Chloe—"

"Just go. The sooner you do, the sooner I can get the hell out of here, go to bed and sleep off yet another bad Valentine's Day."

She didn't open her eyes, and after a moment, felt him move away. She nodded to herself, refusing to acknowledge the pain in her heart.

IAN SET DOWN A MUG OF hot tea in front of Chloe. As peace treaties went, it was a poor one, but it was the best he could do.

Without looking at him, she pulled the mug closer to her, and as she did, his sweatshirt—too long for her by half—fell back from her wrist. It was rubbed raw, chafed by the damn handcuffs, and he stared at it, feeling sick. "Let me get the first aid kit—"

"I'm fine." She said this curtly, and covered her wrist back up. "Just ask me whatever it is you think I know so I can go home."

"I know you're upset."

"No." But it came out in such a way that made it obvious she was upset and also that she considered him a first-class asshole.

He sighed, and pulling a chair over to hers, he straddled it, then steepled his fingers along the back, setting his chin on them. "Chloe."

She blew on her tea. "Yes," she said, a picture of supreme politeness.

"You *are* upset."

"Okay, yes. I'm usually upset when lied to by someone I've trusted."

"I haven't lied."

"Really?" She leveled her baby blues on him then, eyes that were huge and devastatingly beautiful. Not to mention filled with hurt. "You were actually ditched by a real date tonight?"

Okay, so he had lied. "My partner got sick."

She rolled her eyes.

"Look, the truth is we think the antiquities place is really a front for a fencing business."

"And you believe I'm involved exactly how?"

"It's not that—"

"How, Ian?"

"You've done their accounting."

Her eyes flashed her fury. "And you think I've played with the numbers?"

"Someone did— Whoa," he said, his hand shooting out to snag her arm when she jerked to her feet. "I said someone, not you—"

"I'd like to go home now," she said stiffly. "I want to change and get warm."

"Soon—"

She drew up straight and pulled free of his touch. "Do you have any reason to hold me?"

"What? No, of course not—"

"Then, if you'll excuse me…" And with her nose so high he was surprised she didn't get a nosebleed, she walked to the door.

"Chloe, wait."

She didn't, of course. Wearing his sweatshirt, her arms wrapped around herself in quiet dignity, she walked out of the station, and most likely if she had her way, out of his life.

Damn it.

He couldn't let her go, and that fact had nothing, nothing at all, to do with his case. First of all, she was innocent, he knew that in his gut, and he knew it by looking into her eyes, which were mirrors to her soul, a soul that had never purposely hurt or taken from another human being in her life.

Earlier, Danny had suggested he get himself reassigned, that he couldn't be objective.

He'd vehemently disagreed.

Yes, he'd known her once, known her intimately, but that had been years ago and he should have been completely over her. After all, it'd been *him* who'd walked away that time, him who'd decided it was time to move on.

But that had been before he'd danced with her, touched her, *kissed* her. And now it turned out Danny was right. He couldn't be objective because he couldn't, *wouldn't*, believe she'd done anything wrong.

And since he could do nothing else, he went after her.

8

IAN RAN OUTSIDE THE police station into the now clear night. The wind had chased away the clouds.

And, apparently, Chloe.

He raced through the lot, turning in a circle in the middle, stopping short at the sight of her at the far end, his gut clenching hard.

Her skirt soggy and clinging, his own sweatshirt covering her from fingertips to mid-thighs, her hair damp and hanging in her face, she looked like a wreck, an adorable, sexy wreck.

He'd never seen anyone so beautiful in his life.

"Great exit," she was saying to herself. "But your car's at Ian's, you idiot. Of course, it's at Ian's, because this is Valentine's Day." Sighing, she tipped her head heavenward. "Karma? You listening? You *suck*."

"Does karma ever talk back?" he asked, stepping close.

She didn't jump, didn't scream, just closed her eyes. "Perfect." Then she opened her eyes and looked at him. "Do you believe in karma, Ian?"

"That's not the question I expected you to ask."

She let out a low, mirthless laugh. "Tonight, at the party? I had my palm read. The lady told me some pretty crazy stuff."

She'd been crying, and his heart tipped. "Like…?" he asked very softly.

"Like…" She squirmed just a little, which he didn't understand. He'd expected to be on the hot seat, not her. "She said true love was going to walk into my life. Tonight."

"What did you say to that?"

"I laughed. And then she gave me a warning. She said my karma was going to take a vacation to the Bahamas."

"Harsh."

"Maybe she was mad that I didn't believe her."

"You don't believe in love at first sight?"

She looked at him. "Do you?"

"Yes." He was shocked to hear himself say it, but it was true, he realized.

"How about karma?" she asked. "Do you believe in karma?"

"I believe in making your own karma, by being a good person, doing your best, finding ways to be happy so that life is good."

"What if you're too busy securing your future to stop and smell the roses, and then one day you're thirty and all you have to look forward to on Valentine's Days is a day like this?"

She sounded uncertain and alone, very alone, which he hated. With a sigh, he pulled her close, wet clothes and all. "Was the night all bad?"

She went quiet a moment. "No, not all bad."

He found his mouth close to her face, and kissed her temple, her jaw. "Destiny is your own for the taking, Chloe. You know that, right?" He kept his mouth on her, loving the feel of her skin beneath his lips. "And I'm sorry, but I can't imagine you doing anything bad enough to warrant worrying about your karma going south."

Arching her neck to give his mouth better access, her hands came up to his shoulders as if she couldn't help herself. "Why not?" she whispered.

"Because I know you."

"But your case—Steve and Al—"

"If you had anything to do with this, it was without your knowing it."

Her huge eyes never left his, though some of the tension in her body did. "You really feel that way?"

"Really." He let out a long breath. "Jesus, Chloe, do you really think I could kiss you like I did, and believe you to be a thief?"

"*I* kissed *you*."

"Well, I can fix that." Hauling her up against him, he covered her mouth with his. Like before, it was a sucker punch of need and arousal to his gut.

And something more.

Chloe kissed him back, murmuring her pleasure with a sexy low hum in her throat. "Tonight?" she whispered. "When you found me in that office?"

He stroked his thumb over her lower lip. "Yeah?"

"I'd gone in there because I'd heard a noise."

"Me."

"Yes." She shivered, and he ran his hands up and down her arms to warm her. "I found something," she said. "A set of files. Files I didn't know about that show far more income than has been reported."

"Good. That's really good, Chloe, but right now I want to get us out of here and into dry clothes. Can I do that? Take you home?"

She looked at him for a long moment, and he hoped to God she saw a man she could trust. When she finally nodded, he felt like he'd won the lotto. He steered her toward his car, which Danny had left in his spot.

Inside, he directed the heater vents her way and drove her home. He parked in her driveway and walked her to the front door, but when she moved to let herself in, he stopped her, his hands on her chilled arms as he looked into her eyes. "You asked me about karma," he said carefully, watching her eyes flicker with her own unsettled feelings on the matter. "And I said we make our own. I mean that, Chloe. So much so that I'm about to make mine."

"What—"

He put a finger over her lips, then, looking deeply into her eyes, he murmured, "Let me be with you tonight." Then still holding her gaze he replaced his finger with his mouth and let his eyes drift shut, because having his mouth on hers again was so exactly what he needed he could hardly stand it.

Chloe held herself still at first, not because the kiss wasn't stop-her-heart yummy, but because his words had been so unexpected.

No. Not unexpected, but *wanted,* wanted more than anything, and she hadn't been able to see that they'd ever be here again, wrapped tightly in each other's arms, mouths fused, soft, sexy little sounds escaping their throats… "Inside."

"You read my mind."

They fumbled to open the door, both their hands trying to work the key at the same time. She pushed his hands away, which left them free to touch her, a situation he took full advantage of, gliding his hands up her rib cage, to beneath her ribs, the tips of his fingers just brushing the undersides of her breasts…

Knees wobbly, she finally got the key in. "There—"

Which was all she got out before he lifted her over the threshold, kicked the door shut and turned to press her back against it, taking her mouth again.

And again.

Mmm…

"I've got to tell you," he managed. "Ever since I saw you tonight, I—"

He broke off when she pressed her mouth to his throat and just breathed him in, inhaled him. "You what?"

"Wanted you." His fingers tightened on her. "Jesus, I wanted you."

"You never even let on—"

"I was trying not to be me, remember?"

"Your eyes gave you away."

"Yeah?" Sliding his fingers into her hair, he gently tugged her head back and stared into her face. "What did my eyes tell you?"

That you love me. Her breath caught on that. She'd have to be crazy to admit that out loud, that fantasy. No way would she make herself that vulnerable. "They told me that we have a connection."

"Always have. No matter how I ran." He stroked his finger

over her cheekbone. "I know it's too late for this, but I'm sorry about how I left you. You deserved better. I was afraid back then, afraid of what we had. I've lost that fear, Chloe."

Oh, God. What was he saying? She didn't want to have to beat back the knot of hope currently blocking her air passage. "Ian—"

"I know, too little too late, right? But if you can't believe me, Chloe, and you don't believe in karma, then maybe you can believe in letting people right their wrongs, fix their mistakes. I want to make this right."

She pulled his head to hers for another mind-altering kiss, where there were no misunderstandings, no mistakes.

All that existed was now, how he made her feel. He had his hands flat on the door on either side of her head, his mouth hard on hers, and she lost track of everything but this…God, this…

"My room," she said between kisses.

"Again, just what I was thinking." Still holding her, he turned away from the door. "Which way?" he asked, nipping her lower lip with his teeth.

Oh, God. She sank her fingers into his hair and returned the little love bite, thrilling to his rough groan. "Down the hall."

In the hallway, he stopped to press her back against the wall, then plundered and pillaged her mouth, her neck, tugging open his sweatshirt, yanking down the tank and her bra to latch on to her nipple.

She cried out, fisted her hands in his hair and panted for breath. "First door," she gasped.

He headed toward it with such fierce intent, she would have laughed, if she could breathe. In her room, he turned to the bed, but she directed him to the bathroom because that's where she kept a—

"Condom," he said, reading *her* mind this time.

"Top drawer—"

He set her on the bathroom counter and pulled out the top drawer. After grabbing a foil packet, he opened it while she yanked open his shirt and brought her mouth to his chest.

Somehow his shirt melted away, and then hers. Her skirt followed, as did his pants. Then he stepped between her legs, and holding her thighs wide, he drove into her, the power of his stroke making her gasp with unspeakable pleasure so that she arched back. He promptly attached his mouth to her exposed throat, sucking on a patch of her skin there as he took her. It was just as she'd craved—Ian, six-plus feet of solid, warm, hard, ungiving muscle, wrapped around her, *in* her.

And there was nowhere on earth she'd rather be. *Please let this be real....*

By his third thrust, she was trembling, on the very edge. His hands tightened on her thighs, opening her further to him, and rearing his head, he captured her gaze in his. "This is real, Chloe."

Oh, God, she'd spoken out loud?

"Whether the fortune-teller said it or not, this is real. You and me."

And then he sank into her again, and then again, until she was hovering on a plateau, held there, suspended, lost in the way he looked at her, touched her, said her name in that low, raw voice. He filled her senses as he reached between them and stroked her with a knowing thumb, so that she came all over him, wildly, messily, gasping for breath. Then he started all over again, and this time, they both went over together.

"So real," he said on a thread of breath, sinking to his knees, pulling her down with him.

They lay there on the floor, gasping for breath, their bodies damp and cooling, hearts thundering against each other for a long time. Chloe ran her hand up the muscles taut in his back, unable to hold back her smile as he finally lifted his head.

"What are you thinking?" he murmured.

"Thank God some things never change."

He let out a low, rough laugh, a glorious sound, then slid down her body, dropping kisses as he went, on her breasts, her belly, and then... *"Oh!"*

"So you still like that," he whispered against her. "Let's see if you still like…" And he brought his fingers and tongue into the action. "Yeah?"

She couldn't answer, she was far too busy being whipped back into a frothy frenzy. And afterward, when she was still trembling, he rolled, pulling her over the top of him so that she straddled his hips.

Bending over him, she set her hands along his jaw and kissed him deeply. "What now, cowboy?" she purred.

His hands went to her hips. "Well, you could ride me off into the sunset."

Which she did.

THEY MADE LOVE UNTIL close to dawn, and then finally collapsed into her bed. Snuggled in his arms, Chloe lay there with one of those stupid I've-had-amazing-sex grins on her face. She absorbed the warmth of him next to her, and let her fingers drift over his skin, feeling the tough sinew beneath. "You kept in shape."

"I still play ball. For an old guys' league."

"Old guys, huh?" Didn't feel older, just built. Seriously built. She grazed her lips over his throat. "You still got the moves?"

He let out a soft chuckle against her temple and wrapped his arms around her. "You tell me."

Oh, yeah, he had the moves, and he spent the next twenty minutes proving it yet again.

They fell asleep in each other's arms, and for a woman who'd been so fiercely independent for so long, it felt incredibly good.

Ian's pager went off at dawn, and he got out of bed. Hair tousled, an extremely male, satisfied smile curving his lips, he grabbed a two-minute shower and came out of the bathroom with a pair of knit boxers low on his hips.

She fought the urge to tug them back down.

"Be careful," she whispered.

"Always." He leaned over the bed, his hands on either side of her hips and kissed her until her toes curled.

"I wish I'd tossed your pager out the window."

"I'll be back as soon as I can," he promised.

"Take my spare key on the desk in the living room by my laptop—in case I'm at the office."

He smiled his surprise. "You sure?"

So damn sure. "Yes."

"'Kay." And then he kissed her one more time before he left, a kiss that left her body humming.

She sighed dreamily, then tried to go back to sleep. She couldn't. Instead she got up and headed to the shower, where she leaned back against the tiles as the hot water pummeled her deliciously sated body.

She was *still* grinning like a fool.

A fool in love.

Finding the energy, she reached for the soap, shoved her hair out of her eyes and—

Stared down the barrel of a gun.

She thought maybe she gasped in terror. She definitely staggered backward, coming up against the tile.

"Hello, Chloe," Steve said from behind the gun.

9

IAN GOT TO THE OFFICE and took one look at Danny's tight face. "What?"

"They lost Steve and Al."

Ian went still. "What? The text message said—"

"Yeah." Danny was tall, six-five, and as the point guard on Ian's winter basketball league, that height came in handy. It did not come in handy for pacing the small, tight office, and he banged his head on the hanging light. "Damn it!" He rubbed the spot. "They've still got Al in their sites somewhere in Mexico City. But they lost visual of Steve at some point after midnight. Never picked it back up again."

"And we're just finding out? Christ, that was—" Ian looked at his cell phone for the time "—eight hours ago. He could be anywhere, he could be going after anyone he thinks will lead us to him. He could be—" He went still, galvanized by a sudden fear. "Here."

"What?"

"He could be here by now. *Shit.*" He ran toward the door.

"Where are you going?" Danny asked.

"Chloe's."

STEVE LOOKED THE SAME AS always, like he'd raided a techno geek's closet. He wore a short-sleeved plaid shirt, baggy pants that failed to hide that he looked as if he'd made a few too many visits to Krispy Kreme and white athletic shoes with black dress socks. Still, for being fashion challenged and carrying an extra forty pounds, the guy was quick. He reached into the shower for Chloe, who cringed back, wincing, expecting to be raped, maimed, murdered—

The water shut off.

She cracked an eye. Steve was holding out a towel, which she snatched and wrapped around herself. *"What are you doing here?"*

"Came for tea and crumpets." He grabbed her wrist in a tight, unbreakable grip.

She resisted but he simply tugged her out of the shower. "How did you get in?"

"Turns out fencing antiques isn't my only talent. I can pick a mean lock."

"W-where are we going?"

"To talk." He didn't let go of her until they were in the living room. There, he shoved her to the couch.

Standing over her, hands on his hips, scowl on his face, he looked big and tough and mean, and nothing at all like the quiet, hardworking man who'd brought her his books to reconcile once a month.

"What have you told them?" he demanded.

The towel he'd given her just barely wrapped around her wet body, and she was holding it tightly, hoping everything was covered. "Told who?"

Steve pinched the bridge of his nose, sighed, then, looming over her, he held the barrel of the gun so that it was an inch from her temple. "One more time. What have you told them?"

Oh, God, oh, God. "Um, the police?"

In answer, he pressed the gun to her head.

"Nothing!" she cried, trying to sink back against the couch as far as she could go. "I didn't—"

"I know you sneaked into our office. I know you found the second set of files."

"I wasn't sneaking, I heard a noise, and I went to investigate—

"Liar." He grabbed her by the nape of her neck and hauled

her upright. The gun flickered in front of her eyes, then settled against the side of her head.

"Please," she whispered. "Please don't."

"Here's the thing. Al's going down, okay? They have his prints on the bodies."

Oh, God. *There were bodies?*

"They can link him to things that they can't link me to. Only they know he didn't work alone." He smiled into her panicked face. "I'm thinking you got greedy, see? You were working the books, both sets of them, and you saw our profits. You decided to come onboard. You demanded it, in fact, or you'd turn us in. The two of you cut me out first, of course, which makes me the victim—"

"No—"

"Oh, yes." At that, he hauled her across the living room, to her desk, which her laptop sat on. He flipped up the top, opened a Word document, and then shoved her into the chair. "Start typing. To Whom It May Concern."

She stared up at him in horror.

He waved his gun. "Hel-lo-o-o-o?"

She jumped and put her fingers on the keyboard. *To Whom It May Concern...*

"The guilt is too much. I've betrayed Steve—" He broke off when she didn't type, and pressed the cold metal of the gun to her temple. "The guilt is too much," he repeated with a patience that belied the tight grip he had on her.

Heart in her throat, her vision hampered by her own tears, she began to type, but then Steve went still. "Did you hear that?" he whispered.

She hadn't heard a thing over the booming of her heart in her ears, but there...she heard the front door handle rattle.

Ian.

Before she could process the thought, Steve yanked her out of the chair and back against him, the gun once again settling against her temple. "Don't make a sound," he hissed, and pulled her around the desk and back against the wall, where they'd be hidden from anyone coming in the front door.

The handle rattled again. She heard a rustling and envisioned him searching his pockets for the key she'd given him. She looked at her desk. Next to the laptop was the key.

In true Ian fashion, he'd forgotten it.

"Chloe?" he yelled through the door. "Are you still in there?"

She opened her mouth but Steve tightened his grip. She felt the gun against her head, bruising her temple.

"Chloe!" He pounded on the door.

And then…silence.

She went still, trying to hear something, anything, but then she knew. He was running around the back, where he'd come in the kitchen door. There'd be a fight, with no guarantee of the outcome.

She couldn't let that happen. "I feel funny," she whispered to Steve.

"Ah, hell. Don't you dare puke." He loosened his grip and she whirled, grabbing the laptop off the desk as she did. Using her momentum as Steve aimed the gun at her, she cracked him right in the face with the hard plastic casing.

The computer fell to the floor, leaving Steve, who'd lost his hold on her, standing there with a stunned look on his face. The gun lay uselessly on the floor beside him.

Run, Chloe told herself, but her feet didn't move.

Steve, still staring at her, blinked once, then fell backward to the ground, hitting with a sickening thud that didn't bode well for his head.

The kitchen door burst open and Ian came running, skidding to a stop at the sight of her standing there in nothing but a towel, over Steve's prone body.

"I'm fine," she told him, then pointed to Steve. "But him, I'm not so sure about."

Ian rolled Steve over, secured him with a set of handcuffs, kicked the gun away from him, then surged to his feet and reached for Chloe, who'd never been more happy to be held by someone in her entire life.

More officers came running in, including Ian's partner, and for a moment, everything became wild and chaotic all over again. Questions were asked, answers given and then more questions.

Chloe's head whirled with all she'd been through since yesterday evening, but Ian hadn't let go of her except to pull off his shirt and put it on her. He was holding her so close she hadn't yet managed to get out of the towel and into some clothes.

"I can't believe I almost let him get you." Ian ran his hands up and down her yet again, as if to reassure himself she was really here, alive and whole.

"It's over," she said, now comforting him. "And we're okay."

"Yeah." Ian stroked her hair and glanced over her shoulder at Steve, who was still looking dazed as the cops pulled him to his feet. Paramedics had arrived but he wasn't going to the hospital, or if he was, it'd be a short trip on the way to jail, where he'd soon enough be reunited with Al, his brother and partner in crime.

When everyone eventually piled out of the house, they were finally alone. It wasn't for long—Ian had to go into work to face the mountain of paperwork—but for now, Chloe just held him, never wanting to let go.

"I wanted to be the one to save you, you know," he said.

"You did."

"No. You didn't need saving."

"Of course I did." Emotion swamped her. "I needed you to save me from certain incorrect notions. Such as the world is black and white. But I now know it's not. There's gray, a lot of it, along with…"

He seemed to hold his breath. "With…"

"Love." She smiled tremulously and set her hands on his jaw.

He wrapped her close. "God, I love you, Chloe. Always have, always will."

"Now see, that's working for me." Her voice was husky with

all the emotion swamping her. "I love you, too, Ian. I always have, always will." She let out a soggy laugh. "I guess this means my karma couldn't have really taken a vacation to the Bahamas, right?"

He still had his arms around her tightly. "I thought you didn't believe in karma."

"Maybe I was just scared of it." She cupped his face. "I've faced scarier things now. And I've learned life's too short not to live it to its fullest."

"Well, then—" he smiled and slipped a hand beneath the shirt he'd given her, and then tugged on the towel beneath "—let's get to that living...."

TALL, DARK & TEMPORARY
Crystal Green

To Jill, Jacquie and Brenda.

Thank you for inviting me to battle
Madame Karma's curse!

1

"DID YOU KNOW I'm cursed?"

Seated shotgun in the Jeep Grand Cherokee, Erin Holland capped off the impetuous comment with a laugh and turned away from her date to peer out the window. Outside, the gray Pacific Ocean lengthened against a moody sky. The odd hot spell that'd consumed southern California last week had gone back into hiding, leaving behind the regular February grumble of weather.

After a beat passed, she glanced at her date again. She wasn't sure why she'd even been talking to him about her psychic reading from last weekend. "Have you ever been to a fortune-teller?"

Wes Ryan steered with effortless grace. Heck, that's how he did everything—effortlessly, but with an edge of deliberation and cockiness.

He grinned at her, slow, assured. "Nope, never." Wes turned back to his driving. "How did she curse you?"

"*She* didn't curse me. Not really. She just said I'd need to…" Erin paused, second-guessing the wisdom of telling him everything. Why had she even brought all this up? Instead, she was vague. "I doubted her prediction, and she said that my negativity would curse me unless I decided to go with the flow." There. "That's all."

As Wes absorbed that, Erin took a second longer than she should've to linger over him.

The first time she'd seen him—Wes Ryan, the notorious player who ate women for breakfast, lunch and dinner—she'd been hooked. He'd been standing a few yards away at a party when she'd glanced over to find him leaning against a wall, beer bottle tilted in his hand as he watched her talking with her friends.

Maybe it was because he was the perfect man for her current situation: anticommitment, only interested in thrills and feel-good chills. Or maybe Erin had just been a one-man girl for so long that the notion of no-strings-attached sex excited her. Either way, she'd decided then and there to return his forthright interest, locking gazes with him until her skin heated.

It hadn't been love at first sight or anything—God, she wouldn't allow herself to fall for anyone again for at least another couple of years—but it was definitely lust. He had a primal way of holding himself, taut yet easy, his black hair kept long enough to get a little wild. He had olive skin, dark eyes that narrowed in cheetahlike hungriness, a nose that arrowed just above generous lips and a dimple in his chin.

Exotic. Suave. All male.

Her blood pounded, thickening until her limbs felt heavy. She started to ache between her thighs, so she turned back to the car's window, instinctively removing herself from temptation even though she'd knowingly—and very willingly—put herself in its bull's-eye this weekend.

A romantic getaway. A three-day cruise down to Ensenada, Mexico.

She shifted, suddenly nervous.

"So," Wes said, "what exactly are you supposed to be flowing with? What's this prediction you didn't believe?"

Erin forced herself to relax. *Enjoy.* "Well, she said business is going to prosper. That was the first part."

"What's so hard to believe about that? The candy shop's already doing really well."

During their previous, very casual, very lighthearted dates these past couple of weeks, Erin had told him about her and her best friend's plan to franchise Yes, Sweetie, the candy store they'd conceived long ago, while roommates in college. Their dream. But, now, just thinking about the business risk made her fidget, and that's not what this weekend was about. She was supposed to be getting away from it all. To have the fun she'd been lacking up until this point.

"But, then—" Erin added, intending to tell him only this little bit more and that would be it "—there was Madame Karma's prediction about my having a long, long life."

"I'll have to check out your palm to second that opinion, I suppose."

Erin felt him inserting a finger into her hand, which she'd been resting in a loose fist on her lap. His touch tickled, and she laughed, opening for him. The contact was innocent yet sexual enough to heighten the ache between her legs.

"Shouldn't you concentrate on driving?" she murmured, her pulse wavering.

"How can I?" True to his reputation, he moved his finger from her palm to her leg, sliding toward her inner thigh.

The ache turned sharp, damp. Her heartbeat picked up dangerous speed, warning her to slow down.

"Hey," she said, casually directing his hand back to his own side of the car and pointing to a road sign announcing that the Long Beach cruise terminal was ahead. "We don't want to miss our turnoff because you can't keep your hands to yourself."

She could feel his gaze on her, heavy and enticing. But she knew better than to look at him. He could seduce with just one long, hot stare, and she'd *already* almost given in so many times, but…

Well, she guessed she'd be giving in soon enough, right? That's why she was here—to indulge in good times with a man who had a reputation for guaranteeing that a woman came out of the bedroom happy. Heaven knew she needed some variety after being with the same man for so long.

"What else about this prediction?" he asked, eyes on the road now, obeying like a good boy. "It doesn't sound hard to buy into so far, especially for a girl who was open-minded enough to visit this Madame Karma in the first place."

"Actually, *she* came to the Fairfax building complex, where my shop is. She had a table set up at the combination Valentine's Day party and renovation celebration last weekend. It drew a nice crowd and we did great business."

"But *you* still went to *her*. Am I right?"

Erin clasped her fingers into her palm, reliving his touch. "Cheryl, that wench, basically forced me to the Madame's table. Getting our palms read would be hilarious, she said." At Wes's blank look, Erin added, "Cheryl. You met her at the shop last Tuesday when you picked me up for dinner?"

"Sorry, it took a minute to click. Cheryl. Long blond hair, freckles, big smile. Best friend. Partner in crime and business. Yeah, I remember."

Erin paused. Cheryl was such a big part of her life, and Wes's unfamiliarity with her drove home just how new they really were to each other.

And I'm taking a weekend trip with him, she thought, heart stuttering.

Wes was speaking again. "So wasn't there anything more colorful to this prediction, like a passion-filled adventure on the seas—"

"You wish she'd predicted that." Erin managed a laugh, but she really didn't want to talk about it.

Because, before the storm had descended on the complex in Baxter Hills that day, Madame Karma *had* made a prediction about more than just business or a long, long life....

The older woman had patted Erin's palm, the lines around her eyes deepening with the "good" news. "Love must be in the air today because I feel like I've said this so many times, but you can stop looking for the man of your dreams. You've already found 'the one.'"

In the next chair, Cheryl had clapped Erin on the shoulder, beaming with her patented big smile. "Congratulations. Hopefully 'the one' will actually find his way to the altar before six years go by." Mischievously, Cheryl had turned to Madame Karma. "The last one took his sweet time."

Erin had addressed Madame Karma, too. "William and I never even sent out wedding invitations, and that's why we broke up. Our engagement was, like, an endless trek across the desert of all relationships." But why had she even explained? "Listen, I know everyone wants to hear that kind of great news about a love life, so you feel compelled to say it, but…"

"Oh, no," the elderly fortune-teller had said. "I'm not wrong."

Erin had shaken her head. "You don't understand. I'm not in the market for 'the one.' Not for a couple more years at least." When she'd gotten over the disappointment of William, her college sweetheart. The man who'd taken her so completely for granted that he'd thought marriage would come when *he* was ready. Which had turned out to be never.

But that was okay. Five months ago, she'd realized William wasn't the guy for her and had called it off, yet that didn't mean she was looking to settle down with the next candidate. She'd made herself a promise to experience life as a single woman for the first time since…ever. She'd been shackled to William for so long that she'd missed out on dating and doing all those mysterious things available women did, and now she just wanted to enjoy all the *Cosmo* girl fun she'd lost out on over the years.

Yet there was more to it than even that, she knew. She also wanted to avoid the profound emotions that would only lead to getting hurt again, and Wes could give her that. Someone so temporary would allow her breathing room from the anguish she'd just about recovered from with William.

But there Madame Karma was, telling Erin that Wes was "the one." God, it was the last thing she wanted to hear.

Cheryl, who had her own long-term boyfriend, was a big supporter of Erin's new crusade. "See, Madame Karma," she'd said, leaning over the fortune-teller's table, "Erin here is in transition."

Erin had smiled and nodded.

"What can I tell you, then," the fortune-teller had said. "Your transition man is the one you're meant to be with."

At that, Erin had made a sound that smacked somewhere between disbelief and panic. Didn't Madame Karma know how much she *needed* Wes to be insignificant?

The psychic had sighed and risen from her chair, her gypsy skirt swishing around her legs as she began moving away from the table. "I guess *you're* going to give fate a hard time, too."

Cheryl and Erin had exchanged puzzled glances.

Madame Karma had gestured toward the sexy coffee shop, Constant Cravings, where Erin and Cheryl got their daily doses of caffeine. A creamy latte called Goes Down Easy was Erin's current addiction.

"That woman in there…" the fortune-teller had begun.

"Lacey?" Cheryl asked.

The fortune-teller nodded. "She and her boyfriend were the first to scoff."

Erin and Cheryl mouthed, "Boyfriend?" to each other. Lacey Perkins was as single as they came. Sure, Evan Sawyer, the building manager, seemed to enjoy harassing Lacey about her window displays a little too much, but…

"And," Madame Karma had added, "then came the next non-believer, the accountant."

Accountant, accountant…

"Oh," Erin said, gesturing toward the fourth floor. "You must mean Chloe Cooper—"

Madame Karma was on a roll. "Let me tell you something, just so you can avoid the trouble *they'll* be having…" Here, the fortune-teller leaned forward. "If you don't go with what's supposed to be, each and every one of you will jinx your own fate. You reject what love has in store for you, and you twist karma around until it comes right back at you with negative energy."

Cheryl, always up for a lively discussion, had raised a finger to offer her own point of view on the matter, but Madame Karma left in a rush of patchouli before Miss Debate Team could say anything.

That hadn't stopped Erin, though. "But Wes is just a transition man," she'd repeated to no one in particular, staring at the fountain burbling in the courtyard, yet not really seeing it.

Now, as Erin watched the harbor come into focus outside the car's window, she knew she really shouldn't tell Wes any of this. Truthfully, there was no reason to bring it up since their future was limited anyway. Those were the established parameters of this fling; she'd been absolutely honest about it with him. Sure, they laughed a lot and even enjoyed a few heated makeout sessions in which she'd always needed to put on the brakes. Yet it was all good: he was giving her the confidence to build up to a relationship again someday and, in return, she provided him with…well, she guessed companionship. She didn't think he minded though, because he wasn't built for the long-term.

As he guided the car into a parking structure, easing it along the curb where porters waited to collect luggage, Erin told herself that all she knew about him were superficial details anyway: at thirty, he was a successful day trader who'd branched out into real estate these past few years. That made him a slightly older man with the kind of experienced joie de vivre she craved. And he'd proven it with surprises like a picnic at the Hollywood Bowl one night—not your average date. He lived well and played hard, and she lapped that up, enthralled by this new way of experiencing life. This wonderfully carefree way.

After Wes cut the engine, they got out of the car and unloaded. He handed their baggage over to a porter. As Erin watched him move—boy, she really liked to do that—she shivered, and it wasn't just because the weather was sullen.

No, not at all. It was because the porter had piled their bags on top of each other, just as if they belonged together. That luggage would be going to the same room, where Erin and Wes would finally be sleeping in the same bed.

She closed her cashmere sweater around her. What was she

doing here again? To her, sex had always been entwined with what she thought was love. Sex was revealing yourself to someone else, lying next to them with your skin bare. Vulnerable. Open and offered to them. But she was working on changing that, too—serious philosophy. It only led to heartbreak, and she didn't need any more of *that*.

As Wes parked the car nearby, Erin waited, the wind chuffing at her.

But, minutes later, when she saw him sauntering toward her— all tall, muscled, athletic grace—that ache between her legs swelled, twisted, throbbed.

She wanted him, period. And, really, there was nothing wrong with giving in to what her body needed, just as long as it didn't include anything like a commitment. She'd save all that serious stuff for "the one" when he actually came along.

Wes grinned, and she held out her hand to take his.

"Ready?" he asked.

No.

Erin wanted to smack herself. *Fun. Enjoy. Come on.*

"Yup, let's get on board," she said instead, brushing against his leather jacket and taking in the musky, rugged scent.

As they left to embark, the wind seemed to carry the fortune-teller's words of warning: *You reject what love has in store for you, and you twist karma around until it comes right back at you with negative energy….*

2

DURING WHAT SEEMED LIKE AN endless check-in process, Wes had tried to think of everything *but* what would happen once they finally did get to their cabin.

First case in point: as his and Erin's ID cards were issued, he wondered where he'd be able to access the Internet just as soon as they disembarked back in Long Beach Monday morning. There was a certain blue-chip stock he wanted to jump on, and business waited for no man—not even on the tail of a pleasure cruise.

That got his attention off of Erin for about, oh, fifteen seconds.

Try again.

As they waited to board, organized into schoolyard lines under the huge terminal dome, he decided to focus on the frat boys in their see-how-wacky-I-am hats and Hawaiian shirts, ready for a booze cruise.

And that ate up about ten seconds.

The rest of the time, his mind and body were all Erin's.

Hell, he'd been a goner ever since laying eyes on her at Caleb's party. Caleb Dougherty, Esq. was Wes's lawyer and friend, and the party had been the first time the Esquire and his new girlfriend had gotten all their pals together in one place.

Erin had been talking near the food table with a couple of other women, and the minute she'd thrown back her head to laugh at a joke, Wes's gut had clutched into itself, his veins fizzing from a blast of lust and energy. There was something about the way she smiled, something he couldn't get a grip on, something that urged him to look away before it was too late. But he couldn't look away—not for the life of him.

From that point on, he knew he wasn't ever going to take no as an answer from her. So, as usual, he'd set his sights on what he wanted, then had charmed her—because that's what guys like him did best—and had made her laugh and glow the rest of the night. Afterward, no other woman had existed for him, because he'd become just short of obsessed with having her.

When she'd finally said yes to a date, she'd made it clear that he'd be just some sort of rebound fling, and he'd accepted that. Yet, afterward, her casual definition of what they were to each other started to eat away at him. But why did it bother him? Hadn't he earned his reputation? Hadn't he even reveled in it for years?

Gradually, he realized that, this time, it wasn't just about sex. There was… What? He didn't know. Hell, maybe he did, but he wasn't ready to face the niggling "something" that'd been hovering at the edges of his conscience for a while now. "Something" about the way he'd been wasting his life away night after night, never moving ahead while the world evolved around him.

"Something" that made Wes want to convince Erin that everyone was wrong about him.

After Erin ran up to the spa to make a massage appointment for later that day, they arrived at their stateroom. He used his ID card to unlock it, opening the door for her and closing his eyes as he caught a whiff of her scent.

Sweet, he thought. Like raspberries, but with a little bit of something kicky, like lime. She smelled like a sorbet of mixed flavors.

"Wow," she said, moving around the bed to peek out the long porthole window. It offered a view of the dock, the gray of the afternoon. "This room's bigger than I thought it would be."

"You expected a cell?"

"Sort of. I had these visions of bunkbeds chained to the walls and a blue Porta Potti."

"That shows zero trust in my taste."

"And I should definitely know better."

There it was—that glowing smile. It lit up her skin with a blush, gave her gray eyes sparkle. But that was just the beginning of her appeal, really. She had blond hair chopped into layers that came to just below her chin; brown streaks made the style hip and sultry. Then came the cuteness: a button nose and a heart-shaped face that reminded him she wasn't like a lot of the women he usually dated. His type was supposed to be sleeker, like a sports car that took curves instead of created them. But maybe that was part of Erin's draw: her insistence on taking things slowly made him want her that much more with every ticking, shuddering second.

Unable to help himself, Wes allowed his gaze to travel down her petite body—breasts that were a little too large for her stature, a tiny waist, slim hips. Even dressed in jeans and a T-shirt with a fifties-style sweater, she brought out every carnal instinct.

But wasn't he supposed to be showing her that he was above this? That he could be more than just the go-to guy for amusement?

Damn, it was hard to be a gentleman sometimes, especially now, with her standing next to a bed that dominated the room.

She seemed to realize it, too, her gaze falling to the mattress, then lifting to him. She really blushed this time, and his groin tightened.

He needed her. In so many ways.

Their luggage had already been dropped off by the porter, and it was waiting on the bed for them to unpack. Hesitating, Erin's hands hovered over her red faux alligator bag, as if she hadn't fully committed to being here with him yet. But hadn't he sensed this a few times before? Reluctance?

His heart sank. Was she hesitant about jumping into bed with a man she'd only known two weeks—or jumping into bed with *him?*

She stared at her luggage, took a breath, then unzipped her bag with a verve that seemed a little too emphatic. Her smile seemed determined, and it threw him off balance.

Not knowing what to think, Wes closed the door. "You pack pretty light. For a girl, I mean."

"How would you know?" She playfully narrowed her eyes. "Just how many women have you traveled with?"

Enough. And they'd always gone with him on short trips that he was now regretting weren't longer. Somehow, Wes thought that Erin had guessed this already. She had a way of seeing right into him that was uncanny. In fact, he'd never met a woman who made him feel like maybe he didn't have to put on an act because it wouldn't work anyway. And the thing of it was, she *still* wanted to be around him.

He didn't understand any of it.

"How about we don't talk about other women right now?" Wes said, coming closer to the bed.

She caught her breath. Knowing he had that kind of effect on her turned him on.

"How'd you fit your formal wear into one bag?" he asked.

In answer, she casually pulled out a teeny-tiny baby doll piece of fluff. Lingerie, sheer and seductive.

Imagination kicking into overdrive, Wes's cock nudged against his fly. His throat closed up.

"Formal wear," she said, as if musing over the very idea. "Where *is* my formal wear…?"

Then, she tugged a long wispy dress out of her bag—a bohemian print that was meant to retain a few wrinkles. He could tell that she'd chosen to pull out the more demure evening garb to taunt him.

Then, slowly, devilishly, she slid out another length of sinuous material.

Back to the lingerie.

Wes blew out some oxygen. It was almost like she was performing a striptease, but she was taking things out instead of off. In essence, every movement whispered, "This is what I brought for you. Are you ready for some of it?"

When she pulled out a heart-shaped red lollipop—a treat

from her shop, no doubt—she gave him a wicked smile and rested the candy against her lips.

He didn't dare ask what she had in mind. In spite of all his best intentions, he got closer, reaching for the sucker.

"Hey," she teased, raising the candy over her head. "Not so fast."

When he didn't say anything—*couldn't* say anything—she cocked an eyebrow.

"And if you don't like lollipops, I've got more for you. What do you want? Taffy, chocolate…? I have it all."

Yeah, she did. By now, his penis was pounding with the blood rushing to it. He wanted to feel himself inside her, surrounded by her slick heat. He didn't want to taste sugar as much as her skin, her breasts, her sex.

Uninhibited, he reached out to run a thumb over her lower lip. Soft, warm. She closed her eyes, taking him into her mouth as she dropped her sucker-clasping hand to her side.

"Erin," he whispered, weaving the fingers of his other hand into her hair.

She took his thumb further inside, sucking, biting. He moved his finger with her motions, entranced. His veins enlarged to accommodate the blood pumping through them, until it felt like he'd explode from the pressure.

Unable to stand it, he bent to her, removing his thumb and taking its place with his tongue, sliding her a long kiss that stretched time into slow, erotic pulses. He explored her heat, pressing her body against his so she could feel his erection, feel what she did to him.

She responded with a vicious eagerness, engaging his tongue with hers, rubbing her hips against his groin until he moaned with pleasured pain. When she slid her hand between them, testing his hard-on, he clutched at her.

It seemed like he'd been waiting months for this, not weeks. He was ready to rip off their clothes and enter her, but he didn't want that. It couldn't be that fast and anonymous, not this time.

"Hey," he said against her mouth, thinking that she was different now that they were on this trip alone. Less inhibited?

She drew away, laughed, her breath warming his lips. "I'm trying to beat a curse here, 'kay? Play along, please."

A curse. Again, he wondered exactly what that old fortune-teller had told her—what Erin had left out earlier when she'd related her story. What did a curse have to do with what was happening right now?

"You're not cursed with me," he said, smoothing his hands below her jaw to frame her face. Such a beautiful face.

Something within her eyes shifted, white flecks among the gray clicking into a different position, like lenses changing focus.

Then, with even more determination, she undid the top button of his fly.

He stopped her, confused not only by her, but by his own refusal to accept the sex and move on.

"You don't want this?" she asked.

"Hell, yeah, but…" He sucked in a breath.

She'd cupped him in her hand again, her fingers brushing over his balls. His cock strained to burst out of the denims.

"I've wanted this, too, Wes. And now's finally the time for it."

He couldn't get any air into his lungs, yet he tried to talk, anyway. Why was she acting like this was some sort of mission? This wasn't like the Erin he knew—not that he was complaining. He just hadn't expected this strong of a come-on.

But it was working all the same. Was it ever.

She was moving one finger back and forth, as if experimenting with how much he could take. On the fringe of losing it, he pulled her back against him, kissing her roughly.

Then, outside of his kidnapped brain, he heard something like a voice amplifying around him, a physical thing pressing in and trying to force him apart from Erin. Something on the loudspeaker? Hell, it wasn't registering….

Abruptly, Erin pulled away. "You've got to be kidding me!"

Dizzy, he tried to haul her back against him, but she shook her head, pointing to the ceiling. Eventually, the loudspeaker voice filtered through the haze of his animal need.

"…mandatory emergency drill. Please secure your life jackets—"

"Shit," Wes said, his erection at full rev now. "I don't suppose we can ignore that."

"Mandatory."

Flushed, Erin laughed in frustration, but he sensed something else in the gesture. Relief?

What the hell?

Backing away from him, she straightened her sweater, her smile shaky. "Cursed. Didn't I tell you the negative stuff was on its way? You're onboard with a cursed being, Wes. You'd better bail now."

His nethers were killing him, but cool as rain, Erin went to a corner table and lifted off the top to find the life jackets.

Using a wall for balance, one hand holding himself up while the other pressed against his crotch, he attempted to contain the ache.

And she thought *she* was cursed?

3

AFTER THE DRILL, THEY decided to grab something to eat since Erin's massage appointment was in only a half hour. Fortifying themselves had been her suggestion because, based on what'd happened before their *playus interuptus,* she had the sneaking suspicion they would need to store up on energy for when she returned to the cabin.

She'd surprised herself with her attempt at seducing Wes. Heh, yeah, *attempt.* That was an understatement. She'd gone at him with all guns blazing, and he'd been just as open to the attack as she'd hoped. But then they'd been forced to do that drill and...bye-bye bedroom Babylon. Hello, fortune-teller curse.

Of course, it could've just been a coincidence that their intimate activities had been thwarted at a most awkward time. In the heat of the moment, after she'd disengaged from Wes, she'd forgotten herself and actually joked about a damned jinx being the reason for the interruption. She'd only been letting off steam, but she couldn't help wondering if Madame Karma was on to something....

Nah. She and Wes had the whole cruise to get it on and, in effect, allow *her* to get on with life as she wanted it. The farther she inched away from the disappointment of William, the better. One setback was no biggie. Sure, Wes had been forced to carry his life jacket in front of his jeans en route to their drill-meeting station on the ninth deck, and Erin herself had been flushed with such lingering desire that the color was like a scarlet letter on her skin, but they had hours, days to make up for the temporary inconvenience.

They walked to the Lido restaurant after having dropped off their jackets in the cabin, Erin linking onto Wes's muscle-corded arm.

A curse. Ri-ight. Nothing to fret about.

It was just the sense of supreme relief she'd felt when the purser had called them for the drill that was worrying her more….

Dismissing the thought, she climbed the stairs with her date, mahogany wood surrounding them. The ship, *Lady Oriana,* which would sail from Long Beach to Ensenada then back before Monday morning, was a study in Victorian romanticism. With its stained glass, brass railings and an atrium in the entry parlor, the vessel offered many amusements: the spa, a disco, a coffee nook, upscale shops, a casino and even a library. Of course, the upper deck had the requisite pool with water slides and a hot tub.

As they passed by the pool, which rested empty under the salt-tinged breeze, Erin's body hadn't lost any of its melted surrender yet. Just the feel of Wes's biceps brushing against her breast as they walked side by side churned the hunger in her belly.

They entered the restaurant, which had a buffet set out. In spite of the many choices, all Erin saw were the French fries and shrimp cocktail. Breaking away, she made a beeline for them.

"I can't believe," she said while piling her plate high, "that the food is here for the taking. This is awesome."

Wes had snagged a burger plus a hot dog plus a giant baked potato. Real man food.

"You sure you're gonna fit all that in your tiny body?" He reached out, wrapping his fingers around one of her biceps, squeezing slightly.

She flexed for his benefit. "Check it out—I'm buff, huh? I could so kick your butt."

"I'll remember that."

"I'm not kidding." Even with plate in hand, she aimed a jesting kick at his leg but intentionally missed. "You got lucky that time, but I'll bet I'm really intimidating to you now."

He raised an eyebrow, then ambled toward a table, all loose-limbed stalk. But his grin gave away his amusement as they sat down.

"Guess I should watch myself around a karate master like you," he said.

"Kickboxing classes do have their advantages. I'm telling you—meeting me in a dark alley? Not a good thing."

He just laughed, watching her as he bit into his burger. She watched him right back, her gaze fixed on his mouth. Mmm.

When her perusal traveled back up to his gaze, his eyes had gone smoky, and she knew he was remembering what'd happened back in the cabin.

She stuffed a load of fries down her gullet. Food: the glutton's answer to a cold shower.

He rested his forearms on the table, assessing her.

"What?" she said around her fries.

"You. Most girls are afraid to eat around a guy. You're not. *At all.*"

She swallowed. "Why should I be? Food's great."

Maybe she was imagining things, but she thought she read some buried message in his dark eyes. *You're pretty great, too,* they said.

Don't think things like that, she mentally chided him. *We're not supposed to get all "you're so great" about each other.*

She cut off this line of awareness at the pass. "So…"

He went back to eating, obviously reading her loud and clear. "So, what?"

Then the small talk started up again and, phew, they were back to a place of comfort—joking and just enjoying being around each other.

She quizzed him about how he liked to stay in shape, too. He gave her the rundown on his favorite adrenalizing sports—surfing, hang gliding, motorbiking. Then they talked about the Lakers, neutral ground. He had season tickets and promised he'd invite her to the next home game.

"Only if you go to the theater sometime with me," she said cheekily. "Trade-off."

"I can do theater."

She widened her eyes as he nonchalantly polished off the last of his hot dog. Noticing the inspection, he furrowed his forehead.

"Sorry." Erin shook her head. "Most guys I know would kick and scream their way to a show."

Guys like William, the ex. Since he hadn't been much for compromise, she'd elected to do what *she* wanted to do with Cheryl and other friends—things like theater, chick-flick DVDs, shopping. William wouldn't have been caught dead doing half of what she enjoyed, so it only made sense that they'd ended up kaput. The sad thing was that, at the beginning, they'd had so much in common…until they'd grown apart. Scary to think that could happen with any couple.

Unbidden, a surge of latent anger lit through her, but she extinguished it, having no use for the emotion. So what if he'd taken away most of her confidence and moved on without her? So what if he'd wasted so much of her time?

Wes polished off the rest of his food, then said, "I have a couple of sisters, so I guess that taught me a little art appreciation. It's not all so bad—sometimes you see something pretty good on stage."

"Like what?" Now she was leaning her forearms on the table, genuinely interested.

"I remember thinking *Phantom of the Opera* was decent. Kinda foofy, but that chandelier coming down from the ceiling was good. And…what was it called? That show with the leggy Swedish blond…"

"*The Producers?*"

"Yeah, I suppose that was okay." He grinned. "I wish there was less singing and more naked women in those things though."

"Perv." She gave him a light push. "But…seriously? You enjoyed that 'stuff'?"

"*Enjoy* is a strong word." He noticed her astonishment. "What? Am I losing manhood points by the second?"

"No, not at all. I'd love to…hang out…with someone who can

appreciate both the stage and the hoop." And, one day, she'd settle down with a man like that. One day.

"Well, don't think I have a chick gene or something, all right? There were just a lot of cultural things going on in Boston, and my parents wanted me and my sisters to be 'well rounded,' but…"

He glanced away, as if he'd revealed too much about himself.

"But…?" she repeated.

"Let's just say I didn't end up as well-rounded as they'd hoped. The folks didn't exactly throw a party when I caught the travel bug, came out to California on a whim, then ended up bugging out of UCLA just a few credits short of graduation. Having a dropout in the family wasn't in their plans."

Besides the basics, they'd never really talked about family before. All she knew was that his mom was from Italian stock while his dad was a good old American mutt, like her own parents.

Why bother getting the scoop on more? Erin had thought. Light conversation was what had allowed her to say yes to him in the first place. She'd just hoped everyone really knew what they were talking about when it came to his reputation for not getting serious.

"But—" he added, his mood shifting as he leaned back in his seat casually, as if none of this even mattered "—even though they disapproved, it all ended up good. I didn't feel like wasting my time on a business degree when I could be out there actually starting my *own* business."

"Day trading?"

He nodded, seeming a bit uncomfortable at the acknowledgement of his success. Maybe he was one of those people who didn't like to crow about how much money he earned. Made sense. Wes was more the type to show than to tell.

"And things took off from there," she continued.

"I guess." He pushed his plate away.

"Your buddy Caleb told me that you have a knack for pulling out of investments, then redistributing your profits at just the right time. You don't need a diploma for that."

He shrugged.

"What do your parents think about how well you've done?" she asked.

"They say they're proud. I didn't mean to make you think they weren't. They just…I don't know. They have their way of doing things and I have mine."

She wanted to ask him so much more, but that'd be lethal. A transition man wasn't supposed to offer a big connection; the more the two of them mined each other, the harder it'd be to move on to the next experience life had in store for her.

Not that she didn't wonder what it might be like to dig deeper….

"How about you?" he was asking, watching her from his careless position as he reclined back against the chair. "You said your parents are from the East, too."

"Milwaukee. Not so east." She stirred Ketchup with a French fry. "They moved to Arroyo Grande before I was born. It's near Cal Poly, San Luis Obispo."

"Where you went to school with Cheryl." He tapped his head.

"Good memory." She smiled. "A few years ago, the *Ps*—my parents—retired and went back to the homeland with the rest of our extended family. They were getting some pressure to rejoin the fold, and guess who's getting the same pressure right now?" She made a "tah-dah" motion.

"You're leaving California?" he asked.

"Oh, no. It's just that…" She hesitated. "Since I broke it off with William, they think I'm not mired here now. They think my life has become this blank slate that needs to be filled. What they don't get is that this is my home. I have a business here, friends…"

Others.

She kept her gaze away from Wes, not wanting to see how he was responding. While they were so close to the subject of family, she thought about how they'd react to Wes. God. Her mom would weird out because Wes wasn't the wonderful William, whom Erin had "tossed away without thinking everything through." Her dad would be more tolerant, but he'd still be suspect about Wes's charm. Heck, maybe dads were like that with all boyfriends, but since William hadn't possessed much charm, she wasn't sure. And as for Erin's older and younger sisters? They'd tell her she was wasting her time on such an obvious lothario.

But none of them knew Wes. Not like she di—

Wait. Erin didn't know this man at all, and she wasn't ever really going to.

"And what about William?" he asked.

At the name, anger reared up again. She didn't want the ex to enter into this weekend, into her idyll with a man who'd so often made her forget what she'd left behind.

"Aren't exes a taboo subject on romantic cruises?" she asked, trying to inject some levity into the conversation again.

"Taboo then."

A beat passed, the clank of silverware covering discussions from the other tables. The almost imperceptible roll of the boat brought Erin back to the moment. Cruise. An affair. An escape.

Her stomach turned because, now, she couldn't shake William's memory. It pressed down on her shoulders, and she shrugged, trying to jar him off.

"Erin, are you okay?"

"Not used to the motion of the ocean, I think." Before he could say anything else, she added, "I should get going to my spa appointment."

She stood, hoping to leave her ire behind. God, this was what her one and only big relationship in life had left her with? And that was just another reason she didn't want to get involved with anyone right now. The negativity, the disappointment.

But she couldn't leave Wes like this. It wasn't fair. Not to either of them.

Summoning a smile—which was always so easy around this man—she leaned down, resting her lips against his ear. Wow, he smelled so good—rugged, like surf and clean air.

"I'll see you back in the room in an hour?" she asked, pulse picking up speed.

He turned his face so that his mouth touched her jawline. Softly, he kissed her in answer, his hand skimming her hip as she moved away.

When she left, she didn't look back.

Just like she planned to do when her time with Wes was over.

4

ERIN TOOK AN ELEVATOR TO the spa on the twelfth deck, her head more clouded than she'd thought possible on a party weekend. Wasn't she supposed to be relaxing by now? Wasn't she supposed to have become the *Cosmo* girl at this point?

Well, she was going to start, dammit.

She checked in at the front desk, filled out a health and waiver form and then greeted her masseur. He was a slender man named Justin with dark skin and a soft voice, but he snapped his gum as if creating punctuation marks. He guided her to the private room where she'd strip and indulge in her first massage ever— a hot-stone treatment.

Before leaving, he went over the health form with her then slammed the door on his way out. Wow, weren't masseurs usually more gentle? But she didn't let that matter. Nope. Instead, she took in the small, dim room, candlelight flickering amid the smell of herb-laced oils and the sound of ethereal music. In the corner, a minifountain burbled water over rocks.

When was the last time she'd pampered herself? The candy shop had consumed so much of her and Cheryl's attention for the past few years that she hadn't taken the time. Also, William had thought massages were a waste of money, so she'd abstained, even though he never would have known what she spent her money on: though engaged, they hadn't gotten to the point of combining their bank accounts, much less picking out china patterns.

Frustration sneaked up on her again, so she redirected her energy, taking off her jeans, sweater, shirt and underthings. She'd always been modest about her body, but now, with her newfound freedom, the idea of being buck naked in front of another person seemed liberating.

She slipped under the sheet, lying on her belly and resting her face on the doughnut cushion, where she could see the tiled floor. Her breasts pressed against the table, making her ultra-aware of them.

Eyes closed, relaxing, relaxing. The music swept over her, and she allowed herself to wallow in bare-skinned joy at being away from work, being with Wes.

She imagined him naked, too, ready to slide under the sheet with her, ready to press his skin against hers. The nebulous friction of her fantasy made her damp, her clitoris thudding.

Justin took a while to return, but when he did she'd gotten herself so mentally worked up that she had a hard time coming down.

Chill out, she told herself. *Save yourself for the cabin.*

As the door eased shut, the sound of waves frothed from the music speakers. The sheet slithered down her back, her masseur resting it just at the curve of her butt. She felt a little naughty doing this, as if she was were an artist's model seductively flashing a room. She could hear him stepping away to rub oil over his hands, then approach the table again, silent.

But that was fine. A chatty massage didn't sound appealing. All she wanted to do was wilt, free her mind.

When he skimmed the warm oil over her back, she sighed. His hands were big, strong, slightly callused. He worked the slickness in, spreading it over her like cream to be licked off later.

Over her shoulder blades, up to her neck, down, down, near her waist, over the small of her back, to the top of her butt…

With the power of his downward stroke, he pushed away the sheet, palms molding her butt, his thumbs sweeping lower, down inside her inner thighs.

Whoa…

Erin jerked her head off the cushion, looking over her shoulder. And there, with an arrogant grin, stood the anti-Justin. Wes.

Automatically, she reached for the sheet and covered most of her body. It was different with Wes—she didn't know why—but she felt exposed now. "You've taken up massage in your spare time?"

Wes, who'd shed his leather jacket somewhere along the line, stood back and folded his arms across a wide, T-shirted chest. A dark lock of hair covered his brow, making him a nasty boy.

"I followed you up here and…struck a deal with little Justin, that's all."

"A deal."

"I'm a regular wheeler dealer." He grinned. "It's my talent in life."

Wes didn't add that it was also the bane of his existence. He'd always been blessed with a silver tongue, but that was part of the reason people never took him seriously. With as few words as possible, he'd always created his own reputation before anyone else could label him to their satisfaction. Problem was, at some point, he'd started to believe all the things he'd made himself out to be, and he'd dreaded the day when someone would call him on it.

Yet that was the thing about Erin. She'd probably be the one to do it. He both looked forward to it and feared it. Just wanted it to be over and know that she didn't think any less of him for the truth—that his polish would wear off all too easily if tested.

As he drank in the sight of her on the table, candlelight licking her skin, he thought she definitely was worth risking his ego. The sheet didn't cover much: most of one ripe breast was exposed, as well as her ass. Damn, the curves of those bared cheeks, smooth and firm, had felt so good. He was dying to get back to work again.

"You're gonna get Justin fired," Erin said, but she didn't seem displeased.

"That's not what he said when I handed him that wad of cash and told him to take a break." Wes cocked his head. "Well, okay, he *did* say something about getting into big trouble if his boss ever found out, but he was convinced once I added a bit more incentive to the pile."

Erin shook her head. "You devil."

Wes unfolded his arms from across his chest. Lust was spearing his gut, thrusting with every passing second. "Turn back over, Erin. Give me my money's worth."

"Hey, you say that like I'm a—"

"You're not." He hadn't meant to put it in those terms. He would never treat her that way; it stung that she thought he might, mostly because he knew his previous encounters with women were no better than meaningless transactions, anyway.

Voice low, he said, "Let me make you feel good, Erin."

For a moment, she didn't move. That same shift clicked the colors of her eyes into a different mode. There was something going on here, and he had no idea what it was. But he wanted to bring back the twinkle in her eyes, the delight she always wore when they bantered or simply relaxed around each other. He wanted that more than just about anything.

She must've seen that, because she did turn over, inviting him to continue.

He hesitated, but then, driven to his limits—and what guy wouldn't be with his dream girl naked in front of him?—he rubbed more oil on his hands. Carefully, he stroked up her back again, shaping his fingers to her like air over dunes, traveling and mapping.

As he worked the tenseness out of her muscles, he grew hard, anticipating what the foreplay could eventually lead to. A meeting of their bodies…maybe more.

She moaned as he used his thumbs to knead the back of her neck.

"You put in too many hours at the shop," he said.

"Shh."

He laughed quietly, retaliating by coasting his hands beneath her body and cupping her breasts. Soft, erotically swollen. She arched her back in response, allowing him room to slip her nipples between his fingers.

She gasped. The sound jabbed into him.

He smoothed down lower, over her flat belly, feeling a thatch of hair wisp against his fingertips.

"I thought…" she said, voice breaking apart "…I'd get…hot stones with this…massage…"

"Saucy," he said roughly, slipping his hands up and over her waist, then her back, then down to palm her ass again. Moving lower, he spread apart her legs, then ran his thumbs into the wet cleft there.

She rocked upward. "Oh—"

He pressed harder, separating her folds, hunger stoked at the sight of her glistening pink sex under candlelight.

Careful, he thought. *Slow.*

Finding her clit, he circled it. She echoed his movements, clutching the table and bunching the bottom sheet.

He worked her, harder but not faster, drawing out her groans until they grew higher in pitch. All the while, his own libido was expanding, pulsing, nagging him to take this further.

"Wes," she said against the table. "Oh, Wes…"

As she moaned his name, Wes's chest tightened.

There was a knock at the door.

He froze in utter disbelief.

Erin jerked away from him, sheened with sweat. It made her skin gold, hazed with a glow.

An erection ruling him once again, Wes covered her with the sheet, cussing under his breath. She'd been saying his name, as if she'd wanted more than just the physical from him….

"One second," he bit out.

A voice from the other side said, "My boss came in, sir. I've gotta—"

"One minute."

Erin had already jumped off the table, heading for her clothes, which were hanging on a wall hook. "If I didn't know better, I'd say it was that curse."

Wes helped her into her jeans. *"I'm* starting to know better. I think you need to fully explain this curse to me, Erin."

Knock, knock, knock.

She tugged her T-shirt over her head, nipples beading against the thin white material. With a jolt, Wes snagged her sweater and wrapped it around her before Justin came in. He didn't give a crap if the guy saw naked women every day, this was Erin, and Wes wasn't about to allow some random man the satisfaction.

Justin's voice filtered in again. "Excuse me, but—"

"One minute!" they both said in stereo.

"The room," Wes said, pained. "Tell me we're going to our room."

Another click of her eye colors—a combination lock securing her thoughts away into a vault.

"Erin? What is it?"

After a beat, she smiled, looking as if she didn't know what he was talking about. "It's nothing." She touched his arm. "Let's just go back…."

Justin had obviously waited long enough because he jammed open the door. The candle flames waved and angled with the breeze.

"Sorry," he said, "but my boss showed up and asked me why I wasn't with my scheduled appointment."

"That's okay," Erin said, tugging Wes away by the hand. "Thanks for trying."

And they continued on to their cabin, where Wes hoped they could prove that there really wasn't any damned curse.

5

THAT WAS CLOSE, ERIN thought as she and Wes bolted into their cabin. Close to getting caught, close to actually getting somewhere. Even now, her skin was still slick with oil, buzzing with the imprint of Wes's practiced hands sliding over her, under her....

At the reminder, she felt a jolt in her sex. She was still primed for him, beating with a plump reminder of what could've been.

As Wes shut the door, the ship's intercom sounded a bell, and the purser's voice came on. "We'd like you all to join us on deck as we depart—"

"No," Wes said, stalking over and guiding her toward the bed. "*Hell,* no."

She clasped his arms and turned their bodies so that his back was to the mattress. "Exactly. No more interruptions."

With verve, she pushed him onto the bed, where the edge of it caught the backs of his knees to take him down. Propping himself up on his elbows, he reclined, obviously entertained by her take-charge attitude.

They both laughed. Then her gaze caught his and—
Ja-joom.

Her heart pistoned, jarred to life by his sitting there, just watching her with such casual, frank interest. Black hair slouching over his brow, eyes liquid with dark yearning, his T-shirt straining over his tight abs while the white material skimmed every cut muscle. He was more than she could handle and, for a flailing minute, she didn't know what to do or how to do it.

Out of the corner of her eye, she could see the ship pulling away from the dock, taking them out to sea. Stranding her with the decision she'd made to get intimate with this gorgeous, hot man who sent tremors to her core.

Not wanting to dwell on what those tremors might signify, Erin pushed all her doubts to the wayside, purposefully moving to the vanity counter, where she'd set down her lollipop earlier.

Shaking with anticipation, she picked it up, making a show of inspecting it: cherry candy, heart-shaped and innocent.

"Do me a favor?" she asked quietly.

Ja-joom. Oh, man, she was really going to do this. Sleep with Wes. Ignore that they had no future and just go for it. Expose herself to a prediction that scared her half to death.

"Name it," he said, tone low and gristled.

Slowly, she began to undo the candy's clear wrapper. "Take it all off."

He slid a curious look at the lollipop, then cocked an eyebrow, clearly up for any request. Rising, he tugged off his shirt, tossing it away to the corner.

Through the window, the harbor glided by: a swollen sky met by wind-ruffled water.

Stomach going goofy—from the thought of sailing, or from nerves?—she went to the window. With a decisive jerk, she closed the curtains, then turned back to Wes.

There. The room was dimmer now, less intimidating. It was a shadowed alcove where she could act out her fantasies without feeling fully revealed or losing her courage under too much illumination.

Tracking her with predatory eyes, Wes had also taken off his shoes and socks while still sitting on the bed. His olive skin looked darker with the lack of light. Exotic, smooth, so masculine.

"And?" he asked, voice edged with the same sexy amusement.

She went hot again, pulse throbbing in a countdown to contact. Instinctively, she ran the lollipop over her lips.

His smile grew.

Moving closer to him, Erin lolled the candy away from her

mouth. Screw all the cautious cells bumping against each other in her body in their attempt to get her to reconsider, to take this slower. She was ready to go.

"Your jeans aren't going to do us much good," she said.

As he stood and eased them off, she went back to the lollipop, tilting her head and licking the sweet cherry, knowing Wes was taking it all in.

He tossed the denim away, the heavy material hitting the wall with a bunched slap. And there he stood: tall, athletic, his penis half-erect from her preshow.

Erin took the entire sucker into her mouth, then drew it out. "Mmm…"

"Erin…" Wes said. It was as if his voice had been sliced open and was bleeding raw desire.

Infused with the confidence of knowing how much he wanted her, she forgot everything else, moving forward and giving him another slight push to get him back down on that mattress, then tossing him a pillow so he could prop up his head. She knew he'd want to watch; she needed him to do it, too, needed to feel naughty and rebellious.

He understood her intentions, shoving the pillow under his head as she put the lollipop back into her mouth with one hand and pressed one of his legs open with the other.

As she pulled out the sucker, she felt the floor roll beneath her feet. Her head swam.

"You okay?" he asked.

"Yeah." Taking a fortifying breath, she crawled onto the bed to hover over him. "You think the water will be rough out there?"

He closed his eyes, as if he couldn't believe she was talking instead of…doing. She couldn't believe it, either, but for a second, she'd felt queasy.

He opened his eyes again, but his hands clutched the pillow under his head. "Ship's too big for you to feel the waves. Don't worry about it."

Don't worry.

Okay.

She ran the fingernails of one hand up over his leg, his inner thigh. He shifted, his cock bobbing. It made her clit seize, paining for him to massage it again. She sucked hard on the lollipop, juices stinging her mouth.

Traveling higher, she found his sac, tracing her fingers over the softness. He bunched the pillow in his fists, groaning.

Lightly, she rolled his balls with her fingertips, fascinated by the ecstatic agony on his face. Then, while drawing harder on the candy, she ran her index finger up the underside of his shaft.

He bucked. "Erin—"

She cut him off with a low sound from her throat—a strangled longing for him.

Wrapping her fingers around his penis, she took him into her fist, sliding upward. She moved downward, up again, slowly, bringing him to absolute hardness. With every carnal motion, she rolled her tongue around the lollipop.

She found that his gaze was on her mouth. Was he picturing her tongue on him?

She coaxed the candy out, a slurp echoing in the room as she nonchalantly held him in her hand.

Slowly waving the sucker back and forth, she felt more flirty and powerful than ever, knowing she had him at her mercy. *This* was what she'd been missing before Wes came along—a sense of mutual giving and getting.

"You wondering what I'm going to do next?" she asked.

A harsh, choked sound was his only response.

On a whim, she took one more taste of the candy, allowing her tongue to linger and invite. A muscle jerked in his cheek as she leaned the sucker away from her mouth and licked her lips.

Then she whispered, "All those long hours in the store. Staring at those creamy candies, the suckers, the bonbons… It does things to a girl. It makes her create diabolical daydreams. New ways to use all those sweets."

She slid her lollipop back inside her mouth, wet it thoroughly, then took it out and carefully placed it on the tip of his penis. She circled the head, coating him with sticky promise.

After she was satisfied, she lowered her mouth, licking the sugar from him, taking her time as he moaned beneath her. Stoked by his reaction, she took it one step further, winging her tongue back and forth over his head to tease him.

By the time she came up for air, he was breathing hard. "You…learn that from your L.A. friends?" he asked, clenching his jaw.

"Nah, I'm not so L.A." She repeated the process by sucking on the candy again, then this time very deliberately bathing his entire length in lollipop-slickness, avoiding getting too close to the dark patch of hair nesting his erection. "The place is Cheryl's home base. I just moved there to open the business with her."

Business. Why the heck was she talking about it again?

She bent to lay her tongue to him, this time concentrating on his shaft. Greedily, she tasted him up and down as he encouraged her with building groans. Cherry, skin, Wes….

Stimulated by his enjoyment, she took him all the way into her mouth, swirling her tongue around him, up and down, sucking, lingering, getting a sugar rush that hummed in her veins.

Oh, he tasted so good…delicious…

His hands bunched her hair, and when he came, he filled her mouth. She savored that, too, swallowing. She rubbed her cheek lower, against his inner thigh. His leg hair crisped against her skin, the scent of sweet male satiating her.

Dizzy, she rose away from him. Sweat beaded his chest, his upper lip, and he was gasping for air, just as she was. Her pulse jackhammered from her chest to her sex, tearing her into a thousand pieces, making her tummy roil again.

"Come here," he whispered raggedly, reaching for her.

Her stomach jumped, but she obeyed, falling over him, mouth seeking his. She grinded her hips against his to alleviate the pressure that'd built between her legs. Even though he'd climaxed, he was still going strong. She rocked against him, wishing she didn't still have her jeans on, wishing he was inside of her.

As they devoured each other, nipping, sucking, tonguing, the world rolled inside Erin's head.

Words flashed through her, blinding her sight with neon distraction: *You can stop looking for the man of your dreams.*

She tried to shut out the fortune-teller, instead reaching for her zipper to undo it. Fun, freedom, immunity from seriousness, that's all she wanted right now.

You've already found 'the one.'

Panic began to overtake Erin, materializing in clumsiness as she fumbled with her jeans. The sea seemed to lift the ship, and it got to her, making her come up from Wes for a deep breath.

Again, a wave seemed to rock the boat, and Erin's head went tight.

You reject what love has in store for you, and you twist karma around until it comes right back at you with negative energy.

Closing her eyes, Erin backed away from Wes, holding her forehead. "Dammit."

"Hey…" he said, cradling her face.

But she pulled away, lying on her side until the ship stopped moving. "Are we in bad weather or something? I…"

She stopped, the taste of candy suddenly like copper in her mouth. Wes was just a short fling, no more, that's all either of them wanted from each other—

Wes was stroking her hair, obviously concerned. "The ship's not moving. What's wrong?"

The answer was clear.

Cursed.

Her karma truly *was* bent out of shape, and seasickness was the price she'd have to pay this time.

6

IT'D BEEN A ROUGH NIGHT.

And it hadn't been because Wes had stayed up half the time making sure Erin was taken care of, either. No, he hadn't minded running a washcloth under water so he could put it on her forehead. He hadn't even minded going to the gift store for aspirin and those "seasick" bracelets, which were like sweatbands with a bead that pressed against the pressure points on your wrist to cancel the nausea.

Uh-uh. The night had sucked because, once again, he and Erin had been getting so damned close to what he wanted. But it'd also been much too far away.

Fighting his pent-up, eternal state of arousal and the hope of the closeness that might come out of all this, he left Erin sleeping and went to a buffet, bringing back some breakfast for them to share. But upon his return, he found her out of bed and in the shower. So he left the pastries and took a quick trip to the fitness room, where he worked off a load of frustration on a rowing machine.

Of course, that didn't do crap. He was still wound up and ready to blow. Last night's candy-coated games and intimacy had only given him a taste of what was in store with a woman like Erin, and it wasn't enough.

Not nearly enough.

When he came back to the cabin, Erin was off somewhere, so he showered and, by the time he stepped out of the small bathroom, she'd left a phone message for him to meet her for a fresh-air

Ensenada jaunt. She said she'd be in the atrium, where she was accessing her business e-mail via a bank of computers. He didn't feel the same compulsion, seeing as Wall Street was closed.

No, he felt a much different urgency. But when he saw her in the Internet Café, her complexion was still a little wan, so he didn't suggest going back to the room. She was right: the fresh air and solid land of an off-ship excursion would do her good.

Now, as they checked out and strolled down the gangplank to encounter the cool, misted air outside, Wes told himself that, yeah, this really *was* the right thing to be doing: being a gentleman and not jumping all over her when she was under the weather.

A gentleman, he thought, biting back a smile. Sure.

Immediately off the deck, they entered a building with a sign that said Welcome To Ensenada and that held an assortment of tourist shop stalls. Some sold imitation designer watches, some sold salsa and colorful Mexican blankets.

Erin meandered over to a table decorated with a selection of leather bracelets. Lingering over a particular one with flowers, she held it against her wrist, smiled a little, then put it back down.

"You don't like it?" Wes asked, surprised to find that he was actually into watching her shop. But, hell, didn't every one of her moves hold him in thrall?

"It's not me, I think."

He glanced back at the bracelet, straightforward in its elegance. She'd look great wearing it, even though the band was simple and no doubt inexpensive. She was worth diamonds, he thought, but there was something about her that made him think more of a buried earthiness where diamonds would be *discovered* and later polished to a shine.

When Erin wandered over to a toy stall, he quickly asked the shopwoman, *"¿Cuánto?"* and paid the ten American dollars she asked for. No normal wheeling and dealing today.

Tucking the purchase into his leather jacket pocket, he

grinned at the woman, thinking that Erin would be surprised later by seeing the bracelet. Misinterpreting his gesture, the shop-keeper blushed and tucked a strand of black hair behind her ear.

Oops.

Wes turned around, joining his… What *was* Erin to him? Girlfriend? Bed buddy? More?

He turned over that last possibility in his mind as Erin bought something from a different shop. Seconds later, she turned from the salesman to show Wes what it was, her gray eyes twinkling.

"It's for one of my nephews," she said, showing him a small jack-in-the-box.

A nephew. A sign of everyday life outside of this cruise. For some reason, the mention of that sort of thing scared Wes, maybe because it drove home that she'd become far more important, far more *real*, to him in just a couple of weeks than any other woman in the course of his lifetime.

"How old is he?" Wes asked as they started to walk toward the building's exit.

"Three. Look." She turned the side crank on the box, and "Pop Goes the Weasel" chimed out. She hummed along with it.

But when it came time for the surprise to burst out, she stopped.

"Hey," he said. "Don't tell me *that's* cursed, too."

She cracked up, and he reached over to complete the song. When it ended, the clown exploded out of the container, and she flinched.

She put a hand to her chest, laughing. "I'm not so good with…well, things I can't predict."

For some reason, there was more to what she was saying than the literal. He thought about her fidgeting whenever she talked about franchising her candy shop, thought about the look in her eyes every time they started to kiss.

"It's just a toy designed to scare kids," he said. "What's to jump at?"

"Hmm, you make me wonder if I'm going to mentally scar my nephew forever."

She tucked the toy into her shoulder bag, looking as if she might just reconsider giving it to the boy. She was also avoiding the real subject, but he let her get away with it, even as it ate away at him.

They left the building, finding themselves on a crowded sidewalk where they caught a bus to the town of Ensenada itself.

When they got there, they discovered a one-road strip teeming with street vendors, restaurant/bars and fellow cruisers who'd braved the iffy weather to explore outside.

They sauntered past a closed antique store, a place that sold metal sculptures, and one of many joints that offered cheap beer and booze to the delight of the college kids who'd embarked on this weekend getaway.

A little girl managed to persuade Wes to buy some gum, and Erin held back a grin.

"Easy target," she said.

Stuffing his hands inside his jacket pockets, Wes fought his own smile and then they disappeared inside a minimall full of more stores. There, Erin delighted over some teeny leather purses and bought about five of them for her nieces who lived in Milwaukee.

As she scampered around the shops, oohing and ahhing over the shawls and kitschy T-shirts, Wes noted she'd made a sudden recovery now that they were away from the ship. Maybe it was because she was back on land.

Or maybe…

He didn't want to ask himself if Erin was playing some kind of cock-teaser game with him by coming on this cruise and then avoiding what staying in a single cabin meant to a couple.

He blew out a breath, walking onto the sidewalk while waiting for her to buy a stack of those T-shirts.

Then it hit him: the niggling feeling he'd been so reluctant to identify.

He disliked what he'd become in life. Months before he'd met Erin, he'd started feeling uncomfortable in his careless skin: all the parties, all the dates, had started numbing him. Every weekend was the same old, same old, filled with cocktails, flirting, then a trip back to his condo. Rinse, lather, repeat. He'd gotten sick of himself.

But when he'd seen Erin across that room, laughing, full of life, he'd been attracted to what he'd never had: true feeling. And when he'd talked to her, she'd forced everything he'd been questioning into clear focus: he was disgusted with what he'd made of himself so far. Yeah, he was well off with the money, but what else? What really mattered? In her genuine way, down-to-earth, candy-shop-owning Erin had given him a glimpse into what could be. And when she hadn't fallen all over herself to hop right into bed with him, he'd been intrigued, challenged, enlightened.

She could change what isn't working, he'd thought, revitalized and even a little afraid of that conclusion.

But he was just Erin's freakin' "transition man." There'd been no bones about that from the beginning due to that breakup she never wanted to talk about.

Rain began to sprinkle down from the sky, and Wes looked up into the gray.

What was he doing here?

"Wet alert!" Erin said as she barreled out of the minimall onto the sidewalk, clutching her teeming shoulder bag, grabbing his arm and hustling him to an overhang in front of a restaurant.

She was laughing again, infectious and cleansing. But he couldn't smile with her this time. He was still swamped in his idiot, life-altering brooding.

"Hey, there." She tugged on his arm, eyes wide and silvered with happiness.

Happiness? Why? Had he done something to make her that way? Was that his purpose as a "transition man"?

Erin wasn't giving up. "What's going on?"

He shook his head, extremely unwilling to get into it. He didn't want to hear what she would say, didn't want to know once again that he was just a passing thing. Hearing the truth—that she thought he could never change out of "transition" and into something else—would stab him.

The scent of spices floated out from the restaurant, woven with the heavier warmth of tortillas and beer. She tilted her head at him, as if trying to read what was going on under the facade he battled to uphold.

Then she stood on her tiptoes, placing a soft, unexpected kiss on his mouth.

The light pressure tore through him with more power than any climax. Shaken, Wes grabbed onto her hip, needing an anchor.

"Hungry?" she asked, her breath moist on his lips.

All he could do was nod, still overwhelmed by such a little gesture. He was hungry. Too hungry for her.

But she was talking about burritos and enchiladas, not anything else.

As she pulled him by the hand into the restaurant, he knew that maybe she could fill herself up with some lunch, but it wouldn't help him one bit.

Because it wasn't food he needed.

7

AFTER DALLYING AWAY the entire afternoon—eating, shopping, then drinking at the exuberant Papas and Beers bar—a much healthier Erin finally agreed to go back to the ship an hour before it set sail again.

Why return early? She didn't know. After last night's fiasco, she had no doubt that the curse was going to mess up any attempt at nookie anyway. And that had brought her to a definite conclusion: why not try to have fun in other ways when it was obvious that karma had it out for her in the bedroom? Surely she could at least show Wes a good time without the curse interfering. And, all in all, she was having great fun with him: he was everything she'd hoped for.

As they got ready for an early formal dinner seating—Erin had begged Wes not to miss it since she really, *really* wanted to try escargot—she watched him closely. He'd been quiet all day, and why not? He'd invited her to be with him for a reason and, even though she'd insisted on paying her own way when he'd brought up the desire to treat her to an all-expenses-paid weekend, there was some expectation on his end. There had to be. But he was being a gentleman about it, not pushing the issue.

And that surprised her. Wasn't *the* Wes Ryan supposed to pretty much take what he wanted? That's what they said, anyway. But how much of this man was just reputation? More importantly, how much of him was something more? How much of him was contained in that mysterious undertow she'd glimpsed in his dark eyes every time he thought she wasn't looking?

Even with all the questions dogging her, dinner was just as wonderful as she'd expected. The escargot was nicely textured and prepared, but there was also *lobster.* Oh, lobster. Wes liked watching her devour it, so she played to him, catered to his visual fantasies as a substitute for what they'd been missing so far. And even though they chatted with the other guests seated around the table, it felt as if Wes were the only one there. The whole time, she was aware only of him: his masculine scent, his thigh inches away from hers under the table.

Afterward, to work off the food, they decided to stroll on the decks under a night sky that had somewhat cleared. A lazy wind ruffled Wes's hair as he halted, then leaned back against a deck rail. Behind him, the water whispered by as the *Lady Oriana* meandered to sea. He was dressed in a crisp white shirt, which was opened at the collar, black pants and dark Italian leather shoes.

As Erin rested on the rail next to him, facing the ocean, she plucked at her seasickness bracelets: baby-blue sweatbands that clashed ever so slightly with her Roma-print evening dress. "I haven't eaten this much during a twenty-four-hour period since…I don't know. Maybe Christmas with my family? My mom's a mad cook."

"But does she fire up the Cherries Jubilee tableside?" he asked, referring to their dessert treat that night.

With his careless assurance, Wes turned to rest his side against the railing, slanting his body toward hers. Erin's skin prickled, hyperaware with the trace memories of last night. His remembered kisses dusted over her face, neck, chest…

The ladies' man would be expecting the same tonight, too, now that she wasn't sick anymore. But he would want it to go further, to a natural conclusion that made her pulse tremble.

She kept her eyes on one of her seasickness bracelets. "I just want you to know, Wes, this was a good idea—to relax for a weekend away from all the hustle and bustle back home. I'm having a great time."

He didn't say anything for a moment. But then he reached over and slid a finger under her bracelet. At the feel of his skin on her wrist, her belly twisted, injecting her with nervous anticipation, a yearning so strong she could barely contain it.

Smoothly, he moved his finger out from under the elastic, then cupped her hand, turning it over so her palm was facing the sky. As he stroked the underside of her hand, his warm skin was rough, striking friction against her flesh.

With his other fingers, he traced down her palm—her lifeline. She shivered. He seemed to know how to apply the right amount of pressure.

"Looks like Madame Karma was correct about that long life," he said, voice soft and low. He brushed over another line on her palm. "But what's this? Not a business line… Huh."

His touch sent a fizz of electricity under her skin, sizzling every cell to steam.

"What do you see?" Oh, man, why was she asking? She couldn't get into what the fortune-teller had said about "the one." She needed to cut off this conversation now. But how could she when he was dragging his thumb down over her wrist, just above the bracelet? Her knees almost buckled. Blood rushed downward, flooding the area between her legs with heat.

"I see," he said, swirling his thumb lightly over her skin, "that your karma curse goes beyond just a long life or the candy shop. There's something you're not telling me."

Part of her wanted to explain everything and allow him further inside of her, but the other part held her back: she wasn't *supposed* to be worried about this kind of thing with Wes. He wasn't supposed to be interested in that way.

The part that'd been so affected by her breakup won. She steered the subject away from anything that had to do with intimacy.

"Nope, Madame Karma was just all about business and lifelines. And if I've screwed up my chances for making the candy shop the best it can be by not 'going with the flow,' I've got to change that." *Stick to business. Don't mention the love part of the prediction—don't you dare.* "Cheryl's not only my greatest friend, but she's also my partner, and I can't allow my own personal bad luck to drag her down, too, especially…" Erin trailed off, nerves twanging.

Great. Even business talk was making her anxious. Was there anything that *didn't* these days?

Wes stopped flirting, clasping her hand instead. "What is it?"

Biting the inside of her lip, she continued, thinking it was actually kind of nice to have Wes as a sounding board for this since it was hard to lay all her fears out for Cheryl.

"Cheryl's really gung ho about the franchising, but I'm the one who's dragging my feet. *That's* why karma's messing with me."

Bull. She knew better.

"Expanding isn't something to look so down and out about," Wes said.

"I'm scared." There. She'd voiced it. And she wasn't just talking about the shop, either.

"Scared of what?"

She risked a peek up at him. "Of failing, I suppose. I guess moving toward franchising would…" She stopped, made a confused face because what she was about to admit didn't make much sense when expressed in words. "I guess taking this next step would mean that this is it, this is my life, and if the attempt fails, where do I go next? What do I do? And—" she swallowed "—would I be able to handle the fallout?"

"Right. Those damned transitions."

As the words hung there, the wind seemed to cuff around them, avoiding them as much as *she* wanted to.

But Wes wasn't letting it go. "It's more comfortable to be safe, to stay with what you know. Comfortable but not fulfilling."

She looked out to the sea: the moon-glowed water, the endless spaces of unknown territory. They were officially talking about more than just her shop now; he was hinting at how her fear extended from business to personal, and he sounded as if he cared about transitions way more than she'd ever guessed he could.

But why would he give a damn about being a transitional link in her life? Wes Ryan, the player, wouldn't be that invested in her.

Or…would he?

When she glanced up at him, he was watching her so intensely that her breath caught in her lungs, chopped off. All she could hear was the thud of her heartbeat, its rhythm escalating.

"You just don't want to risk making the wrong choice," he said, "right?"

The mere mention of it made her ill because she'd come so close to making the wrong choice with William. It'd take time to summon the will to try again.

But Wes wasn't done. "In fact, I'd go so far as to say that you're afraid to turn anything in your life into something bigger."

He couldn't be serious. He couldn't be offering himself up for something more than a light affair.

It struck her: maybe Madame Karma's prediction hadn't been so ridiculous after all.

Oh, God. Freaking out now…

"Wes." She straightened up, no longer so relaxed. "There're some things in life that are best left to the status quo. Maybe sometimes things are better left alone."

He slid a look at her—a look so laced with buried meaning that she straightened, heart beating in her ears.

"I've always been good at making people think they've gotten the best part of the deal, Erin. That's how I got through school—with the right excuses to my teachers, with smiles and promises. And that's how I've made my way in business and life, especially with women. I've enjoyed my share of them, but I've never been very honest. Not with them, not with myself."

"Wes—"

"Wait. Just hold on, okay?" He took in a breath, then huffed it out. "I've attempted to get serious with a partner two times. With the first, she turned out to be a Clippers fan," he said, his expression wry, "so that didn't work because when they played the Lakers—hell, the competitive spirit between us got ugly."

He assessed Erin with a gaze, searching for something she wasn't giving him. Couldn't give him.

Then, obviously not getting what he wanted, he continued. "After that supremely deep relationship, I waited, then tried again with a woman who was great at first, but ended up being prone to asking why I needed to have my space every so often. *That* lasted eight days, and it was eight days too long. But at least I tried, I told myself. At least I tried. Then I saw you at that party."

Below them, the ocean splashed and broke apart against the ship. That was the only sound right now, because she wasn't about to reveal anything about her own fractured past. It'd only make her angry again, whipping up all the ugliness she'd been running from.

"So that's my story," Wes said. "I've been wondering about yours, Erin."

"Why?" Defensive. Already, the negativity was gathering. She wasn't sure being with another person brought out the best in her.

But Wes wasn't giving up. He was holding on to her hand, clearly determined not to let her go. The realization spurred her to fear, cornered her, forced her to do something rash and effective.

Distance, her buried ex-girlfriend mentality told her. *Create some distance, because he's getting too close.*

"You really want to know about my little history?" she asked, voice on edge.

"Yeah." Wes looked hopeful and, somewhere inside, there was a distant sense of her heart softening.

Can't happen. You can't *let that happen.*

"All right, here's my rather pathetic résumé." She'd gone rigid, as cold as self-preservation needed to be. "High school? Dated normally, if not frequently. College? Met the supposed man of my dreams and lost my virginity to him, thinking he'd be my life. After college? Engaged to the guy. For six years. And when I finally realized he didn't actually want to get married, I did the bravest thing I could and broke it off. I realized how, over the years, I'd stopped loving him somewhere along the way.

Actually, my family ended up more devastated than I was, and that hurt me more than any breakup. I didn't like what I'd brought down on them." She cleared her throat of the emotional debris. "And now? Dating normally again, making up for all the time I wasted."

It was the first time she'd gone into such detail with him, and he looked as if she'd pressed a just-extinguished match to his skin. It didn't burn so much as leave an ash mark that shocked more than hurt.

Gradually, he regained composure, back to the confident player he presented to the world. Problem was, Erin knew there was more to him than that.

"You've already found 'the one,'" Madame Karma had said.

No. God, no, she wasn't ready, didn't want to know that he could be affected by her and her by him.

"Why don't you just come out with it?" he finally said. "Tell me that I'm the type of guy who isn't good for anything more than a few weeks of…fun."

When she didn't answer, his shoulders lost their arrogant line. His gaze lost some of its confident shimmer, too.

The change bent her heart into a shape that didn't belong in her chest; the warp of it made clear to her what she really wanted to feel for Wes—if she could just allow herself to do it.

But she wouldn't. It'd destroy her right now. So she brought back the angry girl who'd been left in the dust by a man who never did value her.

Her body language shouted defensiveness, and Wes clearly didn't have any trouble comprehending. Without a word, he left Erin standing there, the breeze whispering something that sounded like "curse" in her ears.

She tried to tell herself it didn't matter, that this jinx was actually a good thing.

Because, maybe, just maybe, this curse was fate's way of protecting her from making yet another huge mistake.

8

WES DIDN'T KNOW HOW MANY hours he stayed away from the cabin. Two? Three? It didn't matter.

All he knew was that every time he found himself stopping to take stock of what'd just happened with Erin, realization crystallized his brain.

The ocean, he kept thinking, staring out at the black depths. It was his life. And he was this damned ship, floating and drifting even when it was anchored.

Erin might as well have told him that he was just an object to her—a plaything that existed only to amuse. And, truth be told, the old Wes would've been more than happy to oblige. But, just this once, he'd allowed himself to think he could be meaningful, and it'd backfired in his face.

So why try with her again? Why not just go back to what he was comfortable with? Life had been good to him this far, so why was he pining for something else that could turn out to hurt him much more in the long run?

Forget Erin, he told himself, abandoning his most recent spot by the deck railing. *Forget your damned crusade to matter to her.*

He finally went inside, making his way to the ninth-deck casino. Going back to the cabin would only be an exercise in futility, and who the hell needed more "curses," character assassination and cock-blocking?

As he entered the gaming area, complete with slot machines and blackjack tables, he told himself he was happy to be back to normal.

Whatever normal *was* these days….

He watched all the silk-and-satin people laughing at a roulette table, women in pearls hanging over men with loosened ties and slicked-back hair. Music from the disco next door pounded through the area—something hard, something that was bound to make females writhe on the dance floor with sinuous invitation. Maybe he should go over there.

But when he spied three women near the roulette wheel giving him the eye, Wes hesitated. Two brunettes and one blonde.

Blonde. Short, sassy hair, just like Erin's style….

Wes turned away from them. Deciding to get a drink, he ambled to the bar and ordered a whiskey straight up. While he waited for it to arrive, he surveyed the lively room some more, avoiding the trio of lustful temptation because he didn't want to be reminded of what awaited him back in the cabin.

Or what didn't await him.

Ding-ding-ding, went the machines. Hooray, went the people at one blackjack table as a dealer busted.

All the sounds and sights melded into a gray blur. Even his whiskey, when it was served, tasted dull.

Where had his capacity for pleasure gone? And why couldn't he stop himself from wanting to just go back to his room to be near her?

Down the bar a few seats, Wes became aware of a pickup in progress. As he absently sipped his drink, he saw that an older man was lounging on a stool, ice rattling in his cocktail glass as he talked to two women who had to be in their twenties. The girls were glamorous in that way women were when they looked at a fashion magazine and dressed the way it told them to for a night on the town: big hair, glitter on their smooth skin, skimpy halter dresses with short skirts. The man, though, was a different story: pewter hair, bourbon-heavy gaze, his collar opened enough to show a tanned, gray-hair-sprinkled chest.

Wes negligently listened in on the conversation, having nothing better to do.

"…was in Hawaii on a layover when I met two women, just as pretty as you, in the hotel bar," the man said. "The big island is full of beautiful girls. Is that where you're both from?" His voice was slightly slurred, but friendly.

One of the girls, a redhead, who looked like the ringleader, answered. "We're from Chula Vista, near San Diego," she said, tone halfway to disinterested.

But the guy wasn't gauging that. He also wasn't catching the glance the women shared as he continued his story. It was a glance that predicted their escape from the barfly, a glance that made Wes feel sorry for the older man. Wes wanted to tell him to turn back to his drink and stop making a play for this prey; he was embarrassed for him.

"Yeah," he said, "I was a pilot for years. Traveled a lot of places…"

The girls nodded, trading another loaded look.

Ready to go? What do you think? How're we going to get away from him?

"Oh!" the redhead interrupted, looking toward the casino's exit. "I see Debbie!" She turned to the man. "Our friend's outside waiting for us."

The pilot stopped talking, finally getting it.

"It was nice talking to you," said the quieter girl.

"Yes, nice meeting you," said the redhead as she linked arms with her friend on the way out. "Have fun tonight."

The older man didn't even have time to respond before the duo darted away. As they left, they giggled to each other, loudly enough for the pilot to hear.

Mortified now, Wes waited a few moments, scanning the room again and pretending to be so absorbed in the activity that he hadn't heard the exchange next to him. When he finally chanced a look at the pilot, the older man snagged his gaze.

Wes's world seemed to web into cracks. In the pieces, he saw himself in the other guy—Wes Ryan in twenty-five years, wrung out, an object of scorn for all the single girls he'd still be trying to hit on.

Slowly, the pilot turned toward the bar, hunching over his drink.

Shaken, Wes quietly ordered another round for the man, paid for it and left.

The walk back to the room was like a trip through a silent maze. Or maybe that's just how it felt, because frat boys wove down the corridors and parties spilled from open doors. But Wes didn't absorb any of it.

When he finally got to his cabin, he unlocked the door, slipping inside the darkness and standing there until his eyesight adjusted. Erin lay in bed sleeping, one arm sprawled over his pillow, her face angled toward the half-curtained window.

After stripping and putting on a pair of pajama bottoms, he slipped into bed, covering himself with the sheet. Tenderly, he took Erin's hand from his pillow, holding it to his chest as he faced her.

He wished she'd just open her eyes, as he already had, and really see him.

But she never did.

9

ERIN AWOKE TO THE SOFT morning sun peeking through a slit of curtain. The light had the quality of dawn to it: weak but promising.

She blinked, suddenly aware that she wasn't alone in bed. Turning her head to the side, she felt her body tighten at the view of Wes, one muscled, dusky arm sprawled above his head in slumber. His hair was tufted over the pillow in lazy disarray, a shadow stubbling his jawline. The bed sheets had bunched down to just barely cover his belly; a trail of hair hinted at what the sheet covered.

Erin ached to slide her hand under the linen and explore him. She could almost feel his length in her hand, could imagine coaxing an erection with long, sultry, persuasive strokes.

Clit stiffening, she touched herself instead, slipping her fingers beneath the sheet, between her legs, into the crease of her sex. She pressed where it pained her, then rubbed until she grew damp. Burying her face in the crook of her arm, she quietly fantasized that it was Wes stimulating her….

But it wasn't.

She lost momentum and, in pure frustration, stopped altogether, disgusted with all her hang-ups.

Damned jinx. It wasn't even letting her have sex with herself.

Disgruntled, she stealthily got out of bed, careful not to disturb Wes as she stepped into the shower. She made the water brisk. Very, very brisk.

After a token few seconds of symbolic cold showering, she

adjusted the spray to get hotter. At the same time, she couldn't help but wish that last night's falling out had never happened, that he would just join her, fitting his body to the back of hers, his penis prodding her between the thighs. As he grew harder, she'd grow wetter, spreading open for him until he thrust inside, tearing her apart and making her forget about…

Ack!

The water had gone cold, so she shut it off. *Thanks, curse,* she thought. *Can't you even allow me to fantasize properly?*

Confusion made the rest of her routine clumsy. Her stomach clenched as she replayed the confrontation over and over. Boy, she'd been a real winner, picking a fight with Wes to keep her own heart safe. Smart, real smart. Just remembering the disappointment on his face when she'd pretty much told him that he couldn't be taken seriously devastated her— and puzzled her.

Dammit. She didn't want him to be more than a fling. Why couldn't he have just stayed that way?

Last night, after returning to the room, she'd punished herself mentally while waiting for him: hours of cussing at herself and wondering how she could repair the damage, if at all. Finally, eyes burning, she'd fallen into deep, blessed oblivion, touching his pillow and realizing on the cusp of unconsciousness that she wished it were Wes instead.

As she combed out her hair, she carried on with her self-chiding. If Wes had found another way to amuse himself last night—*God, what if he had?*—she… Well, she wouldn't blame him. Right? Definitely not. In fact, if she were him, she would've lost patience with this whole sexless cruise a long time ago. But he'd stuck it out, much to her surprise. Until last night, that is.

Did he really feel something for her?

You're not ready for that, Erin, said her protective 'fraidy cat within.

Yet, when she came out of the bathroom to find Wes lying

on his stomach with a pillow over his head, her heart wrenched with reminders of how good he'd been to her, how patient, how affectionate.

If I take this chance with you, will I end up right back where I was after William? she asked Wes silently while watching the rise and fall of each breath he took. *Except will I come out too bitter to recover this time? Or should I go with what my deepest hopes are telling me? Should I trust you?*

Erin must've stood there for a long time just looking at him, the sunlight slanting over his bare back like a clock hand stretching from one hour to another.

Ultimately, she gathered her guts, then scribbled a note telling him she'd be at the Lido restaurant with her usual morning coffee.

But what if he was too ticked off to meet her?

Yessss, 'fraidy cat said. *Then you're safe.*

She left the cabin, steeling herself for his decision either way.

WHEN WES FOUND THE NOTE, he quickly got ready, images of that pilot at the bar still haunting him. To make things even more nerve-racking, he had a million questions, too.

Why did Erin want to meet with him away from the cabin? To smooth things over without the diversion of sex distracting them, or to break things off, period?

If Wes had any say in the matter—and he damned well did— all the curses and barriers to being with her would end right now.

He took the stairs to the appointed Lido restaurant and, there, on the nearly deserted deck, he found Erin, dressed in white jeans and a sweatshirt with the Yes, Sweetie candy shop logo on it. With the ship anchored far away from shore, the ocean's breeze tousled her short blond hair.

Fluid ecstasy shot through his veins, pumping him with an emotion he'd never given a name to before. But, now, he thought he knew what it was—or what it *could* be, if he were only given a chance to make it solid.

He walked to the table, sat down, hoping she was feeling the same thing at seeing *him* first thing in the morning.

When they locked gazes, something exploded in the space between: a loaded shift of awareness that made her gray eyes go silver. A magnificent smile lit over her lips, and she perked up in her chair.

But then her smile turned shy, as if she remembered all the awkward anguish from last night. "I got out of bed around six. I thought you might want to sleep in, so I came up here to wait."

Wrong. She'd run away from him. Or maybe that goddamned curse had struck again, and somehow forced her to leave the cabin before they might have made love. Who the hell knew.

He blinked. Had he just referred to "making love"? Wes hadn't ever really thought of it that way before. "Screw," "boink," "get nasty"—he'd referred to sex every which way but this.

"I didn't need to sleep in. It's not like I did anything to exert myself," he said, hoping she understood what he was hinting at: that he hadn't fooled around on her last night, even though many scantily clad opportunities had been running around that casino.

Relief seemed to blanket her, and she chanced a wider smile. "So…" She put down her coffee cup. "It's Fun Day at Sea. You up for some miniature golf? Some drinks by the pool while we listen to the reggae band?"

She paused there, pursing her lips. Neither of them should even dare mention sex right now, but it still flapped in the air like a torn, hardly forgotten banner.

"Or maybe," Erin added, "we just need to talk."

Nerves screeching—this was it, everything he'd been waiting for—he leaned forward. "I'm sorry you thought that all I had in mind was a weekend-long bangathon. Maybe I can't help coming off like a wolf. Don't get me wrong—I was hoping we would get around to it…." He sighed. "But that's not entirely why I asked you to come."

"Actually, Wes, I think asking me to come is what all my issues are about." She traced the edge of the table, but then lifted her head, as if forcing herself to face whatever was going on in that head of hers. "This curse thing has really thrown a wrench in all the fun I was ready to have with you. Believe me, I was planning to spend a lot of time in that bed, but—" She motioned around with her hands, yet that didn't conjure up an explanation.

He wished he could help her figure out her own mind. Hell, if he could somehow erase all the discomfort she was obviously feeling right now, he would. He'd take it all on himself.

Her lips parted as she seemed to read that on his face. "Wes…" She trailed off.

"Why don't you just tell me what's happening?"

Erin hesitated, knowing she had to come clean. But the bald truth would change everything. It would officially turn a good-time affair into the real deal, and from that point on, it'd go downhill. It'd bring all that helplessness and anger back because she didn't know how else to handle the sort of rejection William had introduced into her life.

But…what if that *didn't* happen?

You've already found 'the one.'

Once again, she glanced at Wes. He was watching her with barely contained…what? What was it?

And why wasn't it scaring her more now that she was confronting it head-on?

Bolstered, she knew what she had to do: take control of this curse. Stop being life's little pawn. Make a decision and move out of the limbo fear had stuck her in.

"I'm so sorry for what happened," she said, choked. "I didn't mean to hurt you. I didn't even mean what I insinuated about your being no more than a player. See, I've had sex with one man in my life, and it's always meant…well, the skies opening, the seas parting. I thought I'd be able to adjust my philosophy with a guy of your—let's face it—reputation, but then emotions entered the equation, and they were never supposed to. Not with someone like the person I thought you were." She stopped.

Wes gripped the arms of his chair. "Go on."

Here it went, here it—

"That prediction? The fortune-teller?" *Go, go, go...* "You were right. It was about more than just business or lifelines."

He waited, but she was so nervous that she stood, fretful.

He got out of his seat, too, somehow understanding her need to move around while doing this.

Without a word, he took her hand, enclosing it in his all-encompassing grip. She held tightly to him, following him toward the stairs.

"Madame Karma also told me that I'd already found 'the one,'" she finally said.

His fingers tightened around hers.

She rushed on. "And I couldn't accept that because the prediction meant that you were a candidate for being 'it.' I thought you wouldn't be relationship material and that I'd get hurt all over again."

"'The one,'" he said, smiling now.

Her heart skittered, her breathing shallow. But why was this so scary?

Or *was* it...?

"I guess what all this is leading up to," Wes said, "is that I wasn't the type of guy who was suited for the position of 'the one' and you're fighting the prediction—hence, the curse."

They were at the bottom of the stairs now, on their cabin's floor. She turned to him, recognizing the fear in his own eyes. He was afraid she'd reject him, wasn't he? Or, even worse, he didn't like that she'd thought so little of him.

Moved, she stood on tiptoe and kissed him softly, just as she impulsively had that day in Ensenada as rain had pattered above them on the overhang. That afternoon, it'd felt natural to express affection for him. It'd felt right—until she'd started thinking about it again.

So stop thinking, she told herself.

Warm, good... Her mouth lingered against his, her breasts skimming his chest, beading the tips of them with tight yearning.

She pulled away slightly, keeping hold of his shirt. Finally, cathartically, she told him about the world's longest engagement with William and how it'd chipped away at her, year after year; how it'd made her doubt that she had it in her to ever try again, especially if failure meant another spirit-crushing breakup.

"I never want to be that hopeless woman again." She let go of his shirt but kept her hand on his chest. "So when you asked me out, I was looking forward to the freedom of being with a guy who didn't expect anything from me but all the easy stuff: the sex and laughter. And, most importantly, I didn't have to expect anything from you, only to be disappointed when I didn't get it."

A relieved breath escaped Wes, and he shook his head, tucking a strand of hair behind Erin's ear. She leaned into his touch, craving more, startled to find she was unafraid to accept it.

"And here I was thinking it was about me," he said. "I thought that you felt I wasn't good enough."

"It's not that you weren't 'good enough.' You were what I thought I needed. But what you *really* were scared the dickens out of me so I tried not to deal with that side of you."

"So…" He swallowed. "It turns out that *you* made this curse, Erin. You and your psychological obstacle course."

Whoa. She braced herself to withstand a flood of terror at this realization, but it never came. No, there was only a rise of soft heat consuming her from the toes upward, covering her skin, engulfing her.

"*I* was using the curse to keep myself from having to make any decisions about you…?" It made sense now: at first the curse had been built on coincidences, such as the emergency drill. And she'd been all too willing to embrace it, giving it new life from there, starting with her so-called seasickness.

He began guiding her into the corridor, where the early-morning quiet still hovered.

It didn't take a genius to guess where he was taking her. But what if he was wrong? What if the curse wasn't just her creation? What if—?

"Damn the curse," he said, as if reading her mind. "It was nothing. Even if a tsunami turns this ship over, you're mine."

His determination shot a thrill through every extremity, tingling her skin as he shut their door behind them.

Before she could catch her next breath, he'd pressed her against the door, his penis already hard against her belly. Her insides went squiggly, and she latched her mouth to his, seeking to share the pleasure.

They devoured each other, desperate and hungry, tongues tangling as her skin flushed with wet heat. She tried to yank off his shirt; he tried to undo her jeans. Her head hit the wall, but she didn't feel any pain, just adrenaline-fueled, deep-seeded delight.

Moment by beating moment, that delight melted down, over her flesh, into her belly, like the thaw of ice cream on a sweltering day.

Hadn't the fortune-teller said that going with the flow would correct any warped karma? Was that happening now that she'd opened up?

Yes! Hallelujah—

That's when the intercom sounded for an announcement.

10

AT THE INTERRUPTION, ERIN started banging her head against the wall.

"*Hell,* no," Wes said as the purser began to ramble over the intercom.

But the moment he heard the phrase "shipboard games," he carried on. Screw the curse—it was crap.

He lifted Erin up, and she squealed in surprise. It obviously turned her on, too, because she twined her arms around his neck and kissed him senseless.

Blood chopping and all systems "go," he spun her toward the bed. But in their passion, he didn't know his own strength, accidentally knocking her against the vanity counter. Her cosmetics went clanging off the surface, yet it didn't matter as he set her down there, her legs wrapping around him and drawing his cock against the warm center of her.

Hot. Dammit, he could feel how much she wanted him, even through their clothes. His growing erection ticked against her as they grinded, kissed, lapped each other up in long, slow, demanding thrusts and sucks.

He was so starved for her that his penis was already wet at the tip. In reaction, he tugged off her sweatshirt, tossing it away. Then her bra. Her sneakers and pants.

All the while she panted, watching him with a smile.

Not just sex, he thought, gaze caressing her full breasts, her tiny waist, her white lace panties. This was going to be more than just physical. And the fact that he hungered for that excited him to amazing heights.

He shucked off his own clothes, leaving himself bare to her. More bare than with any other woman in his experience.

As she ran a gaze over his body, there was more than lust to her look. A profound craving—that's what it was. An invitation to make her happy beyond just this, and he could give that to her. She made him believe it.

On a groan, he moved forward, dipping his fingers down the front of her panties. As he skimmed over her curls, down between the slick folds of her sex, she purred, shifting with satisfaction. It goaded him, sending a violent throb through his cock, making it go stiff.

He whispered in her ear, breath stirring her blond hair. "You're so pretty down here…pretty everywhere."

She mumbled something unintelligible into his neck, biting it. He flinched with the tickle-harsh contact, then smoothed two fingers inside of her. Circling, stirring, he worked her until she arched against his palm, her own hands bracing herself on the counter.

He found her face flushed pink, dewed with new sweat as she closed her eyes and bit her lip. Her intensity turned him on even more; it slivered his heart, making him feel wildly possessive for the first time in his life.

Ripping off her panties, he got to his knees, pulling her forward and adjusting her legs around his shoulders.

"Oh—" Her eyes shifted to gray for just an instant but then she relaxed, smiling again. The color turned silver, etched with encouragement.

He spread her open with his fingers. Damp blond curls surrounding pretty pink, just as he'd said. Voracious, he licked upward, reaching her clit. There, he laved, then spun his tongue around as if making cotton candy.

She dug her fingers into his hair, pressing, urging. He took one of her lips into his mouth, then angled his head to the side, kissing her, seeking entrance with his tongue. In, out, around…

Rocking against him, she groaned, becoming drenched. But just as she seemed about to fall over the edge, he sucked her other lip into his mouth, slowly drawing back at the same time until it slurped out—his own favorite candy to enjoy.

"Wes—"

Without pause, he rose up, sliding his hands up her hips, her waist and then to her breasts. Her distended nipples were dark and ripe: cherry decadence. Taking the fullness of them into his palms, he weighed their heft, eased his thumbs over their centers, then took one into his mouth to gnaw gently at it.

This time her cry was strangled. He guessed she was ultra-sensitive there, so he doubled her delight by trailing his fingers down her belly, brushing over the soft skin, the hint of pubic curls.

Low sounds, like impatient winces, came from her throat. He laved her other breast, slipping his hands between her thighs again, working her clit until she scratched at his back.

"Now," she insisted. "Do it now."

His cock pounded, making it almost impossible for him to fumble out a condom from the vanity counter where he'd stuffed a string of packets earlier. He managed to sheath himself.

Finally, he took her by the hips, their gazes meeting.

And the curse?

Screw it.

Tested beyond endurance, he tugged her forward, impaling her on his erection. She leaned back her head, grunting softly with the sudden act of taking him in. She was tight, wet and hot.

"Erin…?"

"Gone," she said. "It's gone…"

She began to churn against him, tightening her legs around him to bring him deeper.

Now it was *his* turn to groan, enveloped by her. And he welcomed it, finding freedom in the captivity—a heightened joy that'd escaped him until he'd accidentally found it.

Grinding, she brought him to the point of a primal yell. He pushed into her again and again, their rhythms syncopated as they eventually slowed down, rolling like waves under a ship, rocking it side to side.

Tenderly, he nuzzled her, and she responded in kind, embracing him as if she'd never let go.

But then the waves grew rougher, slapping against him, stripping him raw, rushing and invading until they tore at him from the inside out.

He came with a searing release, falling over her as she sank back against the mirror. His breath fogged the glass, blurring his image as he burrowed against her neck and held on to her with desperate fury.

She gently kissed his ear. "I could get used to this," she said, voice quivering with emotion.

As he gathered her closer, skin plastered against skin, the mirror unfogged.

Revealing the Wes Ryan he'd been looking for.

Epilogue

Two months later

When Erin saw Wes come through the door of Yes, Sweetie, where she'd been tasting new candy for the inventory, she ran out from behind the burnt-oak counter, practically bowling over the barrels of bulk candy. She crashed against him in an exuberant embrace.

"Finally!" she said, digging her fingers into his wild hair and bringing him in for a kiss.

"Mmm? Mmmm." His surprise turned into obvious pleasure as he soaked into her, fitting their mouths together and probably tasting the root beer candy she'd just been noshing on.

She tasted him, too, luxuriating. Then, with cheeky suggestion, she sucked at his lower lip, pulling away at the same time.

They laughed as she leaned her forehead to his cheek. "You know how to keep a girl waiting."

"Isn't that the secret to maintaining a spontaneous, exciting relationship?"

He led her over to "The Candy Bar," a more popular hangout now that Constant Cravings, the business complex's former coffee shop, had relocated. Another java house had taken its place, but had enjoyed little success. Here in the wood-planked room of The Candy Bar, amid the smells of saltwater taffy, licorice and bubblegum, patrons could partake of hot chocolate: white, dark, laced with vanilla—however they wanted it. Every drink came with candy, so it wasn't odd to see both adults and children using the bar: even now, there was a crowd of preteens sharing an iPod, but there was also a customer with liver-spotted hands lingering behind a newspaper at the other end.

"Of course—" Wes said, removing a newspaper from a barstool and taking a seat "—I'm no expert at this relationship thing, so what do I know?"

"You're a natural, so stop being coy." Absently, Erin played with the leather bracelet Wes had given her after their first time together. When he'd tied the simple piece of jewelry around her wrist in the afterglow, it'd been the most priceless thing Erin could've asked for.

Wes pulled her onto his lap. She'd really missed him, even if they'd seen each other this morning when he'd tumbled out of bed early. In fact, it'd been the crack of dawn when he'd started east-coast business on his personal computer, where he'd remained trading even after Erin had gotten ready for work. She didn't stop by her own place much now, had her own armoire at Wes's condo, actually.

Who would've predicted that she would agree to her own closet space with him so soon? But he was her "definite man," and it made sense to be halfway moved in with the guy she loved.

A chipper voice interrupted the canoodling. "Keep it PG, kids," Cheryl said.

From Wes's lap, Erin turned to her best friend and partner in the franchise they were creating. "Don't you have some paperwork to go over for our franchise venture?"

Cheryl scrunched her nose at Wes. "Control your woman, please?" She shot a pseudo-mean look at Erin, grabbed some empty mugs, then took off toward the back room.

From the teeny bopper end of the bar, giggles sounded. The newspaper patron turned a page, ensconced behind the inked barrier.

That reminded Erin…

She tugged over the morning edition Wes had discarded on the bar's surface. She'd been reading it earlier while taking a break.

"You're not going to believe what I found today," she said, opening to the Baxter Hills announcements page. "Look."

Wes scanned the paragraph she'd indicated. "Evan Sawyer and Lacey Perkins announce their engagement…"

"Remember?" Erin just about bounced on Wes's lap. "They're the other couple that dissed Madame Karma's prediction. They managed to beat the curse, too, just like Chloe and Ian." The accountant and Erin had started talking more, ever since the fortune-teller crisis. They'd even bonded over their shared experience, Chloe inviting Erin to her own engagement party.

"'Curse'? Did you say the word *curse?*" Wes asked. "I thought we were never going to mention the damned thing again."

"Don't call it damned!" Erin whispered. "Don't curse the curse. You don't know what can—"

Wes cut her off with a kiss—a deep, long, limb-melting press of his lips. At the end of it, he sucked *her* lower lip in a sexy promise of what would happen when they were finally alone again.

"I love you," he said, "but stop fretting. You know what fretting brought on back when you were having those issues—"

Now she kissed him, shutting him up for good.

As they fused into each other, the preteens giggled even louder at the kissing adults and sprang from their stools, leaving the candy shop as if they had much better things to be doing.

And, at the other end of the bar, the shop's newest customer, Isabelle Girard, aka The Legendary Madame Karma, peeked out from behind her newspaper at Wes and Erin.

She smiled, then went back to her horoscopes and hot chocolate, pleased at seeing yet another prediction come true.

* * * * *

Happily ever after is just the beginning...

Turn the page for a sneak preview of
A HEARTBEAT AWAY
by
Eleanor Jones

Harlequin Everlasting—Every great love
has a story to tell. ™
A brand-new series from Harlequin Books

S pecial? A prickle ran down my neck and my heart started to beat in my ears. Was today really special?

"Tuck in," he ordered.

I turned my attention to the feast that he had spread out on the ground. Thick, home-cooked-ham sandwiches, sausage rolls fresh from the oven and a huge variety of mouthwatering scones and pastries. Hunger pangs took over, and I closed my eyes and bit into soft homemade bread.

When we were finally finished, I lay back against the blue-bells with a groan, clutching my stomach.

Daniel laughed. "Your eyes are bigger than your stomach," he told me.

I leaned across to deliver a punch to his arm, but he rolled away, and when my fist met fresh air I collapsed in a fit of giggles before relaxing on my back and staring up into the flawless blue sky. We lay like that for quite a while, Daniel and I, side by side in companionable silence, until he stretched out his hand in an arc that encompassed the whole area.

"Don't you think that this is the most beautiful place in the entire world?"

His voice held a passion that echoed my own feelings, and I rose onto my elbow and picked a buttercup to hide the emotion that clogged my throat.

"Roll over onto your back," I urged, prodding him with my forefinger. He obliged with a broad grin, and I reached across to place the yellow flower beneath his chin.

"Now, let us see if you like butter."

When a yellow light shone on the tanned skin below his jaw, I laughed.

"There…you do."

For an instant our eyes met, and I had the strangest sense that I was drowning in those honey-brown depths. The scent of bluebells engulfed me. A roaring filled my ears, and then, unexpectedly, in one smooth movement Daniel rolled me onto my back and plucked a buttercup of his own.

"And do *you* like butter, Lucy McTavish?" he asked. When he placed the flower against my skin, time stood still.

His long lean body was suspended over mine, pinning me against the grass. Daniel…dear, comfortable, familiar Daniel was suddenly bringing out in me the strangest sensations.

"Do you, Lucy McTavish?" he asked again, his voice low and vibrant.

My eyes flickered toward his, the whisper of a sigh escaped my lips and although a strange lethargy had crept into my limbs, I somehow felt as if all my nerve endings were on fire. He felt it, too—I could see it in his warm brown eyes. And when he lowered his face to mine, it seemed to me the most natural thing in the world.

None of the kisses I had ever experienced could have even begun to prepare me for the feel of Daniel's lips on mine. My entire body floated on a tide of ecstasy that shut out everything but his soft, warm mouth, and I knew that this was what I had been waiting for the whole of my life.

"Oh, Lucy." He pulled away to look into my eyes. "Why haven't we done this before?"

Holding his gaze, I gently touched his cheek, then I curled my fingers through the short thick hair at the base of his skull, overwhelmed by the longing to drown again in the sensations that flooded our bodies. And when his long tanned fingers crept across my tingling skin, I knew I could deny him nothing.

* * * * *

Be sure to look for A HEARTBEAT AWAY,
available February 27, 2007.

And look, too, for THE DEPTH OF LOVE
by Margot Early, the story of a couple who must learn
that love comes in many guises—and in the end
it's the only thing that counts.

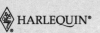
HARLEQUIN®

EVERLASTING LOVE™
Every great love has a story to tell ™

Save $1.00 off

the purchase of any Harlequin Everlasting Love novel

Coupon valid from January 1, 2007 until April 30, 2007.

Valid at retail outlets in the U.S. only. Limit one coupon per customer.

5 65373 00076 2   (8100) 0 11302

HEUSCPN0407

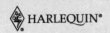
HARLEQUIN®

EVERLASTING LOVE™

Every great love has a story to tell™

Save $1.⁰⁰ off

the purchase of any Harlequin Everlasting Love novel

Coupon valid from January 1, 2007 until April 30, 2007.

Valid at retail outlets in Canada only. Limit one coupon per customer.

RETAILER: Harlequin Enterprises Limited will pay the face value of this coupon plus 10.25¢ if submitted by the customer for this product only. Any other use constitutes fraud. Coupon is nonassignable. Void if taxed, prohibited or restricted by law. Consumer must pay any government taxes. Void if copied. Nielsen Clearing House customers submit coupons and proof of sales to: Harlequin Enterprises Ltd. P.O. Box 3000, Saint John, N.B. E2L 4L3. Non–NCH retailer—for reimbursement submit coupons and proof of sales directly to: Harlequin Enterprises Ltd., Retail Marketing Department, 225 Duncan Mill Rd., Don Mills, Ontario M3B 3K9, Canada. Valid in Canada only. ® is a trademark of Harlequin Enterprises Ltd. Trademarks marked with ® are registered in the United States and/or other countries.

52607370

HECDNCPN0407

This February...

Catch NASCAR Superstar **Carl Edwards** *in*

SPEED DATING!

Kendall assesses risk for a living—
so she's the last person you'd
expect to see on the arm of a
race-car driver who thrives on the
unpredictable. But when a bizarre
turn of events—and NASCAR
hotshot Dylan Hargreave—inspire
her to trade in her ever-so-structured
existence for "life in the fast lane"
she starts to feel she might be
on to something!

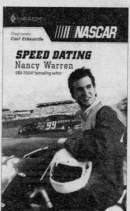

REQUEST YOUR FREE BOOKS!

2 FREE NOVELS PLUS 2 FREE GIFTS!

HARLEQUIN®

Blaze®

Red-hot reads!

HB07

Silhouette®
Romantic
SUSPENSE

Excitement, danger and passion guaranteed!

Same great authors and riveting editorial
you've come to know and love
from Silhouette Intimate Moments.

> *New York Times*
> bestselling author
> Beverly Barton
> is back with the
> latest installment
> in her popular
> miniseries,
> The Protectors.
> HIS ONLY
> OBSESSION
> is available
> next month from
> Silhouette®
> Romantic Suspense

Look for it wherever you buy books!

HARLEQUIN®

Blaze™

COMING NEXT MONTH

#309 BEYOND DARING Kathleen O'Reilly
The Red Choo Diaries, Bk. 2
Hot and handsome Jeff Brooks has his hands full "babysitting" his P.R. agency's latest wild-child client, Sheldon Summerville. When she crosses the line, he has no choice but to follow....

#310 A BREATH AWAY Wendy Etherington
The Wrong Bed
Security expert Jade Broussard has one simple rule—never sleep with clients. So why is her latest client, Remy Tremaine, in her bed, sliding his delicious hands all over her? Whatever the reason, she'll toss him out...as soon as she's had enough of those hands!

#311 JUST ONE LOOK Joanne Rock
Night Eyes, Bk. 2
Watching the woman he's supposed to protect take off her clothes is throwing NYPD ballistics expert Warren Vitalis off his game. Instead of focusing on the case at hand, all he can think about is getting Tabitha Everheart's naked self into his bed!

#312 SLOW HAND LUKE Debbi Rawlins
Champion rodeo cowboy Luke McCall claims he's wrongly accused, so he's hiding out. But at a cop's place? Annie Corrigan is one suspicious sergeant, yet has her own secrets. Too bad her wild attraction to her houseguest isn't one of them…

#313 RECKONING Jo Leigh
In Too Deep..., Bk. 3
Delta Force soldier Nate Pratchett is on a mission. He's protecting sexy scientist Tamara Jones while hunting down the bad guys. But sleeping with the vulnerable Tam is distracting him big-time. Especially since he's started battling feelings of love…

#314 TAKE ON ME Sarah Mayberry
Secret Lives of Daytime Divas, Bk. 1
How can Sadie Post be Dylan Anderson's boss when she can't forget the humiliation he caused her on prom night? Worse, her lustful teenage longings for him haven't exactly gone away. There's only one resolution: seduce the man until she's feeling better. *Much* better.

www.eHarlequin.com